Toothpicks And Wicked Tricks

The Tooth Fairy Chronicles

Book Five

Victoria Rocus

Serenade Publishing

For every fearless woman holding this book...the female fighters, the girlies with grit, the ladies of lenity, the sisters sporting spines of steel, the mamas meeting mayhem with mettle, and the badass babes who never bow. Hold the line, my fellow Valkyries...we got this.

GLOSSARY AND PRONUNCIATION OF ANCIENT OTHERWORLD GAELIC

Aine - (awn-yah) – meaning radiance or splendor; Rosie's late mother's name

A mhic daor – (ah-mick-dair) – "my dear son"

Asgard - (As- gart) – A *Nordboerne* Otherworld Elven kingdom north of *I Idir* and ruled by Odin; currently not on friendly terms with *I Idir's* monarchy over their opposing stand on Mundanes crossing the Veil. Pronounced (As-garter) by its citizens.

Athair - (ă-hair) - "father" - when capitalized, used as a formal title

Bairn - (bĕrhn) - "baby"

Birgit – (beer-gît) – a variation of the name Bridget, meaning "help" or "salvation; The name of Dylan's *scathach.*

Blaincead – (blan-keed) – blanket

Bru na Boinne – (brew na bun-yay) – the ancient home of *Boann*, the Celtic goddess of fertility, poetry and knowledge who it is said created the River Boyne

Buaf – (boo-êf) – toad; the name given to the orphaned kitchen boy at *Dun Siorai*

Caic tarbh – (cak tarb) – "bullshit:" a crude term implying an untrue statement

Caoin leanbh – (kween la-nov) a "cry baby"

Caomhnoir ainmhithe – (kweeve-nar an-i-vee) – translates to "animal watcher;" in Otherworldly magical terms it refers to an animal guardian

Cillian Mac Badh – (kill-ee-an mc bod) -translates to "bright-headed" in reference to war or strife. Cillian *Mac Badh* is the young heir to House *Badh,* a cousin to the Queen of *I Idir,* and Declan's long-time nemesis.

Claiomh – (klave) – a sword

Crann Bethadh - (Krŏn Bĕ-hĕ) - "Tree of Life" - the royal seat of The Morrigan, Queen Maeve, built out of a giant, ancient oak; sometimes referred to as "The Raven's Nest"

Deaglan - (Dĕk-lĕn) - "full of goodness" - the Otherworld spelling of Declan

Deamhan – (june) - demon

Dearthair – (JAW-haw-ihr) - brother

Dubnos - (dŏv-nus) - the Fae version of the Underworld

Dun Siorai - (Dune Shear-ē) "Eternal Fortress:" House *Nuada's* ancestral home

Fanacht curtha – (fun-knot cur-ha) – "Stay put"

Fear go fear – (far ga far) "man to man"

Fealltoiri – (fel-tars) - traitors

Fear na bainnase – (far na ban-uhs) – bridegroom

Fiali – (faw-lee) – weeds

Formorians – (fó-mor-ee-ans) – an Otherworldly race of violent, monstrous giants who are always at battle with the Fae.

Gancanagh - (ghan-kan-ah) - "love talker" - Celtic incubus

Gleann Glas – (glôn glas) – translates to "Green Valley" in the Old Language and is the name of the Asgard city closest to *I Idir*. Its citizens call it *Groenn Dalr*, which eans the same thing in the *Nordboerne* tongue.

Ghrain – (gren) – sun

Go Leor – (guh loo) – "Enough!" as in a command.

I Idir - (ē ēdar) "In Between"- the Fae kingdom in the Otherworld ruled by The Morrigan, Queen Maeve, as its monarch.

Laghairts – (lie-erts) – lizards

La Mo Chroi – (low mo kree) – "The center of my heart;" term of endearment Declan uses to describe Rosie.

Leanai – (yan-lee) – children

Liathroid – (year-oid) – a ball

Lugh - (loo) – a god-like warrior king in ancient Otherworldly history; patron of the arts

Mac - (mc)- "son of"- a title given to an eldest son and heir of a Ruling House

Mathair - (mă-hair) - "mother" - when capitalized, used as a formal title

Mo aingeal alainn – (mo an-geh-l al-in) – "My beautiful angel;" a term of endearment Declan uses for Rosie

Mo ghra amhain – (ma graw ahon) – "my only Love;" a term of endearment Declan uses for Rosie

Mo Shiorghra - (mō hear-gra) - "My Eternal Love" - a fated mate in magical Fae tradition, wrought by a magical spell.

Mo una beag – (more oo-nah beg – "my little one" or "my little lamb" – term of endearment used for a small child and infant; Lady *Nuada* calls Dylan by this title.

Nazar – (nah-zer) – a gemstone amulet used to temper negative magical energy.

Neamh chinnteacht – (now shin-ta) – the Otherworld version of "limbo," residing between the sphere of the living and the Afterlife. Can sometimes refer to the absence of registered time; a space in which time stands still

Nia – (nee-AH) - nephew

Niall (of The Nine Hostages) – (nile) – an ancient legendary king of the Otherworld who secured peace by taking hostages from warring Houses. *Siobhan* Donnelly Fitzpatrick, Declan's mother, is descended from his line.

Nil – (nil) – translates to "do not;" used repeatedly (*"nil, nil, nil"*) it is warning to stop a certain activity as an adult might say to a misbehaving child.

Nuada - (new-a-da) - the name of an ancient Celtic king who possessed a silver arm: a major House from his bloodline within *I Idir's* Ruling Council.

Oidhre fealltach – (eye-da fel-ta) – a traitorous heir

Oisin – (uh-sheen) – a male name of Celtic origin that translates to "little deer"

Ruoshui – (rue-shay) – translates to "Weak River;" the name given to the river that seperates *Asgard* from the Jade Kingdom. The "Weak River" flows with water so lacking in gravity that even a feather won't float upon it, thus keeping the "unworthy" from entering the Jade Kingdom

Riail an Tiarna – (ree-al en cheer-na) – "The Lord's Rule;" an ancient law of *I Idir* allowing a House's reigning Lord to override the decisions made by the lower-ranking heads of households within his bloodline.

Scathach - (skah-hak) – an elite group of trained Fae female bodyguards hired by Ruling Class Houses to care for their infant heirs. These positions are usually passed down

Seamus – (shay-mus) – the Otherworld name for "James" or "Jamie;" the name the kitchen boy, *Buaf,* gives his dog.

Seanathair – (shin-a-ver) – grandfather; capitalized in formal terms

Seanmathair - (shin-ma-ver) – grandmother; capitalized in formal terms

Sidhe - (shē) - the term used for the Fae race in Celtic mythology, as well as the forts and mounds they once lived in during ancient times; the *Sidhe* possess higher levels of magical skill, and thus are considered part of Fae higher society

Siobhan - (shiv-awn) - a Celtic female name meaning "gracious gift"; the name of Declan's mother

Soith – (soyth) – a vulgar term meaning "bitch"

Tachran – (tock-run) – a toddler

Torthai cloiche – (tar- hee clay-her) – "stone fruit:" a pitted Otherworldly fruit similar to Mundane peaches or apricots

Tuatha de Danann - (two-ha de dan-an) "The Shining Ones"- a magical race of ancient, metaphysically gifted Fae with royal bloodlines. They compose *I Idir's* ruling council under the Monarchy of The Morrigan, Queen Maeve

Tuismitheoiri – (two-mush-hor-ee) - parents

Ulchabhan – (úl-who-on) – owl

Uncail – (un-kil) - uncle

GLOSSARY AND PRONUNCIATION OF NORSE

Alfheimr – (alf-hay-mer) – ancient home of the earliest *Ljosalfar* (Light Elves) and now considered a sacred place to the *Nordboerne* folk; knowledge of its location is limited to a small group of high ranking *Asgard* elites

Berkano (ᛒ) – (ber-ka-no) – a rune within the Elder Futhark alphabet usually meant to refer to a change or rebirth; relating to Otherworldly *Nordboerne* spirituality, this rune represented the Birch goddess and was often used as a symbol for fertility.

Dagaz ('ᛞ') – (DAY-gahs) the seventh rune of the Elder Futhark meaning a change or new enterprise.

Dokkalfar – (dol-kal-far) – translates to "Dark Elves" and refers to the *Nordboerne* Elven race of darker-skinned inhabitants who lived unground or in cave homes built within the sides of the earth in the upper most Northern areas of *Asgard*

Dokkr Bygo - (DAWK-kur Bjó) – translates to "Dark Settlement," the name given to an ancient community in the most northern territories of *Asgard*, near its border with the Jade Kingdom. It is home to a sect of *Dokkalfar* Elven people who still practice the forbidden *Jotun* dark sorcery.

Dyr – (dh-eer) – the *Nordboerne* word for "deer"

Elder Futhark Runes – (el-der foo-thark roonz)

Elder Futhark Runes – (el-der foo-thark roonz) – ancient *Nordboerne* runic alphabet used mainly by the *Dokkalfar* people living in the northern regions of *Asgard*. The alphabet consists of 24 runic symbols that have differing meanings based on their context.

Freyja – (FRAY-uf) – an ancient *Nordboerne* goddess of fertility, sex, and battle who is the twin sister of the god *Freyr*; the *Dokkalfar* worship her as the patron of *jotun* magical arts

Groenn Dalr – (groy-n dahl-r) – translates to "Green Valley;" the name of a larger-sized *Nordboerne* town in *Asgard* that sits near the border of *I Idir*. Called *Gleann Glas* by the Fae, the community is known for its exquisite metal work

Jord – (yord) – an ancient Mother goddess of the *Nordboerne* race; mate to *Odin* and mother of *Thor*

Jotun – (YOOT-uhn) – a type of dark sorcery believed to have been first established by a race of ancient people, the *Dokkalfar*, who worshipped the goddess *Freyja*; it uses "soul magic" as part of its ritual, and the practice of it has officially been outlawed in most Otherworldly kingdoms

Ljosalfar – (lyohs-ahl -farh) – fair-skinned Elven folk descended from an ancient race physically and magically similar to the *Sidhe* Fae; the *Ljosalfar* and the *Dokkalfar* make up the majority of the citizenship of *Asgard*, though over many centuries, a small portion of the *Ljosalfar* have

taken up residence and built family units in *I Idir* among
the Fae

Mannaz (ᛗ) – (MAN-naz) – the *Elder Futhark* rune for
man, but can also mean "enemy" depending on the
context in which it is inscribed

Margyr – (mar-gheer) – a Norse mermaid or sea spirit

Nordboerne – (NOR-bo-ren) – translates to "people of the
North," and refers to all the races, Elven and other, who
can trace their bloodlines to the ancient kingdom of
Asgard

Orskots-Helgr – (OR-skots hel-gruh) – translates to "home
away from home;" the ironic name for the run-down
Dokkalfar inn where Rosie and Declan spend the night on
their way to *Dokkr Bygo*

Pethro (ᛈ) – (PET-hro) – an *Elder Futhark* rune associated
with mystery, hidden things, and secrets

Sal Bjofr – (sahl byor) – translates to "Soul Thief," and
refers to Master Brendan, who used powerful, dark *jotun*
magic requiring the energy essence of a recently deceased
soul for his castings, and who may have passed on his
knowledge to others

Seior – (SAY-der) – the style of magic practiced by all
types of *Nordboerne* people; similar to *Sidhe* personal
magic but associated with a larger degree of ritual spell
casting and differs spiritually from the darker magic of
Jotun

Valkyries – (VAL-kuh-rees) – *Nordboerne* warrior women

TOOTHPICKS 1

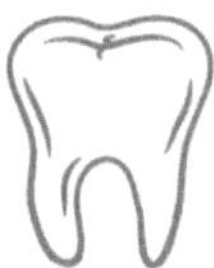

Half-Hearted Forgiveness

MY FEET, arms and hands continue to work as they always have, a reality my short-circuited and thoroughly confused brain can't even begin to comprehend. How can I still hear Dylan wailing in the background or see the absolute horror in *Buaf's* little boy eyes? Why is it even possible, in the midst of this terrifying situation, that I am able to note that my stomach is making embarrassing rumbling noises, or that the wire boning in my corset is knife-poking me in the ribs? Considering the extent of the living nightmare in which I now find myself, all of these physical sidebars should...to my mind...cease to matter.

I get that it's not uncommon for people to use the term "living a nightmare" to describe the awful, gut-wrenching experiences in their life. Those awful, but altogether unavoidable, situations that lead to anxiety and despair. Hell, I'll admit that even I've coined that same dramatic phrase on multiple occasions; for example, those months when my mom was dying of a mysterious Fae blood disease, or while watching my dad slowly lose everything he was to the plague of Alzheimer's. And I'd be remiss to not mention those terrifying six weeks when my beloved Tax Man was taken prisoner by the North Koreans, me not knowing if I'd ever see him again.

While all of those previous life experiences were gut-punching miserable, I, myself, was not the center character in them. Those terrible things were actually happening to someone else, and my pain was just the unfortunate reaction to witnessing it. What's going on right now, me being falsely accused of a heinous crime while at the same time having the one person in my life that I trusted most turn his back on me, is the worst "nightmare" in the entire scope of my 34 years of existence. I could pinch myself black and blue in an attempt to "wake up" from this horrible dream, but the outcome would still be the same.

As soon as we walk out the door of our family suite at *Dun Siorai*, I shake the Black Knight's hand off my elbow. "You don't have to manhandle me, Lord Knight. I'm obviously not going to run away," I snipe.

"I apologize if you feel I'm 'manhandling' you, Lady *Mac Nuada.* That is surely not my intention. However, if you wish for me to move us magically to our final destination, then we will have to be physically touching." The Black Knight puts a hand out for me to take. I ignore it. "The alternative, Lady Rosalinda," he explains, "is for us to do the 'walk of shame' past the gawking staff and out through the front gates to the waiting carriage. I would think you'd prefer to forgo that spectacle given the propensity for communal gossip by the Fae. Also keep in mind that as a personal favor to you, I am breaking all kinds of *I Idir* protocol by offering to move us magically."

He's correct on that point. I'd rather not be made any more humiliated than I already am. I reluctantly take the Knight's hand and feel the current of magical energy layered over it. Unlike in the Mundane world, where the physics of the sun's magnetic field and gravitational pull prevents it, most *Sidhe* Fae can jump by will from place to place anywhere within the Otherworld. The fact that they don't, choosing old-fashioned horseback, carriages and carts in lieu of magical skill, has more to do with protocol, law, and tradition rather than metaphysical limitations. The idea of just "popping into places" is disdainful to the average Fae, mainly those who don't possess this higher level of ability, and considered extremely rude, as well as a serious breach of privacy. However, in this particular case, I'm glad his Lordship is overlooking that culturally dictated tenet.

Before I blink twice, I find myself standing in a large, rather opulent suite. It's absolutely not what I expected when I was told I was being taken "into custody." "Where in the hell are we?" I ask, no longer caring about tiptoeing around Ted Beckett's titles. Any of them.

"One of the guest suites at *Crann Bethadh*," he says.

I look at him as if he's lost his mind. "This is where you usually hold your murder suspects?"

"No. Not usually," he admits, the corner of his mouth turning up. "We have holding cells in the lower level, but you are being afforded the respect and dignity your title affords, Lady *Mac Nuada.* Now, if you'll excuse me, I need to take care of urgent business. I'll return later this evening and you and I will talk. In the meantime, I've arranged for Afternoon Tea, as you didn't have time to enjoy the one at *Dun Siorai.* Please relax and make yourself comfortable."

"Are you freakin' kidding me? You expect me to 'relax' and drink tea? What a ridiculous notion! I've just been falsely accused of murder!" I argue.

"Yes. I suppose that's a lot to ask," he says before completely disappearing without so much as a polite good-bye.

* * *

I spend the first few hours of my imprisonment alternately sniffling and pacing, but mostly dropping f-bombs and vile curses upon everyone involved in my false arrest. Being who I am, I have jiggled and tugged at the main door handle and every one of the several window latches in the suite. They are, of course, all solidly locked, a major disappointment even though I'm not sure how I would have escaped the twelve-foot drop of tree branches that make up the structure of the Royal Seat. Wisps of male conversation outside the heavy door of my luxurious prison also make it very clear that if, by some miracle, I could escape all the locks, I wouldn't get very far before being caught.

I try reaching out to my husband via our telepathic bond lines, but my pleas bounce around in a silent void. Each time I get no response is a sharp dagger to my already aching heart, so after a handful of attempts, I surrender to the silence rather than facing the pain his avoidance causes me. Desperate as I am, I even try reaching out to Herself, but receive no assistance from that source either. It's gut-wrenching to know that I'm completely and utterly alone in my troubles.

Daylight from the tall arched windows turns to the rosy red of sunset and makes the golden accents in the room's decor appear as if they're on fire. I poke at the now-cold remnants of the light meal that was left for me, but all the food tastes like sand in my mouth so I push it away. With nothing else to fill my time, I take a superficial tour of the different rooms that make up my prison; besides the large parlor and dining room, the suite has one larger bedroom and a smaller one, obviously meant for staff, each with an accompanying bath area. The furnishings are top-rate, examples of the exquisite craftsmanship that one would expect from royal appointments. None of it means anything to me.

I curl up in the corner of a tapestry covered settee, my breasts aching and full without my baby to nurse. There should be an extra bottle of breast milk from the supply I left with *Birgit* this morning, but beyond that, I am at a loss as to how they will feed Dylan. Perhaps they will hire a wet nurse, a total stranger, to feed my child. It's a travesty I need to address with the Black Knight as soon as he returns. A father himself, I hold a seed of hope that he will allow me to at least nurse my baby a few times a day. But what happens after that? The possibility that my son might grow up without his mother destroys any shred of strength I've been trying to build. Overwhelmed, I put my face into my arms and weep.

It is the sounds of loud discussion outside my door that puts an end to my private pity party. I pick my head up and wipe my face as the door opens to a woman wearing the Raven colors. She steps inside the suite pushing a service cart in front of her. "Dinner time, ma' Lady," she says, rolling the meal to the dining table while noting the uneaten food from earlier. "Was there something amiss with your Afternoon Tea, Lady *Mac Nuada?* Ya' hardly touched a bite."

"I'm not very hungry. You can just take it all with you when you leave." I reply, putting my head back down and ignoring the intrusion. I'm usually not this rude with people but I can't seem to make myself care. I don't want their food. I don't want their fancy quarters. And I sure as hell don't want anyone's false pity.

"'Tis yar' favorite, Love," says a familiar voice. "Salmon with dill and those wee *pratai* (potatoes) ya' love so much."

I leap from the sofa and sprint to my husband, the bond between us too strong to ignore. Declan opens his arms and I fall desperately into them. Home in his familiar embrace, it still takes only twenty seconds for me to recall his earlier actions at *Dun Siorai.* I stiffen, give him a good, hard push, and step away. I don't need to look down to know that there's a big leaky milk stain on the front of my dress. "How dare you show up here and act as if you didn't shatter my heart into a million pieces. I don't want you here, Declan Fitzpatrick! Go back to that psycho hell you call home and leave me alone. And, if you ever truly held any feelings of affection toward me, you'll send our son to me. It's beyond cruel keeping me from my baby. Cruelty towards Dylan as well as towards me." I pause, then add with the venom I can't hide at the moment, "But that seems to be a family trait among the *Nuada* men, isn't it… ripping infants from their grieving mother's arms."

I can tell my well-aimed verbal strike hits its mark. For the merest of seconds, my fated mate pales and his carefully neutral façade waivers. Then, just as quickly, the cool and completely emotionless Tax Man I recall from our first meeting returns "Ya'll have Dylan back with ya' in a few minutes," he says with a calm I can't begin to understand. "Before these rooms get substantially mar' crowded, I've come ta' explain some things ta' ya', Sweet Rosie Lass."

I turn violently toward him. "Don't you ever call me that again! I'm not your 'sweet lass.' I'm not anything to you." My eyes get teary around the edges, but I'll be damned if I let him see me cry. "I will never, ever, forget how you turned your back on me, Declan Phineas Fitzpatrick. Not ever."

At least now the Tax Man has the courtesy to look very uncomfortable. "Please don' say 'never,' Love. Far' us that's…well…forever. I shudder ta' think that ya'll be angry with me all through eternity, though I am sure ya' believe I deserve such a thing. If there had been any other way, we would have chosen it, but…"

"Wait. We?" I ask. "Who is 'we'?" My over-worked brain starts to put the pieces together. "Are you trying to tell me that my being humiliated…broken-hearted to my very soul and arrested like a common criminal…is one of the damn Black Knight's espionage plans?"

It's obvious the Tax Man is not playing Master Spy anymore. Pure guilt is written in the way he stuffs his hands in his pockets and averts his gaze. I'd like to think my husband and mate is astute enough to know when he's walking a fine line between duty to the kingdom of *I Idir* and a mate's loyalty to his *Mo Shiorghra*. "This treachery goes deep, ma' Lo…Rosie." He catches himself and uses my name instead of his affectionate moniker, knowing I'm not in the mood for his sweetness and romance. What I desire from him…no…not desire…what I absolutely need right this moment is complete honesty. "Marcy Kilcrabtree's murder is only the tip of something, that left to itself, could topple the entire kingdom and the fragile peace we currently share with our neighbors, while openin' the Veil to an intrusion by the vera' people in the Mundane world we've been fightin' to keep out."

I consider whether his Junior Lordship isn't being a bit melodramatic to counter my annoyance with him, but I'm not getting that vibe. Here in this room together, it's hard not to have that deep connection between us, mentally and physically. "So, I'm here at *Crann Bethadh*, with everyone thinking I'm some kind of crazy murderer, as part of a ridiculous plot to save *I Idir*?" I question, letting the words drip with sarcasm.

Declan runs his hand through his hair, the serious "guilt-tell" he never manages to hide from me. "Aye," he says. "We need for people to think that the Black Knight is no longer looking into the woman's death."

I can tell he's not giving me the whole truth. "And? I

know there's more to this story, Tax Man. What aren't you saying?"

He twists his mouth into a tight grimace. "This is a cesspool that's been growin' far' some time now, Rosie, and I am ashamed ta' say that there are those within ma' own House involved. Because of this, for yar' and Dylan's complete safety, I need ya' both away from *Dun Siorai*. *Buaf* as well. I ken' no longer keep ya' all safe there. The security here within the Raven's Nest is impenetrable. You are safer here than anywhere else I can think of."

"Safe from who?" I shout, louder than what's considered polite within the walls of the Royal Seat.

My *Mo Shiorghra* returns my question with a look that breaks my heart. He doesn't need to tell me. I know who he means. "Oh hell, Declan, not this again! From the moment we met I've needed to constantly look over my shoulder for someone from House *Nuada* out to get me. Now you drag our son into all your crazy nonsense! Are we always going to have to live this way? In a constant state of anxiety and fear brought on by your totally dysfunctional family?"

I see his strong façade waiver with each word that leaves my mouth. I'm hurting him. Hurting the soul that makes him who he is. And even though he put me through what he did today, I don't feel good about sticking my sharpened words into him. In an instant, I have a flashback of our first few days together, when Declan was my "security detail" over the trouble with the Chechens. I go back to that very moment he picked up my hand and asked if I really wanted him to find my cut fingers in a box. His face that day was a map of every fear he held. It was days before I knew we were fated mates, but his far-reaching concern for my well-being was hard to miss, even when we were nearly strangers. I see that same expression on him now, only ten times more intense. I try to break the hold that memory has on me with another question. "How long do I have to stay in this frickin' chi-chi, la-de-da, Raven prison?'

My mention of The Morrigan in a less than flattering tone causes my anguished Eternal Mate to slip away before my eyes, replaced with a cranky, overly stubborn husband who doesn't much care for my lack of respect regarding his worries for our safety or the gifted hospitality that The Throne of *I Idir* is offering us. "Ma' Lady, ma' son, his *scathach*, and our new Page, along with his *madra* (dog), will be the grateful and polite guests of Her Majesty until I determine that 'tis safe far' ya' ta' return ta' either *Dun Siorai* or Salem. At this moment, I ken' no give ya' an exact date on when that might be. I expect you to act fully in the context of yar' title, Lady *Mac Nuada*, without bringin' more heartache ta' yar' Lord and husband.

I've never been good at being "called-out," and the modern, Mundane part of womanhood in me rises up against his patriarchy. "And if I decide I don't want to be trapped here? Since I'm truly not under actual arrest for Marcy's murder, then there's nothing in *I Idir* law keeping me here…your Lordship," I argue, my tone not disguising my disdain over the title. Truthfully, if there was even the slightest chance that Dylan might be in any kind of danger, we both know I'd agree to live in a fortified 4x6 box if it meant keeping him safe, but I'm still smarting from the heartache Declan put me through these past few hours to let him off the hook that easily.

Evidently the Tax Man knows me well enough to understand that I would never risk our son's safety and that I'm just throwing my crabby shit at him. He sighs and raises that one damn eyebrow. "I wholly trust that ma' beloved One and Only will do what is best far' the safety of our family," he answers. "I know ya' will not like hearin this, Rosalinda, but I will do whatever I must to protect the treasures of ma' life. The Universe has shown me how quickly everythin' I hold dear ken' be lost. I've become the Universe's star pupil in the months since you've become part of ma' life. After nearly losin' ya' twice, I will take no chance with yar' safety ever again. I understand yar' anger with me, but it had ta' seem believable that I stood with ma' House over ma' personal feelins' for ma' mate. I want ya' ta' understand that I would never take light the possibility of hurting you, but I make no apologies far' doin' what I felt most necessary. The look on yar' face as ya' were taken out of our home will haunt me for Eternity. But faced with the same situation, I wad' do it all over again to keep you and Dylan secure. I hope in time you will come to accept that and forgive me."

I work at coming up with a snarky retort but I never get the chance. There is noise and shuffling at the door again. "That would be the rest of yar' entourage," Declan says. The door opens and in struts *Buaf* with *Seamus* in tow, followed by *Birgit* with Dylan in her arms. The Black Knight takes up the rear, and addresses my husband. "Is everything…settled in here, Fitz?"

I assume he means me and my reaction at being made

a patsy in his dumb-ass investigation so I interrupt before the Tax Man can answer. "If you're asking if my mate has informed me of your decision to use my poor, clueless self in your latest under-cover, hair-brained quest, rest assured I've been...briefed," I say, staring at him with unveiled hostility.

The Queen's Hand of Justice stares unblinking right back at me, though I can see the tiniest beginning of a smirk at the far-left corner of his mouth. Despite his burning devotion to the people of *I Idir* and his devastatingly handsome good looks, I'm pretty sure I don't care much for this man. "I'm sure you have a plethora of questions, Lady *Mac Nuada*," he comments, not breaking his stare.

I end up being the one looking away first. "As a matter of fact, I do, Lord Knight."

"And I plan on fully answering each and every one of them, dear Lady. Unfortunately, it's been a long day for everyone involved, and I still have an audience with Her Majesty. I'll let everyone here settle in. I will return early in the morning. We'll talk then. If you are in need of anything, just ask the house. It's been instructed to answer your demands." Then with a brief nod of his head, he exits the same door he came in.

It takes an additional three hours to get everyone fed, bathed, and settled in for the night. Simple logistics suggests that *Birgit* and the two children should take the larger of the two rooms, and Declan and I the smaller staff room with the twin beds, as the baby's paraphernalia takes up a lot of space. But there's no way my husband's 6'4" frame is going to reasonably fit on that small cot, plus both *Birgit* and *Buaf* are mortified at the suggestion, so deeply rooted in Otherworld protocol as they are. "We'll be fine here, ma' Lady. It will be cozy and warm," the nanny insists.

Looking huggable in his cotton nightshirt, the little terrier curled up at his feet, *Buaf* seconds the *scathach's* comments. "Aye, Lady Rosie. I ken' no believe someone the likes of me is spendin' the night in the Raven's Nest. Cook's eyes wad' pop out of her skull ta' see me and *Seamus* sittin' here like we was fine, gentry folk. 'Tis also vera' good that me and ma' *madra* (dog) are here in the same room as the wee Lordy Dylan. We ken' protect him from any harm that might come our way," the child explains, holding up a toy wooden sword, the pommel and the grip painted in the colors of House *Nuada.*

I try not to smile at the kid's bravado. "And what a gallant sword that be, Master Page. How, may I ask, did you find yourself in possession of such a wondrous thing?" I ask, guessing it was a gift from my husband.

Buaf clutches the sword to his chest. "This be a vera' special sword, Ma' Lady. It came from the Black Knight himself. 'Tis a magical sword to keep even bad dreams away. The Queen's Hand told me I must keep it near me so I ken' protect ma' Lord and Lady, and the wee Dylan. I will sleep with it right here under ma' pillow."

My shock at the Black Knight's show of kindness must register on my face, because *Birgit* turns to me to explain. "When ya' were arrested, Lady *Mac,* the boy could not be consoled. We caught him tryin' ta' climb out the third story window in an attempt ta' rescue ya'. Almost broke his neck doin' so. When the Black Knight returned to *Dun Siorai* after yar' arrest, he spoke ta' the lad and gave him that sword. Calmed him right down, it did. I know the Lord Knight has a fierce reputation, rightly earned, but the man does have an uncanny way with *leanai* (children)."

The nanny's story grants the Black Knight a few brownie points in my eyes. But just a few. I still don't like him much, and I sure as hell don't trust him. I do, however, smile at the picture of the formidable Black Knight giving a kid a "magic" toy as I head to my own room. I'm thoroughly exhausted, both mentally and physically and in no mood for yet another go-around with my husband, so when I see him curled up on a ridiculously small chaise lounge, his feet hanging off one end and his head over the other, I lose any attempt at patience. "Oh hell, Declan, you look ridiculous! Just sleep in the damn bed already. I'm tired, achy, and beyond crabby, so I'm not up for yet another battle.

"Yar' still angry with me, Lass. I ken feel it down ta' ma' vera bones. Ma' par'self ken' no just lie next ta' ya' pretendin' that all is good between us," he says.

I still haven't begun to work through my hurt and resentment over his part in this stupid spy game, and if he's looking for blanket forgiveness, I'm not ready to give it. "Suit yourself, Tax Man. If you want to offer up penance, then I'm not going to stop you. But you'll only end up with a sleepless night and a crick in your neck. And it will be all for naught. I'll still feel the same way about everything in the morning. Guaranteed."

I take off my clothes, the beautiful dress I put on this morning, now a limp, crumpled mess, and slide into a nightgown that miraculously appears out of nowhere. I crawl in between the linens and close my eyes. After a few moments, I feel the Tax Man take his spot on the other side of the large bed, and I try to relax, hoping against hope that we all can just get some rest and pick through all this shit tomorrow when we're fresher of mind and body.

It doesn't happen. I toss and the Tax Man turns, neither of us able to relax enough to fall into the deep REM sleep we both desperately need. I know what the problem is; the new Eternal bond between us is just too heavy and strong to ignore. The fresh ink on my shoulder blade vibrates with magical energy.

"'Tis no use, Lass," my *Mo Shiorghra* whispers in the dark. "I ken' no ignore the connection between us. The bond is stronger than logic. I vera' well understand that I need ta' respect yar' feelins' and give ya' the space ya' desire, but the burnin' need ta' touch ya' is too great ta' ignore. Would ya' consider consentin' ta' at least holdin' hands? Maybe it will help us both relax."

In the same sleep-deprived position, I reach out and take the familiar hand that finds its way across the great mattress divide and entwine my fingers through his. After that one touch, there's really no turning back. We take down the walls of anger and sorrow and let the magic have its way. Though our coupling is fierce, intense, and lacking in any semblance of forgiveness, at least on my part, it temporarily blocks the pain of the day. As I lay on my back, panting, letting my rapid pulse slowly turn to normal, an unwanted thought comes to me explaining that this might be exactly how my in-laws still managed to create six children together despite the deep animosity that lives and breathes between them. It's a horrible notion and I shudder at the thought of this being the future between my Tax Man and me, a magically forced physical connection that has no foundation in the heart or soul. I vow to try to figure out how to get past this betrayal by my One and Only, and in the back of my head, I hear what sounds like the tinkling of tiny bells.

TOOTHPICKS 2

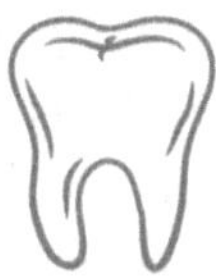

A Cup of Joe Before They Go

LOST SOMEWHERE in the realm of a strange, wispy dream, I feel a very real hand on my shoulder shaking me awake. "Rosie…Love…I need far' ya' ta' wake up," a male brogue whispers in my ear.

Still foggy, I open one slitty eye and look up at my husband. "What?"

"I'm sorry, Lass. I know it's early, but ya' need to rise and shine. The Black Knight is here and he needs to meet with us before his return ta' the Mundane world. Robyn is with him."

I open both eyes and peer around the inky room. "What time is it? It's still dark in here."

"Nearly 5:30. The *ghrain* (sun) hasn't yet risen," he explains.

"Feckin' hell, Declan! Normal people don't show up in other people's homes before the crack of dawn. What is wrong with that man? Doesn't he ever sleep?" I argue.

"I donna' think he needs as much sleep as most people," my husband explains, as if that somehow excuses the Knight's overtly rude behavior. "I know ya' are not much of a mornin' person, Rosie, but this is important and Beck does have a multitude of other responsibilities. We always try ta' cut him some slack." He doesn't wait for me to reply and adds, "I'll tell them ya'll be joinin' us shortly. As a full member of the team, I want ya' ta' hear everything that's bein' said."

He leaves the room and I grumble to myself as I try to find my discarded nightgown, lost somewhere last night in the tangle of the sheets. "Full member of the team, my ass. You all just used me as your pretend murder suspect and didn't even clue me into what was going on." I contemplate just throwing on a robe and wandering out there, but know without doubt that my showing up undressed like that would mortify my protocol-adhering husband. Instead, I shower and dress in record time and join the ensemble in the living room with my still wet hair pulled into a tight bun at the back of my head.

All three men stand when I enter the room. Despite it being such an ungodly hour, they are all impeccably dressed; Beckett and the Doc in their respective Mundane work apparel, and my husband in his usual GQ-style Otherworldly garb. I'm glad I decided against showing up in my robe. "I offer apologies over rousing you this early, Lady *Mac Nuada*, but it can't be helped," the Black Knight says. "I have a full day of Essex County business, and the Doc here has early rounds in Swampscott. I felt it was imperative for you to be on the same page as the rest of the team."

"That would be lovely…for a change," I quip.

Declan pours a cup of Mundane coffee and hands it to me, his way of letting me know I need to rein in my sarcasm, but the Black Knight just laughs. "Touché, Lady *Mac*."

"Call me 'Rosie,' gentlemen. I don't need to be coddled like a child or handled with protocol covered kid-gloves. I realize you both have other pressing matters, so why don't we just get down to the reasons you're here this early," I suggest.

Robyn Brannigan opens the file folder sitting on his lap and hands a stack of papers to Declan, who sits next to me so that we both can peruse the pages at the same time. I grimace at the autopsy photos of Marcy Kilcrabtree. I'm not gonna lie. I hated the woman's guts, but it's still hard to look upon the senseless violence of a life taken. My eyes immediately go to the ring of marks around her slender pale neck as the doctor explains the photos. "The marks on the victim's neck are from manual strangulation. The pattern is indicative of a larger finger spread, most probably belonging to a male of some height and considerable strength. Those marks, along with the petechiae in and around the eyes and the swollen tongue leads me to believe the victim was strangled to the point of unconsciousness before being thrown off the cliff. I say 'thrown' rather than 'pushed' because of the footprint evidence found at the crime scene. There are two sets of distinctive foot prints a few feet away from the edge where we believe a struggle took place, but only one larger pair leading to the cliff's rim, thus giving evidence that the victim was carried by the perp to the edge and thrown down the side, where at some point her neck was broken. The contusions to the body and the head show that she probably hit several rocky outcrops on her way down, one of which was the killing blow that snapped her neck before she hit the ground below."

Between the coffee on my empty stomach and the graphic nature of the discussion, bile churns in my gut like laundry in a washing machine. I grab a dry scone from the plate on the table and force it into my mouth to control my rising acid reflux as Robyn continues. "The tox screen showed no trace of alcohol or drugs, except for a high amount of Vitamin B9, Choline and Inositol, commonplace to prenatal vitamins."

I can't help but gasp. The Doc adds, "Yes. The victim was twelve weeks pregnant with a perfectly normal male fetus. We are in the process of running DNA tests in hopes of getting a lead on the child's father. I expect the results later today. Running Fae DNA requires a higher level of testing, and quite a bit of secrecy, but nonetheless, we should have some answers soon if there is a match to anyone in the system."

"You have a database of Fae DNA?" I ask, shocked at the concept.

"Not a large one," Robyn explains. "But we have data on everyone who works within our intelligence network; members of the inner Royal Circle, as well as all the staff members here at *Crann Bethadh*. Since Otherworldly culture is so family structured, it gives us a decent sampling across a large group of genetics, as many Fae are interrelated within a set of specific Houses and families." The Doc addresses my husband. "As you asked, Fitz, I'm also running the sample Beck took from the boy yesterday. It should be ready by this afternoon as well."

I freeze. Once again, this is a fact I knew nothing about. If the Tax Man has requested a DNA profile on *Buaf,* I am guessing he has strong suspicions regarding the child's parentage and a high level of trust in his compadres. The real question is…are we ready for the impact those results will have? I nervously clear my throat. "So, where do we go from here?"

"As you've probably guessed, we're almost one hundred percent sure the perp is a male of Fae origins, based on the level of strength needed to throw the victim over the edge. Unconscious bodies are dead weight and cumbersome to throw," the Black Knight explains. "The DNA results will hopefully give us some information regarding the father of the baby the victim was carrying. We know the victim was seeing at least two men in an intimate fashion. You can help this investigation, Rosie, by explaining to me how you came to be in possession of that second earring. We know that the earring was not, as the witness claimed, ripped from the victim's ear. There is no evidence of ripping and tearing of the ear's cartilage, which would be present if it was torn from her ear as the witness describes."

I look at my husband. We both understand who I am implicating if I tell them everything I know. "Go ahead, Lass. Tell Beck what you told me about findin' that damn earring. Don't leave anything out," the Tax Man advises.

"Everything?" I ask. "Even about the boots?"

"Aye," he says, his face expressionless. "Even yar' thoughts about the boots."

And so I relate the events of that horrible day, looking above their heads and not at the faces of the Black Knight and Doc Brannigan as I tell my story; of how I ended up in that old dungeon and trapped in that decrepit trunk; of the hard-to-miss sounds of sexual activity between a male and female; my clear description of the boots of the male partner I viewed through the open space between the slats; the manner in which I found the single emerald earring in the hallway of the east wing; and lastly, how I recognized the same boots I saw in the dungeon on the feet of my husband's father.

Declan shows zero emotion as I go through my narrative, though personally, I am silently embarrassed and sad for him. Hearing such intimate details about your own father, details that go against everything fated mates are supposed to represent, would be difficult for most people. In my Tax Man's case, as a true and faithful believer in the Old Ways, his *athair's* immoral behavior toward the mate the Universe had specifically chosen for him can only be woefully repugnant to his only son and heir.

The Black Knight and Doc Robyn listen without comment, their faces as blank as my husband's. When I come to the end of my testimony, "Beck" thanks me for my complete honesty and asks again if I'm one hundred percent sure that the boots I saw on the male in the dungeon were the same one's I saw Lord *Nuada* wearing the following evening. I reiterate that the boots are hard to miss with their distinct silver toes and heels, and thus I am soundly sure.

"It goes without saying that all the information we've discussed here this morning stays between the four of us," the Lord Knight says. "For us to continue to investigate without hindrance, the general population of *I Idir* needs to continue to believe that Lady *Mac Nuada* is the perpetrator of Marcy Kilcrabtree's murder." He turns his piercing blue peepers on me. "I sympathize that this is enormously embarrassing for you, Rosie, and appreciate your loyalty to Her Majesty. Please understand that once we round up all the guilty parties, your help in solving these crimes will become public knowledge and your assistance will be generously rewarded."

"Truthfully, Lord Knight...I don't need any 'rewards.' I would just like for this all to be over so that my family and I can return to our lives in Salem. I have my own responsibilities in the Mundane world, just as you and Doc Brannigan have yours. Surely you can understand that?"

"I most certainly do, Dr. Parker," Beck says, throwing me a bone by using my professional title. "And as soon as it is safe for you all to return to your other life, you'll be the first person I tell. Until then, Her Majesty has only your best interests at heart. In the meantime, please know that your willingness to play your part in all this is noted and greatly appreciated." The Knight addresses my husband, apparently satisfied that his hand-holding of me is over. "I assume you'll continue with your own investigation, Fitz. Your access to private House records is certainly a bonus."

"Aye," says my husband. "There'll no doubt be a mountain of documents to go through, but if there be somethin' of interest there, I'll find it."

"Excellent," the Black Knight says as he rises to leave. "Perhaps your Lady Wife could give you a hand with your search, Fitz." It's a comment I take to mean that the Queen's Hand of Justice would like to see me kept busy and out of his hair. I drop an eye roll that's met with an equally obvious smirk. How the Lady Dear Heart puts up with this annoying man day in and day out is a mystery to me.

As if to answer my silent query, Beck adds. "I have a message to relay from my own mate, Lady Rosie." I feel the heat rise in my cheeks. I thought I was holding a pretty strong mental shield, but perhaps not. I'm a little embarrassed over the possibility that he might have picked up that last thought. Without missing a beat, he looks me straight in the eye and says, "She's asked me to let you know that she would visit you if she could, but that her nasty ogre of a husband has 'suggested' that she wait a few days until the interest in Marcy Kilcrabtree's murder dies down and less people have their eyes on *Crann Bethadh*. Until then, she hopes that you are 'hanging in there' and that you should not hesitate to ask the House for anything you need to make your 'visit' more palatable."

"Please give the Lady Dear Heart my most gracious thanks. I appreciate her kind thoughts and look forward to sharing tea with her soon," I say, looking away first and admitting defeat in the stare game.

"I will certainly convey to her your…'thoughts,' Rosie," he replies, the corner of that damned lip of his turning up. "Expect to see both myself and the Doc here later this evening. Most likely sometime after the evening meal, as I don't dare miss yet another dinner with my family. Until then, I hope the day produces the information we need toward gaining some headway in this heinous case."

TOOTHPICKS 3

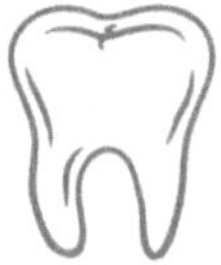

Bad News Travels Fast

THE FIVE OF us spend the rest of the day trying to normalize an abnormal situation. Despite the new surroundings and the fact that our current lodgings are nothing more than an exquisitely decorated prison, our little "family" group moves through the day as if Marcy Kilcrabtree had not been strangled and thrown to her dramatic death just the day before. After an unusually substantial breakfast and his one-on-one time with our son, Declan goes off to relieve his cousin, Duncan, who has been impersonating Lord *Mac Nuada* at *Dun Siorai* under the mantle of heavy glamour magic. He promises to return sometime in the afternoon with the records and documents he wants me to help him go through. Unfortunately, he doesn't go into a lot of detail over what it is we are actually looking for within those old records.

I spend some of the morning with Dylan before *Birgit* settles him down for his early nap, then focus my attention on working with *Buaf* on his studies. The traumatized kid is more than a little distracted and his obvious high level of anxiety transfers to the dog, who paces the rooms like a caged tiger, whining and barking at ever imaginary foe. To drive the child's attention back to his lessons, I promise that if he can conquer the simple addition and subtraction problems I've assigned for today, I will help him create a leather sheath for the gifted wooden sword so that he can wear his newest prize on his belt. In high anticipation of the project, the boy attacks his worksheet with a renewed sense of gusto, finishing all of the number problems well before noon.

Thus, we spend the rest of the day designing the "perfect" sheath for the ruler-sized, toy weapon using a good length of softened leather provided by the magical wards of *Crann Bethadh*. The boy and the dog sit at my feet in rapt attention as I sew the two cut pieces together while my Dylan appears to monitor us from his cradle. This quiet interlude is peaceful and soothing and in direct contrast to the hellish past twenty-four hours. The day flows so easily that I am surprised to find it is nearly tea time when I finally finish the project. Thrilled with his new sheath, *Buaf* and *Seamus* retire to their shared room to play dragons and knights, followed by *Birgit* who takes Dylan for a much-needed diaper change before our early evening meal. I look at the ornate raven clock on the mantle and mentally call out to my husband. *"Any chance you can make it home for tea?"*

A few minutes later, I receive a distracted reply. *"Give me about another twenty minutes or so, Love, and then I ken' join ya' all. 'Tis a lot to go through here."*

Knowing my husband's sense of time is never set in reality when he's in the middle of something important, I consider holding off asking the House for afternoon tea service so things are fresher when we actually all sit down. I'm startled by heavy banging on the suite's door, not expecting that anyone would be allowed to see the "prisoner." "Yes?" I ask through the locked door. There is the rattling of keys and the door swings open and an armed guard wearing the royal colors steps inside. "Apologies far' the disruption, Lady *Mac Nuada*. There is a gentleman har' that insists he must speak to ya' and ya' alone. He claims that he comes on urgent business. As the Black Knight did not notify us ta' expect any visitors, we ken' no allow him inside."

"Who is it?" I ask, as puzzled as the guard.

"It's just me, Lady Rosie," a voice declares from behind the guard's large body. "Rory Dell." He maneuvers around one side of the burly Fae and holds up a peach-colored envelope that I instantly recognize. "I have a message from your sister, Claire. She says it's urgent."

My heart drops down to my toes. My sister is the most pragmatic person I know, and not one for "Chicken Little" reactions to emergency situations. If she says her words are urgent, then they must be. I reach for the envelope but Rory Dell pulls it away. "Mistress Claire says I must wait for an answer. May I please come inside, Lady Rosie? I do not believe you would want any more of your personal business spread throughout *I Idir*."

My husband's assistant is right. More muck about our family circulating the halls of the Ruling Council is the last thing Declan or I want. Plus, only a handful of people know about my Mundane sister in Swampscott, Massachusetts. For the safety of her and her family, I'd like to keep it that way. I speak directly to the guard. "This is my husband's trusted assistant. Lord *Mac Nuada* should be returning to *Crann Bethadh* any minute now. I have no doubts he'd be unhappy to find that his man was turned away."

"I'm sorry, ma' Lady. We have explicit orders not to let anyone in or out," the guard answers.

"I understand. You do have your orders. Perhaps I can call for the *Banphrionsa's* assistance," I say, hating myself for trading in on my relationship with the Lady Dear Heart. However, desperate times require desperate measures. If my sister needs me, I have to know why.

The guard looks uncomfortable, and I can physically see him weighing his options as he shifts from one foot to another. If his expression is any indication, neither he nor his partner want the Princess of *I Idir* involved in the discussion. "You say this man is Lord *Mac Nuada's* associate?" the man asks.

"Oh, yes. He is my husband's Mundane business partner. My Lord trusts him without pause," I answer, striking a wide-eyed picture of innocence. "I'm sure his Lordship wouldn't want family business discussed in the hall."

"I suppose it would be within reason to allow this man entry. For a brief period," the guard concedes as he allows Rory Dell passage into the suite.

"Thank you, kind Sir. I appreciate your wise decision," I say as I literally close the door in his face after Rory steps through. I don't offer him any of the expected Fae hospitality, solely focused on what might be in that letter from Claire. "How long ago did my sister give this to you?" I question, extending my hand to take possession of the envelope that Dell doesn't offer.

The young man doesn't answer my query, his attention riveted to his surroundings. "This is quite the place" he comments. "I've never been inside the private living quarters of *Crann Bethadh* before. Not what I would have guessed a prison to look like. Have you gotten a chance to see Herself?" he asks.

His use of "Herself" to describe the Queen strikes me as odd. It's a moniker used privately by members of The Morrigan's inner circle, which, most definitely, does not include a half-*Sidhe* accountant like Rory Dell. "No. I'm sure the Queen of *I Idir* doesn't have my lowly welfare on her busy mind. Don't think me rude, Rory, but I'm beyond anxious about that message from Claire."

He gives a stiff bow and I wonder if perhaps I've insulted him, though I'd always thought my husband's business associate was a pretty laid-back guy. He hands me the envelope and I work at not ripping it from his hands. Tearing it open, I read the words in my big sister's familiar handwriting:

Rosie Posie,

Dad is failing at a rapid pace. The doctors say he has congestive heart failure and it's only a matter of time. I know the timing is terrible, but I didn't feel like I could keep this news from you. If you wish to see Daddy before he passes, please come as soon as possible.

*I miss you so much. And Declan and Dylan too. I hope you
all can come home to Salem soon.*
Love you,
Claire

I can't help the burning in the back of my throat, the hitch
in my breath, or the tears pooling in the corners of my
eyes. My poor Daddy. The man who loved me, Mundane
or otherwise, from the moment I was born. Now, when
he needed me the most at the end of his life, I was stuck
here in the Otherworld, accused of a crime I didn't
commit, separated from my own flesh and blood, and, in
truth, nothing more than an ugly tooth fairy duckling in a
sea of magical swans.

"Bad news, Lady Rosie?" Rory Dell asks, his
unblinking hazel eyes magnified by the round spectacles
perched on his nose.

"It's my father. He's very ill. My sister says he probably..." I can't bring myself to say the words.

"I'm very sorry to hear that, my Lady. Is there anything
I can do? Do you wish me to take a reply back to your
sister?" the accountant asks. "I do believe she is expecting
one," he states.

I can't even begin to think of what to say to my big
sister. How can I add to her already full plate of trouble by
revealing that I've been taken into custody as a cold-
blooded murder. I do what comes naturally; I mentally
call out for Declan, wanting...no...needing his loving
support as well as the matter-of-fact logic he always
manages to balance in any type of crisis. But my words

seem to bounce around my head as if I were communicating in a rubber room void. I write off the bad connection as being caused by my scattered and unfocused mind, instead picturing my dad in his bed at the nursing home, taking his last breath without me. Somehow, Rory Dell seems to sense this grief in me. "I know you want to be with your *athair*, don't you, Lady Rosalinda? If you desire, I can take you to him,"

"Thank you for the very thoughtful offer, Rory, but this place is heavily warded against any kind of escape. It is the Raven's Nest, for Pete's sake. There's no way I can leave here without anyone noticing and trying to stop me," I explain.

"That's where you're wrong, dear Lady. There's more than one way to skin a magical cat per se… if one knows how," Dell says.

I look at him, not bothering to hide the tiny seed of hope that grows in my heart. "Are you saying you can sneak me into the Mundane world and back without anyone knowing?" I ask.

"I believe I can do just that, Lady *Mac Nuada*. No one will be the wiser, I promise," he says, his eyes glinty in the afternoon light of the parlor.

"I would be forever grateful, Rory. I need to see my dad one last time."

"That is to be expected, Lady Rosalinda. One always owes their *athair* complete devotion and loyalty until the day they breathe their last breath. Your sire's blood feeds your life source." My husband's business partner takes a chunk of a red chalky substance from the pocket of his breeches and proceeds to draw a large circle on the floor in front of us. The air circling the room begins to smell strange to my sensitive nose, a mix of rotten eggs and burning feathers. So intent am I on the odd mechanics of this peculiar spell, I don't notice *Buaf* and the dog enter the parlor at the same moment Rory Dell wraps a strong hand around my arm to pull me into the circle in anticipation of him drawing the final piece to close the casting. Across the room, the terrier begins to bark madly while his young Master screams, "No Lady Rosie! Don' do it!" The boy lifts the sword from the newly made sheath and flings it at Rory and myself with more force than an eight-year-old child should be able to muster. As the toy weapon draws closer to where we are standing, the oak wood of its origins explodes into what I can only describe as a flaming missile. The moment the sword torch reaches the outer edges of the casting circle, the toy itself, along with Rory Dell and the red chalk line on the floor, evaporate into a putrid smelling mist of red dust, leaving me standing there in complete shock.

TOOTHPICKS 4

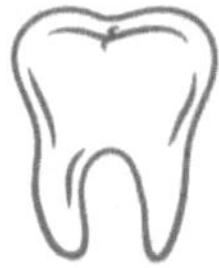

That 'Ole Black Magic

ALL THE DETAILS of what happened directly after my husband's business partner turned into a cloud of smelly red mist comes to me second hand, as shortly after this horrifying event, I apparently took a very un-lady-like nose plant directly into said mess. My last thoughts before losing consciousness were obviously centered on my mate because it's Declan's panicked face I see when my eyes flutter open.

I am told that when he appeared in our "prison" at *Crann Bethadh*, white faced and terrified at the sight of my prone, unmoving self, the panes of every window in the parlor shattered along with two crystal vases and a very ugly statue of an in-flight raven. Once I was able to speak coherently, I related exactly what had happened, not entirely surprised at my husband's disapproving body language over what he called my "less than wise decision in allowin' an authorized visitor inta' the suite after bein' directly ordered not ta'."

Unfortunately, the "supposed" letter from my sister had gone the same route as Rory Dell, news which yet again annoyed my husband's spy sensibilities over the loss of "key evidence." Still, I believed I was doing a fine job of composing myself throughout the Tax Man's interrogation until I got to *Buaf's* part in the unbelievable series of events. The moment had happened so fast that I had difficulty in explaining exactly how the child's toy sword had turned into a flaming magical weapon that was able to save me from what undoubtedly was not a good end. *Birgit* had not been in the room when this all went down, and instead had instantly gone into *scathach* mode the moment she felt strange magic enter the suite, her entire focus centered on protecting her infant charge as she had been trained to do. Thus, she could offer no additional information on the type of magic being used or how it had originated. Despite my pleas to not traumatize the child any further, his Jr. Lordship declared that it couldn't be helped and that it would be a lot easier for the boy if he himself questioned *Buaf* before the Black Knight arrived, who we both knew would not be a happy camper over my serious breach of security.

"Sometimes I think you guys exaggerate the Black Knight's…menace. You all make him sound worse than he actually is for the sake of public propaganda. I don't think he's nearly as scary as he's made out to be," I say.

In return, he gives me that deep suffering look. You know the one; the type that husbands give their beloved wives that indirectly implies that poor little you doesn't know what the hell you are talking about. The one that always drives me crazy. "Beck reigns in his... 'resolve' when the situation calls for it, but ya' shad' never forget that he ken' be as ruthless as needed ta' accomplish his plans, Lass," the Tax Man says. "He is a Master Game Player, second only ta' Her Majesty in that regard. 'Tis best to never underestimate either of them."

"Hmmmm," I say, not convinced.

This time I get the infamous single raised eyebrow in reply, the one I both hate and adore. "Ya' do know what the man did for the Mundane government before commitin' ta' *I Idir*, correct?" he asks.

"Some kind of spy work I presume. Ex-military, from what I've heard."

"More than just spy, Love. Ya' can add assassin to his resume as well. Our Black Knight does no shrink from ending a life if he believes 'tis far' the common good. I am deeply glad he is on ar' side rather than that of the Mundanes. He would be a formidable enemy."

I had, of course, heard the stories about Ted Beckett, Black Knight and *I Idir's* Hand of Justice. I'd always assumed that most of the rumors surrounding the man were greatly embellished and meant to fortify his mystique amongst people who gobbled up that kind of stuff. Now, according to my husband, there were actual teeth behind the tales. Still, I find it hard to mesh the idea of a man, who, as a father himself, would give a frightened child a toy with this new image of a hired killer determined to conduct an intense interrogation on a boy barely out of diapers.

Our debate regarding the true nature of "Beck" comes

to an abrupt end as Lord *Mac Nuada* switches back to his original plan to question the boy himself before the Black Knight arrives. Doing so presents a major challenge, as the terrified child has jammed himself, along with the dog, under the small bed in the room designated as the "nursery." Between bouts of sniffling and weeping muffled under the cover of the mattress, *Buaf* professes to having no memory of seeing Rory Dell in the parlor or of throwing his wooden sword at the man. When Declan tries to bring up the flaming toy, the child cries with heart-wrenching sobs, not so much over witnessing the graphic demise of my husband's business partner, but over the fact that the "bonnie new sheath his Lady made far' him has no sword ta' grace it."

Lord *Mac Nuada* switches to the Old Language, and though they are speaking a tad too fast for me to follow everything as it's being said, I can pick out enough words to follow the conversation. My Eternal Mate is insisting to the child that whatever *Buaf* did with his sword saved the life of his beloved Lady and that Lord *Mac Nuada* and his House will be forever grateful for the young Page's courage. Declan also promises the boy that he will replace the wooden sword with a real one made of forged iron, albeit one with blunted edges and tip until he comes of age, and that his Lordship will personally see to the Page's weapon's training when the time comes.

The ginger-colored terrier wiggles out first, as if to offer reconnaissance of who's truly outside the safety of their chosen hide-away. Seeing only my husband, *Seamus* gives a high-pitched yelp, which in turn causes *Buaf* to belly crawl out from underneath the low-sitting twin bed.

The boy picks up his head and asks, "Did ya' really speak the truth, ma Lord, when ya' said I ked' have ma' own fire-kissed *claiomh* (sword)?"

"Aye," Lord *Mac* replies, first touching his right hand to his forehead and then to his lips, the ancient Other-worldly sign for a promise. "'Tis only a small token for savin' the life of ma' Eternal One and Only." The Tax Man looks over to where I'm standing in the doorway and repeats the same hand gesture he just gave the boy, but this time places his hand over his heart as well, and in my head I hear him say, *"My One and Only for all of Eternity...I ken' no describe the terror in my soul when I saw ya' lyin' so still, Rosie Lass. I donna ever want ta' feel that nightmare again. 'Twould seem that the Universe is forever remindin' me of what a great debt I owe It."* I answer by simply moving my own hand from my forehead, to my lips, and then to my heart.

In the meantime, *Buaf* pulls himself completely free of his hiding spot and sits on the floor next to my husband. "Ya' have been vera' generous ta' me, ma' Lord, but I must ask ya' for one more boon...if it be within yar' reason ta' make it so."

"And what might that be Master Page," Lord *Mac Nuada* questions, the corner of his mouth twitching at the hilarity of the boy's boldness.

The child lifts the sheath attached to the belt at his waist. "The new *claiomh* must be made to fit inta' this sheath and this sheath alone. 'Twas a prize from ma' Lady far' doin' ma' numbers correctly. I shall never be parted from it."

The Tax Man fingers the leather cover, running his

thumb over the amateurish ink drawing of House *Nuada's* sigil on the front of the sheath, an attempt to match the one on my shoulder blade. "'Tis surely a thing of beauty, Master Page, and a rightly earned prize. Ma' Lady is vera' talented. I ken' see why ya' would want ta' hang on ta' it. She brings the magic of love ta' everything she touches," he says as he looks up at me, the pure honesty of that statement reflected in his moss green eyes. "We will make sure the new sword is a perfect fit far' yar' handsome sheath."

Without warning, the child jumps into my husband's lap and throws his spindly arms around Declan's neck. "Yar' the best Lord I know, *Mac Nuada*! The best in all of *I Idir* and I will fight anyone who says otherwise. Someday I will call ya' ma' Liege Lord and I will keep protectin' the Lady Rosie as long as I live! I swear to it, ma' Lord!"

And now it's my turn to weep.

* * *

The Tax Man's intelligence training takes priority over his obsessive need for neatness and order, thus the leftover red dust that was once Rory Dell is left exactly where it dispersed in the parlor earlier this afternoon. This is despite the fact that the weird odor and whatever spell was attached to the circle is giving everyone in the suite mild headaches and a sense of off-balance dizziness, though I appear to be the only one it caused to lose consciousness. Whether it's because I was closest to the magic as it was being cast, or if it's simply because I am the most Mundane person in the room, it's hard to say. Nevertheless, we all give that area a wide berth, going so far as to have our tea picnic style and reclining on over-sized pillows in the Master Suite, much to the delight of *Buaf* and *Seamus*. We try to keep the mood light and breezy as we wait for the Head Honchos to arrive and sort out exactly what occurred this afternoon amid the tightest security in all of *I Idir*.

I watch with poorly hidden adoration as my *Mo Shiorghra* subtly works to prepare *Buaf* for what will undoubtedly be a very stressful experience by encouraging him to speak freely about what was going on in his head when he saw me in the parlor with the strange man. Even *Birgit* who normally keeps her personal thoughts entirely to herself in the way of every trained *scathach*, is smiling and nodding along with Lord *Mac's* easy going, relaxed relationship with the young boy. Not that I ever had any doubts, but seeing the Tax Man with *Buaf*, I realize what an awesome dad he's going to be, here in the Otherworld as well as back home.

Doc Brannigan is the first to arrive. Declan and I note the file folders he's carrying, and despite our burning curiosity to know the results of the DNA testing on both Marcy Kilcrabtree's unborn baby and the orphaned boy, protocol dictates that we wait for everyone involved to arrive. We've been told to expect that *I Idir's* current Merlin (who also happens to be the father of our Black Knight), Ambrose Myrdynn, will also be joining us this evening in hopes of providing some information and history about the strange spell. I'm not too proud to admit

I am starstruck by the man and beyond nervous about what to expect from all of this.

By the time the Knight and his father arrive, the tension in the room is like a too-heavy blanket you can't seem to kick off your feet. *Birgit* discreetly takes Dylan from my arms back to the nursery, encouraging the terrier pup to come with her, but the dog refuses to leave his young Master's side, hugging the boy's leg and daring anyone to shake him loose. "The dog is fine to stay," the Merlin says. He walks over and scratches *Seamus* under his furry chin. "It's been a long time since I've come across such a strong *caomhnoir ainmhithe* (animal guardian)." He directs his question to *Buaf.* "How did you find him, child?"

"I no found him, Lord Merlin. Ma' gad' boy found me," *Buaf* says with wide eyes, overwhelmed by the opportunity to speak to a wizard of such renown. "Cook says he just showed up one day when I was just a wee *tachran* (toddler) and refused ta' leave the estate. We have been a pair since, though 'tis strange that *Seamus* never seems ta' get past his pup stage. I just reckoned he was a late bloomer."

"I see," the Merlin replies. "'Tis often the way it goes with animal guardians.

"Are you saying that this little mutt is a magical enti-ty?" the Black Knight questions.

"Oh yes," the wizard says. "No doubt about it. He's the child's 'watcher.' They aren't as prevalent in the Other-world as they once were, but every Pantheon and every race of preternaturals has some type of canine that acts as a special guardian." Turning to my husband, he adds, " 'Tis a good omen to have a *caomhnoir ainmhithe* attached to one's House."

"So ma' gad' boy ken 'stay with me…always?" *Buaf* asks.

"I don't think much in the Otherworld could keep him away, child," the Merlin replies. "Now, why don't you be a helpful Page and assist your nanny in tending to the baby. Take your 'good boy' with you."

"As ya' wish, Lord Merlin," the child stammers, bowing so low before leaving the room that his nose almost scrapes the ground, with the little dog trotting off behind him. "'Tis no reason for the child to hear the graphic details of what went on here. We can call him back later if we need to question him."

"It's interesting that the dog came to House *Nuada* years in advance," the Black Knight adds. "I'm curious to see how this all fits in regards to this afternoon's events. Perhaps you can shed some light on the security busting spell that took place here at the Raven's Nest, Lord Merlin?"

It always surprises me how these Fae types call their own flesh and blood, their loved ones, by their titles instead of their familiar monikers. This strict adherence to protocol is something I'm still having trouble getting accustomed to, but seems to come naturally to the elite of the Otherworld.

The wizard heads in the direction of the parlor, immediately noting the foul odor. "Nasty stuff," he comments, making a face to match the tone of his words. He waves his hand over his head and kneels down, pinching a bit of the red dust and rubbing it between his fingers. I try not to recall that the ash is all that's left of Rory Dell because the concept makes me queasy. "This explains why he or she was able to get into *Crann Bethadh* despite the layering of wards. This is a style of very ancient Norse *seior*, also known as *jotun* (sorcery) black magic, the practicing of which has been illegal in *I Idir*, as well as most Otherworld kingdoms, for over three centuries, though I am fully aware that secret sects still practice in the remote areas of *Asgard*."

At the mention of *Asgard*, I see the Black Knight throw a weighted glance at my husband before commenting. "I suppose this means Her Majesty needs to rework the wards to include spells of this type."

"Easier said than done," the 26th Merlin says, not bothering to hide his obvious concern. "*Jotun* sorcery is a type of magic practiced long before The Morrigan even came into her power. It will take some heavy research to find a way to counter it."

"Herself is known to hold the ability to work both white and dark magic. Surely this is something she can overcome," his son replies.

"What we have here is the remnants of thwarted 'soul magic'. It's a difficult and highly...distasteful style of conjuring," the wizard explains, "and exceedingly challenging to interrupt."

I can feel the tension in the room rise over the mention of "soul magic." It's a term I've never heard before. "Can I ask what 'soul magic' constitutes?" I query, not caring if I sound like a dumb ass.

"It is a style of hex conjuring that requires an offering of a soul, Mundane or Otherworldly, to the Norse goddess *Freyja* in exchange for the ability to cast a nearly untraceable *Jotun* spell. If the spell had not been disrupted in time, Lady Rosalinda, your final destination from inside that circle would have been wholly unknown. I doubt even The Morrigan would have been able to locate where you'd been taken."

I can hear my mate literally growling over the meaning behind the Merlin's word, while a lamp behind him shatters into a million pieces. No one in the room even bats an eye over it, an obvious sign that all the people gathered here apparently are aware of my husband's new rage 'issues.' "I will find the *jotun* bastard and kill him with my bare hands," Declan vows.

"As is your right, Lord *Mac Nuada*. But before retribution can be dished out, this pot of treachery must come to a full boil," the Merlin advises. "To end it at a simple simmer is a waste of our time and energy. The deceit will only grow more robust over time. No. We must be patient, careful to totally annihilate our enemies once and for all if we are to save our way of life here in *I Idir*."

All this metaphorical talk of boiling pots confuses and annoys me. To hell with Fae word play! For Pete's sake…I was almost taken to *Lugh* knows where! Away from my mate and my son. What I want is logical answers and my fury and fear make me bold. "That is all fine and dandy, gentleman…all these picturesque cooking metaphors about water and pots. But what happened today almost cost me everything! I don't mean to sound rude, Lord

Merlin, but if this magic is so damn powerful, how did a mere child disperse the spell?"

Doc Brannigan, who up to now hasn't said a word, jumps into the conversation "Actually, I think I may have the answer to that," holding up the file folders in his hand.

TOOTHPICKS 5

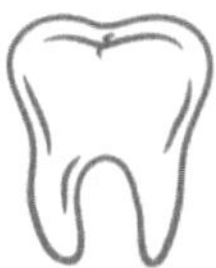

Answers

BEFORE ROBYN CAN GIVE answers to our million-dollar question, the Black Knight stops him, making me just want to go ahead and slap him. "Hold off on the DNA results for a few minutes, Doc. I'm still trying to work out this 'soul magic' shit," Beck says. He addresses his father. "You said earlier that the casting of this spell requires an offering of a soul to *Freyja*. Do you mean a soul in or out of its physical body?"

"The soul offered must be liberated. Free of its earthly vessel," the Merlin replies.

"Then you're saying that Fitz's associate, the real Rory Beck, is dead?"

"Sadly, I believe that's the case." The wizard turns to my husband. "I am sorry Lord *Mac Nuada*. I assume your man no longer walks among the living. Even worse, because his soul was stolen at the moment of his death and used as an offering, it cannot move on to the next plane."

Declan looks physically ill at the notion and I can hear the crystal on the sideboard rattling. "Lord Merlin, is there any way that you ken' free Rory's soul? He was an honest lad. Brave and loyal. His *uncail* (uncle) is a respected member of ma' team. Rory Dell deserves better than ta' wander eternity in *neamh chinnteacht* (Limbo)."

The sorcerer puts a hand on my husband's shoulder in sympathy. "In truth, young Lord, I am not sure if it can be done, but rest assured, I will do my best to find a solution. Perhaps Her Majesty knows more on the subject than I."

Practically tapping his foot in obvious impatience over the side conversation, the Black Knight interrupts. "Getting back to the crime's sequence of events, am I correct in assuming that whoever attempted this casting must have murdered Rory Dell shortly before coming to *Crann Bethadh?*"

"Aye," his father said. "As I am sure you are aware, it is believed that a liberated soul remains on this plane of existence for a short window of time before moving on. The 'perp,' as you call him or her, would have needed to trap the soul and then quickly prepared the additional elements of the casting before coming here to *Crann Bethadh*. There is little room for delays."

"So, the perp would have needed to have had a pretty good idea of the lay-out of the Raven's Nest. This tree dwelling is massive with branches and hallways going off in multiple directions. It would be difficult for someone unfamiliar with its configuration to locate the exact area of the tree where the guest suites are located plus have insider knowledge of where the Lady Rosalinda might be held," Beck explains. "Common knowledge would dictate that she'd most likely be placed in the holding cells. The fact that the perp came directly here indicates that they had confidential knowledge of our plans."

"Ya' think it was someone on the team?" Declan asks.

"Not particularly. But we can't rule anything out at this point. I understand that the Lords of the Ruling Council have freer access to *Crann Bethadh*, and some may have actually been invited to stay within the network of guest suites. How likely is it that young *Mac Badh* has spent enough time here to easily find his way around here? He is, after all, related in some way to Her Majesty."

"Hold on. Are you saying that Cillian *Mac Badh* might be our perp?" I ask, unable to hide my complete shock at a name seemingly pulled out of left field.

"I said no such thing, Lady Rosie," the Black Knight clarifies, not bothering to hide his annoyance with me. I suppose I deserve the terseness of his tone. I blatantly disobeyed his orders by letting someone into the suite after I was specifically instructed not to do so. I can't even consider the notion that I had somehow been part of poor Rory's demise. "However," the Lord Knight continues, "we do know for a fact that the young heir had a sexual relationship with the victim. Having gone through The Ritual at age fourteen, it seems unlikely he is the father of the victim's baby, but with our new knowledge that black soul sorcery is involved, we can't rule out anything."

I sense my husband's anxiety ratchet up over Beck's last comment, and I guess he's thinking about *Buaf's* mysterious parentage, but it's the Doc who says, "I agree.

At this point, we can't rule anyone or any possibility out, but I still believe the results from the DNA can help narrow our circle of investigation. May I suggest we move away from the crime scene where we can open some windows to let in fresh air. Breathing in this soul magic residue isn't doing any of us any good."

Taking the lead, Robyn Brannigan herds everyone to the furthest left corner of the parlor, a space that has westward facing windows. The glass panes slide up on their own, having been magically replaced after Declan's outburst, and we all find seats. It's difficult to reign in my apprehension over what impact the Doc's test results may have on our little family. Robyn leans forward and says, "I have the DNA report back on the male fetus Marcy Kilcrabtree was carrying."

The Black Knight puts his hand out for the file folder. This being a criminal case, it's his right to view the information first, as he is *I Idir's* Seat of Justice. His eyes travel over the documents but his expression gives nothing away. Then he rises and hands the folder to my husband. Maybe it's the lighting in the room, but I actually see a glimmer of sympathy in his eyes and in the grimace he's wearing as he shares the results with Declan. My heart is beating way too hard in my chest and no doubt everyone around me can hear it. I'm pretty sure I know what those test results will show and the thought is devastating. I watch my mate's eyes travel up and down the page and I try reaching out to him through our personal connection but he has his mental shield at full capacity. He flips to the next page and peruses that as well before shutting the folder and handing it to me.

My medical background makes the test results easy to decipher. Marcy Kilcrabtree's unborn baby shares nearly 25% of DNA with someone in the Black Knight's private database, exactly 2284 cm, making the child a half sibling of someone involved. I fight the dread hovering inside me; I don't need to turn the page to see the match. In my heart I already know what I'm going to find typed there. Declan's eyes bore into my back and I hear him say in my head, *"Go ahead and look, Love. There's no hiding from scientific data."* I flip the page and see my husband's name and DNA profile in black and white and the words next to it: **Percent: 98.9 Relationship: Half Sibling**

"That doesn't automatically make his Lordship the murderer," I blurt out. "Even if Marcy was carrying his baby, that doesn't mean he was the one that killed her. The woman was reprehensible. Extremely easy to dislike. There's probably a multitude of people who wanted to see her...gone." I know I'm babbling, plus not helping my own case much. I can't get a read on Declan's emotions, his shield back up immediately after sending me that message. It's obviously not rage he's feeling. There's no breaking glass around me.

The Black Knight is unusually polite in answering me. "You're correct, Lady Rosie. That DNA report in no way proves that Lord *Nuada* killed Marcy Kilcrabtree, or that he was behind the soul magic that took place here this afternoon. However, in a case this important, every piece of evidence is helpful."

Encouraged by his comment, I suggest, "You mentioned that she was involved with *Cillian Mac Badh*. Is it possible that this was a lover's quarrel that went sideways? I wouldn't think the young heir would be thrilled to find out his paramour was…romantically involved with someone else." After I say it, I realize what I'm implying and how it reflects on what my own husband has told me about the parameters of The Ritual casting.

My *Mo Shiorghra* doesn't let my conjecture stand. "Havin' gone through The Ritual ma' self', Rosie, I do not think *Mac Badh* would have had any romantic feelings' toward the woman. Not enough to want ta' go ahead and kill her over her sexual involvement with another man. As I have explained to ya' before, the biological desire is still there after The Ritual, but there is no emotional attachment of any kind involved. Any time spent with Marcy Kilcrabtree would have just been pleasant sport far' *Mac Badh.*"

I can feel the heat rise from my neckline upwards to my cheeks. As far as I'm concerned, in present company, the Tax Man's comment is TMI, but the Black Knight just takes it in stride. "Point taken, Fitz. From my personal experience, greed is a far bigger motivator for murder than sex. Logic dictates a carefully worded discussion with the young heir of House *Badh* is in order, though we'll have to be careful not to step on any Ruling Council toes.

I think to myself that no one seemed to worry about stepping on my own tooth fairy toes, but I'm distracted by Robyn handing my husband the second file which no doubt contains *Buaf's* DNA results. As Declan reads the information within, the three other gentlemen politely look away, talking amongst themselves and refilling coffee cups. Not me. I watch my husband's face for any sign of shock; a wobbly grimace, a pinch of the lower lip, or the widening of pupils. I see absolutely nothing in his expression or body language, but I feel and hear everything that's running in his head; resolve, reluctant acceptance, and an all-encompassing sense of grief. He looks at me and speaks verbally, loud enough for the whole group to hear. "I suppose I've already known the truth far' a while now. I felt a connection ta' that boy the vera' night I rescued him from that hole. I am fully shamed over the knowledge that I put off testin' him far' as long as I did. The lad deserved better from his own flesh and blood."

My mouth goes dry over the million-dollar question and I struggle to push the question out of my mouth. "So…he's your…?"

"Aye. He's ma' half-brother as well. The match is 98.9 percent," Lord *Mac Nuada* reveals.

I can't help sighing in relief, which I realize makes me a horrible person. I honestly feel terrible for poor *Buaf* and the rough start of his earlier life through no fault of his own. But I would be lying if I said that I wasn't immensely relieved that the child playing in the substitute nursery was my mate's sibling and not his son. I understand that Declan desperately tried to reassure me that he didn't believe he fathered that child, but there's a huge difference between "believing" and having scientific tests put any doubts to rest. However, the news that Lord *Nuada* has fathered not one, but two children outside his Ritual bond, leaves a lot of unanswered questions.

With his usual forward bluntness, the Black Knight asks, "Isn't the whole point behind The Ritual to ensure that Ruling Council heirs only have long-term mate bonds, and thus, offspring only with their Universe chosen mates? To avoid the messy problems associated with infidelity or any illegitimate children?"

"That's exactly the point," the wizard says. "And throughout the past eight hundred years, it's worked exactly like it was designed, except for a handful of cases spread throughout the centuries. In each of those cases, the flaw was determined to be caused by a mistake in the application of the casting. I would not be wrong in guessing that this is probably what we're dealing with here. Do you know the name of the ink mage who cast your *athair's* ritual?" the Merlin asks my husband.

"I do. 'Twas the same Master who inked mine…Master Brendan," the Tax Man replies.

The wizard scratched his chin in thought. "As I recall, Master Brendan left the practice and took up the solitary life, correct?"

"So I've been told," Declan says. "Master Finn, the mage who added the Eternal Bond far' ma' Lady and me, mentioned that no one has seen or heard from him for many years. I donna' believe his whereabouts are known."

Addressing his son, the great sorcerer said, "I think it might be worthwhile to track down this ink mage and talk to him. I can't say for sure if he has anything to do with this particular case, but it's imperative that we check out every angle. If this was just an honest mistake in laying out the spell, then it's only regrettable and sad. But if there's more to this, then it is important we get to the bottom of it. The Ritual was instituted under sound reasoning. Now more than ever, *I Idir* needs a united Ruling Council if we are to deal with the Mundane attempts to breach the Otherworld. If someone is purposely thwarting The Ritual casting, they need to be contained and questioned."

"Doc, you said earlier that you might have an explanation for the soul magic in those same DNA results. Why is that?" I ask, uncomfortable in regards to the current topic and its connection to our family histories.

"May I?" Doctor Brannigan asks, as he holds out his hand toward Declan to retrieve the folder. He opens it and turns to a back page. "We know for certain who the boy's father is, but the identity of his mother is unknown. There were no matches in our current database, although that's easy to understand why. The child's maternal profile shows that through his mother he carries DNA markers for both the *Dokkalfar* (Dark Elves) and *Ljosalfar* (Light Elves) races, a very unique and powerful genetic magical combination and one you don't see very often, as the two groups usually do not intermingle. The *Dokkalfar* (Dark Elves) contain themselves to remote northern areas in the *Asgard* kingdom and do not adhere to any laws of the kingdom's governing body. Most importantly, they are known to be strict devotees of the goddess *Freyja*, and purveyors of *jotunn seior* (Norse black magic). It might explain the boy's unique ability to disarm the soul magic."

TOOTHPICKS 6

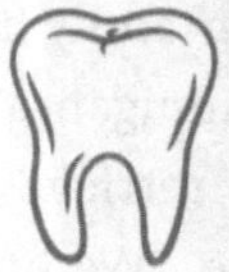

The Ties That Bind

THE ROOM GOES silent in the aftermath of the doctor's explanation. All of us fight the urge to let our eyes wander toward the nursery where the child in question is peacefully unaware of how the life he's known has instantly changed. I know nothing of fact regarding the *Asgard* elven races, except for the bed-time stories most Fae children hear at some point in their early years, with the elves playing the villainous boogeymen of nightmares. The little boy who saved my life today is no monster hiding in the woods, but rather a lost child who had the misfortune to be dealt an early bad hand. "I'm afraid I don't know a whole lot about the *Nordboerne* folk of *Asgard*," I admit. "Especially the Elven people. You mentioned that *Buaf's mathair* was born of both Light and Dark elves? Isn't that rather unusual?" I ask the group's medical expert. "I was always led to believe the two groups didn't get along at all."

"My knowledge of the *Ljosalfar* and *Dokkalfar* history is limited to a basic course study of Otherworld humanities during my time at the Academy. I think perhaps Lord Merlin might be better prepared to give you an answer that has more depth to it," Doctor Brannigan suggested.

"Although there is an abundance of New Age mythology about the history of the Elven races, especially within the literature of the Mundane world, real fact, rooted in documented history, is rather scarce," the sorcerer explained. "The Elven people are thought to be one of the oldest inhabitants of the Otherworld, here long before many of the current pantheons, including our own Queen. The *Ljosalfar*, or Light Elves, were believed to be celestial in origin, beings of light and beauty, not unlike the descriptions of 'angels' in some of the Mundane world religions. They were said to originally live in *Alfheimr*, a paradise-like kingdom known for its pure magical skill and immense range of knowledge.

The *Dokkalfar*, or Dark Elves, were also believed to be of the same origin, and made their appearance here in the Otherworld within the same historical time frame. Despite modern culture wanting to make them dark skinned, most respected writings in the magical community have them being similar in appearance to the *Ljosalfar*, and they were thought, in the beginning, to be the same race of people. At some point early in their history, there was a falling out between opposing parties within the ruling system, the cause of which is only speculation. Rather than bringing war upon their people, the opposing group took half of *Alfheimer's* wealth, and built their own homeland under large earth mounds and within caves where the sun seldom reached, not much different from our earliest *Sidhe* ancestors, thus earning them their 'Dark' moniker.

For centuries, the two groups co-existed peacefully until during the time when the sun appeared in the constellation *Ophiuchus*. With no explanation, the *Ljosalfar* attacked their ground-dwelling fellow elves, unprovoked and under the guise of a peaceful trading visit. History is unclear why the Light elves took such a course of action, though many scholars believe it was because the *Dokkalfar* had come across a method to conjure even stronger magic, a type that came to be known by the name we call it today, '*Jotun.*' From that point on, pure animosity reigned between the two groups, and if a child was conceived between a Dark and Light elf, I would guess that *Buaf's mathair* was either the product of rape, or a love child, the result of some doomed relationship in the manner of Shakespeare's *Romeo and Juliet*. I would also venture to say that her offspring, having such a complex genetic make-up, one consisting of the ancient *Tuatha de Danann* bloodline, along with ancient *Dokkalfar* and *Ljosalfar* genes, would have considerable magical talent, enough, at least, to stop a 'soul magic' casting with little or no training."

"Is the boy's magical skill something we need to be concerned about?" his son asked, security forever first on the Black Knight's mind.

"I think 'concerned' might be too harsh a word," the Merlin answered. "He will undoubtedly need to be made aware of his heritage. I imagine he is very confused over what happened yesterday with his toy sword, and he'll, of course, need proper training and guidance."

"The child is a descendant of House *Nuada*, and within the reins of my responsibility. I will take formal guardianship of my half-brother and see to his magical training. I assume his *Nuada* birthright gives him access to the Academy?" my husband asks.

"Aye," the wizard replied. "And I would be more than happy to sponsor him."

Declan gave a short bow of his head. "That is most gracious of you, Lord Merlin. I am vera' appreciative."

"I realize this is a major assumption on my part, Fitz, but if your Lord *Athair* had planned on claiming the child as his own, I expect he would have done so by now. The boy is far beyond toddlerhood. I don't believe Lord *Nuada* will welcome the news of himself being the father of a child conceived outside his Handfast bond, a child of Elven heritage, no less, becoming public knowledge," the Black Knight stressed. "Not after he's managed to keep the kid a secret for eight years."

"I obviously donna' know ma' own sire as well as I thought I did," my husband says, as the china tea cups and ceramic coffee mugs rattle on the tray. "I have no explanations far' his poor decisions, nor do I wish ta' make excuses far' them, but I agree with yar' comment that his Lordship will not be happy that he has been 'found out.' I understand that Marcy Kilcrbtree's death is a homicide that needs addressin', but I am askin' that ya' keep the mention of ma' young *dearthair* (brother) out of yar' investigation until we know far' sure what's what. I donna' wish ta' put the child in any mar' danger."

"I agree wholeheartedly, Fitz. There's no reason to drag the boy into this adult mess unless we have no other options," the Knight says. "However, despite yesterday's unfortunate breach of security, I still believe your family is safer here than anywhere else." The Queen's Hand of Justice gives me a pointed stink eye and I have enough common sense to appear appropriately chagrinned. "Now that we know what we are dealing with," the continues, "Her Majesty and I can take measures to secure against this new style magic. I'd also venture to say that between your *scathach* and the kid's magical watch dog, any other attempts by this perp to get to the kid here at *Crann Bethadh* would be deemed too risky." The Black Knight puts down his coffee mug on the side table and stands up. "I need to cross back over to the Mundane side. I have at least two full days of headaches there with Essex County business. Let's see what we can uncover in the next thirty-six hours with a plan to meet back here on Thursday evening. I'd like to bring *Cillian Mac Badh* in for questioning, although I need to think on how I want to do that without shaking his House's tree and annoying Herself. Fitz, can you assign Duncan to look into what may have happened to Rory Dell? If he is dead, as Lord Merlin predicts, then we need to let his family know."

"'Tis ma' place ta' speak to his kin. I am vera' close to the family," Declan says.

"I understand your feelings on that, Fitz, but right now that would be a mistake. Too many moving pieces and parts and the last thing any of us need right now is for you to give the North Koreans an opportunity to snatch you again. If necessary, I'll ask Connor to come see you here at *Crann Bethadh.* I've no doubt he'll be as determined as you to bring Rory's murderer to justice. What I really need for you to do, ASAP, is to travel to the Elven community on the outskirts of *Asgard,* undercover, of course, and see what you can find out about anyone who's been practicing hard-core *Jotun* magic. That missing ink mage would be a good place to start. See if you can bring him in for questioning. He might be able to give us some idea of who may be involved in today's attempt against Lady *Mac,* or at least shorten the list a bit." He paused, as if going down a mental checklist. "And while you're there, see if you can track down any gossip about a woman who was pregnant with a mixed-blood elven baby. Something like that would be hard to keep a secret given the Other-world's propensity for gossip. I don't know if the boy has anything to do with the Kilcrabtree case, but that information couldn't hurt to have for an abundance of reasons."

"Aye, Lord Knight. I'll leave first thing tomorrow morn, but I will be takin' my Lady Wife with me," the Tax Man says, causing my head to swivel around in shock so fast I must look like that little possessed girl in *The Exorcist* movie.

Beck's face gives away his opinion on that plan, all pursed lips and narrowed eyes. "I don't think that's a workable proposal, Fitz. Lady Rosie has no daytime magical energy, and even after sunset her skill is very limited. Plus, she's had no formal weapons training nor any self-defense instruction. I see her accompanying you on this mission as more of a distraction and a huge security impediment. I'd prefer that your Lady stay here at *Crann Bethadh* with your son and the boy."

Truthfully, I don't relish my shortcomings being discussed as if I wasn't even in the room, but the Black Knight has said nothing that isn't one hundred percent true. Even I realize that my being made part of *I Idir's* intelligence network was just a boon to my husband so he wouldn't have to keep secrets from his fated mate.

"I fully understand yar' reasoning, Lord Knight, but I'm afraid I must insist," my hubby calmly states. "I have made the error of leavin' ma' *Mo Shiorghra* to the protection of others on three separate occasions and in each of those circumstances, the results were disastrous. 'Twas only through the goodness of the Universe that ma' beloved Lady is still here with me. 'Tis ma' sacred right to protect ma' mate, and protect her I will. No disrespect meant, Black Knight, but I have no doubt that you would do the same far' yar' own *Banphrionsa*."

"He has you there, Theodore," the Merlin laughed. "If my humble opinion is worth anything, I believe the Lady *Mac Nuada* is up to the challenge of a bit of spy work."

I can't help blushing over the wizard's confidence in me. I just wish a little bit of it would rub off on me. However, his father's assurance must be enough for *I Idir's* security expert. "I suppose I'm outvoted on this decision. If you feel you can accomplish what needs to be done in *Asgard*, Fitz, with your mate at your side, then so be it. You're the very best at what you do. I have complete faith in your commitment and loyalty to Her Majesty."

My Tax Man gives a polite bow in appreciation. "Thank you, Beck. I am grateful far' yar' confidence in me.

And I agree that ma' Lady Wife is in need of mar' formal training. I will be looking into finding an appropriate coach far' her, as I donna' think our peaceful family life could handle it bein' me," he adds with a grin.

The other three males laugh in response to his obviously sexist statement. I, however, do not think Declan's comment is all that funny. It makes me sound like a shrew. Which I'm not. If anyone is 'difficult' within our small family unit, it's the Tax Man himself with his obsessive-compulsive, always-right personality. But I'm too excited about getting a chance to "work" with my husband, the spy, so I smile politely at his good-natured teasing.

The group finally departs, with the Merlin promising Declan that he will research all possible ways to free poor Rory Dell's soul from its post-death entrapment. It's not a conversation I want to have before bed, so I change the subject to one that's just as difficult. "So, how do you think we should tell *Buaf* the news? I imagine it will come as a big shock to him. He's bound to have a lot of questions along with a wide range of conflicting emotions."

"It will be vera' difficult, Lass. That is why I believe I should be the one to tell him. Alone. Brother ta' brother, man ta' man. To a *Sidhe* male, the knowledge that yar' own sire dinna' want ta' claim ya' as his own is devastatin' news. It will be easier comin' from his own flesh and blood."

"You do know I work exclusively with children, right? I have a pretty good handle on child development," I say stiffly with an overlay of defensiveness. "I've become rather fond of the child, and I don't feel it's fair of you to shut me out of such a monumental, life-changing conversation."

Declan puts his hand over mine, his long fingers wrapping lightly around my wrist. "Yar' heart, ma' Love, is so givin' and generous. It warms ma' own ta' know ya' will be like a *mathair* to the boy, the only one he's ever really known. But he is also a child of the Otherworld, one whose future is different from the Mundane *leanai* (children) ya' are familiar with. He is grounded in a culture and tradition that even you yarself' are unfamiliar with. Please. Let me give him the news in ma' own way, and then I will send him ta' ya' for the mother's comfort he'll undoubtedly need."

I know my husband's heart is in the right place and that he has the boy's best interest in mind. Still, it stings a bit to be reminded that I'm out of my league when it comes to his Fae heritage. Even my own son has more biological ties to the Otherworld than I do. "Whatever you think is best, Declan. I only want to do right by the poor child."

"As do I, *mo ghra amhain* (my only love). He has suffered enough as it is. I ken' no imagine how hard his life as a *bairn* was at the mercy of the adults around him who were not his kin."

The hard truth of our discussion is interrupted by the noisy chaos from the nursery. I hear my wee baby boy yowling for his night feeding along with the sounds of child and dog wrestling over the hem of his night shirt. Both Declan and I head toward the nursery, me to mother one child while I wait to pick up the shattered pieces of the other. *Buaf* looks leery when his Lord asks him to join him in his study, especially this late at night with the boy dressed in his bed clothes, but is relieved when Declan tells him it is okay to bring *Seamus* along.

While Lord *Mac Nuada* has his all-important conversation with his half-brother, I relate all that was revealed to *Birgit*, who is surprisingly not shocked by the news. When I formally ask her to take on *Buaf* as a client along with our own son, the *scathach* informs me that Lord *Mac* had already asked her before they left *Dun Siorai* and that she had already accepted. That's me...Rosie Fitzpatrick... always the last one to know anything.

Nearly an hour later, the boy and Declan return to the nursery, the boy's little hand in my husband's much larger one. Both of them are red-eyed which squeezes tight at my heart. *Buaf* walks to the rocker where I'm sitting with Dylan, his demeanor oddly shy for such an outgoing child and his steps hesitant. "Ma' Lord is ma' half-brother, Lady Rosie," he says, his voice barely more than a whisper.

"Yes," I say, my heart breaking over the confused little face looking up at me. "I know. 'Tis wonderful news."

"Aye," the boy replies, his unusual gray colored eyes filled with open hope. "It would seem then that ya' would be ma' beloved 'sister'...of sorts. That is...if ya' truly wanna' be such as that."

In the back of my throat, I feel that familiar tightness that signals I'm heading for an onslaught of ugly crying. "I would love to be your big sister, *Buaf*. And Dylan would adore having you as his own '*Uncail*'."

The gunmetal-colored eyes blink. "I dinna' think of that, Lady Rosie...that wee Dylan would be ma' *nia* (nephew)!" *Buaf* perches himself on my other knee and sticks out his finger for the baby to grab. "Hello, nephew! I will be a gad' *uncail* ta' ya'. I will show ya' where to catch the best *laghairts* (lizards), how to answer the hoot of the white *ulchabhan* (owl), and what it means when the wooly caterpillar has a heavy coat. All the important things ya'll need ta' know, wee Dylan." He goes quiet for a minute and then whispers in my ear. "Don' tell his Lordship what I'm about ta' say ta' ya', Sister Rosie, lest he think I am just a *caoin leanbh* (cry baby) and not worthy ta' be his own." I can see the beginning of tears forming in the corners of his eyes. "'Tis all too much. This news of ma' *mathair* and ma' *athair*. I donna' know if I ken' bear it." A lone tear escapes as he murmurs, "I am afraid, Rosie. Vera' afraid."

Buaf is right. It's all too much. Way too much for an abandoned little boy and the woman who will now take over the role of the mother he's never known. There's no holding back as the two of us simply dissolve into a weepy puddle of deeply felt tears at the injustice of it all.

TOOTHPICKS 7

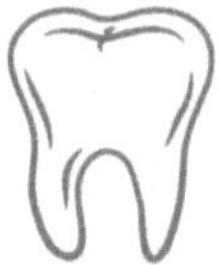

Adventures in Spy Town

AS EXHILARATED as I am about partnering with my husband the spy, the timing of our little adventure is plain lousy. After the life-altering news of the night before, none of us slept very well. In turn, the morning brought on one very colicky infant who refused to be soothed and a normally independent and cheerful eight-year-old who was now a poster child for separation anxiety. These family issues keep Declan and I from getting the early start we'd hoped for, thus greatly irritating the very organized, intelligence officer part of my husband and making the spousal side of him downright cranky.

The ornery disagreement regarding our roles in this assignment doesn't help matters. I'd just assumed I'd get some fun cover story role and that Declan would "glamourize" me using the magic he's so admired for. What I hadn't understood in the months we'd been together was that, though Lord *Mac Nuada* could cast a perfectly believable glamour image for just about anyone, it was up to the recipient to hold the spell for any extended time, as the original casting only lasted an hour or less. Being that we were traveling during daylight hours and I'm a tooth fairy with limited post-sunset magical abilities, glamourizing me wasn't going to be a long-term solution, as there was no way I could hold a spell of that magnitude. Instead, I was forced to go the Mundane route in regards to a cover story and suitable disguise.

It was decided that I was far too "curvy" to un-magically pass myself off as a man, or as my Tax Man commented, "Even a blind man with one hand cud' tell ya' are no lad, Rosie Love." All my secret fantasies of being the pirate girl disguised as a handsome cabin boy while being lusted after by the confused Captain flew right out the window. Since being a male was out of the question, his Lordship, and my superior officer in regards to this mission, determined that I would be the spinster daughter of an old amulet maker delivering wares to his clients in the outer banks of *Asgard*. It was not a disguise that made me happy. The apparel Declan produced for me to wear was ugly, ill-fitting and none to clean. A rough linen headscarf covered most of my head and hid my less-than-Otherworldly, human-shaped ears.

Anyone who knew me would probably still recognize me, which according to my "superior officer" didn't matter much because in the location to which we were headed, no one even knew I existed. It was a true statement, but it sure as hell didn't make me feel good. The Tax Man's disguise, though very realistic, didn't lend itself to any kind of erotic fantasies either, since I've never been a fan of "age-gap" romances. Magically aging fifty years before my eyes, his yellowed, rotten teeth and wrinkled face were not the things that drove salacious daydreams, so I was already disappointed in my first honest-to-goodness spy mission before it even began.

We took off from the Raven's Nest, unnoticed, on a piebald horse who looked as if he was ready for the glue factory, my eighty-year-old "*athair*" hefting me up on the pillion set behind his own saddle instead of my usual spot in front between his thighs. Disgruntled over the whole experience, I questioned how a horse in such poor shape could take us all the way to *Asgard*. Declan laughed and explained that "Hades," as the horse was named, was one of The Morrigan's "gifted" stallions, capable of holding a glamour spell as well as any *Sidhe* practitioner. The realization that even the horse had more magical power than I did didn't do much to help my lack of spy confidence. "Well, that's just peachy keen, Tax Man. The damn horse has more Fae juju than me. I feel bad for you, Sweetie… married to a loser tooth fairy who can't even hold a casting someone else conjures," I tease.

I instantly feel him stiffen in the saddle in front of me. In a voice two octaves lower than normal he growls, "Loser? Is that what ya' really think, Lass? I would burn the world to ash far' ya, Rosalinda Parker Fitzpatrick *Nuada*. Every inch of it with no regrets. In ma' eyes, ya' are a treasure I don't deserve and I expect ta' never hear ya' utter those feckin' false words agin'.'"

I swallow the urge to reply with a flippant remark. I've obviously touched a raw nerve. How does one even react to a comment like that? Burn the world to ash? Hells bells!

That's a bit extreme. I don't have the right words for a moment like this one, so I just wrap my arms around his waist and lay my cheek against his broad back. "I love you, Declan Fitzpatrick, with everything I am. I'm sorry if my teasing ended up hurting your feelings. I won't use that word again. Ever."

"I love ya' too, Rosie Lass. So much so that at times I ken' not even think straight. I never wan' ya' ta' forget that."

"I won't forget," I answer. Overwhelmed by the intensity of his emotions, I try to lighten the mood without setting him off again. "By the way, Tax Man, how come I'm stuck sitting back here and not in front of you like before? I always enjoy sitting with myself pressed against your good parts."

"Ta' a fellow traveler, 'twould look rightly odd, even unseemly, to see a man's daughter sitting in such intimate fashion. We need ta' keep up appearances," my husband explains. "Plus, havin' ya' wiggle and bounce around on ma' cock for six hours would be mar' distraction than a man ked' bear. I have no doubt I would need ta' keep stoppin' in some thick wooded outcrop so I cad' ravage ya' right there on the spot. Hence, since we're held ta' such a strict time schedule, we no have the extra time far' such a luxury. We need to get to the far border of *Asgard* by nightfall. I do not like the idea of travelin' these roads after dark."

To me, the idea of a "ravagin' in the woods" sounded like the best part of this adventure, and since I can't see the expression on his face I can't tell if he's teasing or not. His tone sounds disappointingly matter-of-fact, so I take it as a challenge to figure out another way to convince him that "ravagin" me is a fine idea, even from my less-than-optimal position on the back of the horse. If anything, it gives my mind something to dwell on instead of the uncomfortable chafe of my inner thighs and the teeth jarring thumping of my ass hitting the hard seat of the pillion. In addition, the never-ending silence of wide-open country space is mind-numbingly tedious and I have to keep pinching myself to stay awake.

"Do you think *Buaf* will be able to handle this new change to his life?" I ask, looking for a topic that doesn't dwell on either burning the world to ash or my husband's dick.

"I do not think he has a choice, Lass. It is what it is. He will have to face his path the best he can," Declan replies. "We will help him as the Universe allows, but the journey, and the way to forge it, will be his own."

"I understand all that. But sheesh! He's just a tot. It's a lot for his little mind to work out, although his new identity as a *Nuada* has to be better than a life of servitude, right?" I reason.

The Tax Man sighs. "Perhaps not," he admits. "He is the bastard son of a Lord whose vera' sense of honor is in question. The deeper I dig, the more information I find that my *athair* may have lost his commitment to *I Idir* a long time ago. 'Tis one thing for me as a grown man to defend myself against the rumors and threats. It will be altogether different for a wee lad. He will find that his peers will both shun and test him at every turn. It may be that life in the kitchen as an orphan would have caused him less heartache."

"It's absolutely ridiculous to blame the child for the actions of his parents. It's not like he had any choice in his conception," I argue.

"I agree, Love. But 'tis the way it is. Not only here in the Otherworld, but in the Mundane as well. When I was in college, I saw firsthand how students of different races, religions and even those with less fortune were treated so indifferently, as if their contributions didn't matter. I believe it is a flaw in the soul of both peoples, or perhaps a test to overcome. Neither world seems to have found the answer."

Declan isn't wrong. Growing up, I never found it difficult to get along with my peers. If I was never the Queen Bee in any group, I did have enough friends and acquaintances to keep me from feeling lonely. Still, I often wondered how the attitudes of my fellow friends and students would have changed if they had ever found out that I was part Fae, born of a mother from a completely different dimension that they didn't even know existed. There's not a shred of doubt in my mind that if they had known my secret, they would have looked at me with different eyes.

"In the poor lad's case," Declan continues, "there's yet an additional strike against him here in the Otherworld. *Buaf* will not be accepted by any of his people: The *Sidhe* will shun him because he is Elven. The Elven people will distrust him because he is *Sidhe*. And the *Dokkalfar* and the *Ljosalfar* will look at him as some freak of mixed blood, a constant reminder of the hate between their two peoples. It is a path I would not wish on anyone, especially such a sweet-natured and innocent child. I can't help but sometimes question the wisdom of the Universe."

The conversation is depressing and makes me want to cry, so I drop it, returning to the empty sounds of chirping birds and the clomp of the horse's hooves on the hard-packed soil. For the life of me, I cannot understand the Otherworld fascination of travel by horse-back, especially in a world chocked full of magical ability. Declan has tried to explain that the cultural dictate of not transporting by magic is a way to "even the playing field" among the different races of Otherworldly people with varying levels of power and skill, but coming from a world built on technology, taking hours and hours to get somewhere uncomfortably by horse seems silly to me.

Eventually, sleep-deprived and bored, I give in to the rhythm of the bouncity-bouncity, and slip into a drowsy slumber, waking with a start only when the horse comes to a complete halt. I find myself belted to my husband's waist with an embarrassing wet drool spot on the back of his tunic where my face was pressed up against him.

"Sorry. I must have dozed off. That seems to happen to me when I'm on a horse for long periods of time," I apologize.

"'Tis fine, Love. I'm glad ya' were able to rest. It will be a long day. I belted ya' to me so ya' would not slip off the harse'. Ya' looked like ya' might be wobblin' a bit." He helps me down off the disguised Hades, holding on for an extra moment or two while I stretch my cramped legs. "I thought this would be a good spot far' a break and a wee bit of lunch. It's a deserted and quiet stretch of wood with a runnin' stream for Hades ta' drink. Plus, it's within ten miles of the first town I want to explore so it should be the perfect place far' a short rest."

"Deserted, you say?" I ask with an innocence I'm not feeling.

"Aye," he says. "This is a less traveled route, though 'tis a bit longer than travelin' the main road. I thought it prudent ta' keep ta' ourselves far' as long as possible."

"Hmmm…deserted enough far' ravagin' da' ya' think?" I ask in the heaviest brogue I can muster.

"Aye, that it is," he grins. "But I'm afraid we only have time far' eatin' or ravagin'. You'll have ta' make a choice with the understandin' that we probably won't stop again until early evenin'."

"Oh, no contest there." I state as I stand on my tiptoes and throw my arms around his neck. The Tax Man lifts me up until I can wrap my legs around him. "Easy decision, ma' Lord. I pick 'ravagin', of course. Every time."

"I always knew ma' beloved was wise beyond measure," says my *Mo Shiorghra* as he drops the old-man glamour while together we sink into the thick, soft grass.

TOOTHPICKS 8

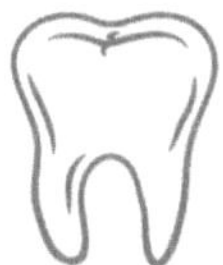

Horsin' Around

THOSE LAST TEN miles might as well have been fifty if my sore ass had anything to say about it. Getting back on that horse after our little "break" was difficult, made worse by the melty-bone -relaxed state I find myself in 'post-ravagin.' I am tired of the constant friction and bouncing long horse travel offers and I looked forward to finally letting my own legs take me where I needed to go. The terrain of *Asgard* isn't much different than that of *I Idir*, though the spring temperature here was a good ten to twelve degrees cooler than back home. It was a condition that the Tax Man remedied by conjuring up a moth-eaten cardigan in an awful shade of puce that reminded me of moldy plums.

"Are you purposely trying to make me look as hideous as possible?" I ask, stuffing the last piece of a hard cheddar biscuit in my mouth and brushing the crumbs off the front of my ugly sweater.

"That's exactly what I'm attemptin' ta' do, Lass, though

it be no easy task without the aid of magic. 'Tis like tryin' to hide a lone rose among a crop of *fiali* (weeds). It's true color and scent will always give the rose away."

I give his middle a squeeze and let my right hand drop just a tad lower. "Such a romantic you are, Tax Man. A girl could get used to your pretty words."

He chuckles and adds, "More than just 'pretty words,' love. I'm doin' the best I can ta' keep other men from noticin' ma' own precious 'Rose.' I'd hate ta' have ta' kill some stranger far' puttin' his hands on ya'. It would surely cause an international incident and Herself would be mar' than a little pissed at me. House *Nuada* has already given Her Majesty enough reasons to banish the whole lot of us."

Once again, I can't tell for sure if Declan is teasing or speaking the truth, as his tone gives nothing away. However, if that new-found rage inside him simmers hot enough to shatter glass, then I have to believe he actually means he would be willing to hurt someone over me. My mind wanders back to his interrogation of Erik Ashton, the traitorous tooth fairy who tried to turn me over to the Chechens and the very same asshole who also shot his cousin, Duncan. Although I was prevented from actually seeing what transpired between the two men, Erik's painful howls and his eventual unconscious state led me to believe that the Tax Man hadn't pulled any punches in dealing with the creep. Literally.

Looking out from my position on the horse's hindquarters, all I can see is miles and miles of open green space, no sign of any thriving metropolis. "Are we getting close, Declan? I'm anxious to stretch my legs."

"Aye. We are about ten minutes away," he says.

Shifting in my seat, I try to see around him, but even leaning far to the left, and then to the right, all I see is more miles of green. "Is this some kind of invisible city?"

My husband laughs before explaining. "Yes, but not in a magical sense. *Gleann Gas, or Groenn Dalr*, as the *Nordboerne* call it, translates to 'Green Valley.' The town is built below the rolling hills. 'Tis hard to see unless you are nearly on top of it. It has kept them 'off the radar,' so ta' speak, far' nearly nine hundred years. It is an interesting place...home to an abundance of artisans of all kinds. They are especially known for their exquisite metalwork in both jewelry and weaponry. I was hopin' ta' purchase the pint-sized sword I promised the lad while we're here, and one ta' perhaps put away far' Dylan when he comes of age. The selection is sure to be better here than in *I Idir*."

"You're just the sweetest Lord anywhere, *Mac Nuada*... a big ole' teddy bear," I comment. "So besides buying souvenirs for the kids, what's our mission in *Gleann Gas*?"

"Do ya' recall that yesterday, before yar' run-in with the false Rory Dell, that I went to House *Nuada's* archive library?"

"Yes. You told me you were planning to bring back some old records back for us to go through together," I say. "Did you find something?"

"I'm not sure. An anomaly of sorts. The accountin' ledgers far' the runnin' of the estate have been formatted in the same manner far' over three hundred years. I remember as a kid sittin' with ma' *athair* while he did his monthly balancin'. Even then I was fascinated with those long lines of numbers. 'Twas likely the reason I honed in on accountin' as ma' Mundane life's work. Back then, I only had eyes for the digits so I never paid much mind ta' the notes in the margins. However, yesterday I noticed somethin' odd. A strange symbol in the bottom left-hand margin at the end of each month beginnin' in September of 1987, the same month and year ma' *athair* became Lord of House *Nuada* at the death of ma' paternal *seanathair* (grandfather) during a skirmish with the Formorians."

"What kind of symbol?" I ask.

"I dinna' recognize it as bein' Fae. Looked *Nordboerne* ta' me, but my knowledge of the old runes is vera' weak. It's one of the things I hope to uncover on this trip," Declan explains. "What is even stranger was the addition of another symbol added next ta' the original one about eight years ago, with a third added goin' back only about three years. Because of what happened to ya' at *Crann Bethadh,* I didna' get a chance to finish ma' exploration so I ken' no say far' sure if the symbols represented payments goin' in or out."

I let the words sink in. "The second symbol was added eight years ago? Do you think it has something to do with *Buaf* and his arrival at *Dun Siorai?* The timing can't be coincidental."

"'Tis suspicious at the vera' least, but we donna' have enough information ta' make such a grand leap. Knowin' what the symbols mean would be helpful. If they are Elder Futhark Runes, as I believe, deciphering them will be tricky as each symbol can carry more than one meaning. Plus, we believe the lad ta' be eight years old, but we have no proof of his true age. Like Mundane and Fae children, Elven offspring can vary in their physical development."

I shift from one aching butt cheek to another. We can't get to *Gleann Gas* soon enough. "I suppose, you're right, Sweetie, but neither of us believe in coincidences, so I feel like there's bound to be some connection to that second symbol and *Buaf's* sudden appearance at the estate. Finding the child's *mathair* would surely clear up a lot of details."

The Tax Man doesn't immediately answer, but when he does, his voice is rough. "Truth be told, Lass, I don' expect to find the woman among the livin'. Offspring are rare among Otherworldly races. Children are a treasured commodity, even among the Elven peoples. They represent a path to a family's future. I don' believe *Buaf's mathair* would have willingly given him up, even knowing the difficulties the boy would face in his life."

I don't like the implication of my husband's statement. If the kid's mother is dead as Declan believes, it makes Lord *Nuada* involved in the death of two women he was in a relationship with and upon whom he fathered children. Any way you want to spin it, it's an ugly thought.

Hades abruptly comes to a stop at the edge of a large overhang. Declan turns the horse sideways so that I can get a better view from my seat in the rear. Below our position, a sprawling town of clay-tiled roofs and cobblestone streets sits among the flora and fauna of spring in the soup-bowl valley. The road leading down to *Groenn Dalr* is narrow and cork-screwed, and I have to fight a sense of dizziness as the magical stallion sure-footedly winds his way down to the city gates, an imposing wood structure with wolf-like creatures carved into the main posts.

We are stopped at the entrance by two armed guards who ask in the guttural language of the land what business brings us to *Groenn Dalr*. Their tone and body language is far from welcoming, a reminder of how chilly political relations are between *I Idir* and *Asgard*. One of the men gives me the once over, then obviously dismisses me as unworthy of his male attention. The Tax Man's attempt to make me appear "unappealing" is apparently right on target, which is a relief, I suppose.

My elderly *"athair"* speaks to the guards in their natural tongue, explaining to them that he hopes to sell his charmed amulets to a few of the magic shops in town. The man grunts in reply but neither of them moves from their position blocking our entry until my spy hubby hands over two small cut garnets of exceptional color. Pocketing the "toll," the security detail finally steps aside for us to make our way into the main town square.

Say what you want about the warrior mentality of the *Asgard* ruling class, the *Nordboerne* people have an amazing sense of beauty and creativity. The town center of *Groenn Dalr* is proof of that, utterly charming, as if the setting had been drawn from some of the Mundane world's favorite fairy tales. The space is dominated by a large working fountain in the town center displaying two exquisitely carved *margyr* (Nordic mermaids) holding conch shells from which water poured into the pool below. The fountain rested in a garden of precisely manicured flowers and shrubs, including several patches of live toadstools in vibrant colors of red, orange and carnelian, all adorably spotted in white dots and known to be incredibly poisonous.

"Oh, Declan! This is delightful! What a lovely town. I'm so glad we stopped," I say.

"I knew ya' would enjoy it, Love. I believe it's one of the prettiest towns in all of the Otherworld. I wish we had time ta' properly see all the city has ta' offer. Alas, we need ta' get ta' the North Border by nightfall, so our time here will sadly be short. On that note, I want ta' remind ya' that we must stick ta' our designated roles as closely as possible. Ya' must remember that we are meant ta' be lowborn Fae and that ya' are ma' spinster daughter and I am yar' curmudgeonly old *athair*. Far' appearances sake, I will need ta' treat you as such. Promise me ya' will not hold it against me."

It's on the tip of my tongue to mention that, in truth, I am already a lowborn Fae, but I know my saying that will only annoy him, so I answer accordingly. "I promise, Sweetie. Cross my heart and..." I stop myself before uttering the last sing-song words of the common Mundane kid phrase. The Fae are extremely superstitious regarding words sent into the Universe. It doesn't bode well to finish the sentence with, "...hope to die." I struggle to replace it with something else that suitably rhymes and is less offensive. "...stick a needle in my eye?" Nope. Too gruesome. "...eat some pie?" No. Too silly. Then a good one comes to me. "...love my guy," I say, completing the phrase.

"I'm gonna hold ya' to that promise, Lass," he says with a laugh. "I am guessin' ya' won't like yar' new spy role vera' much." To prove his point, he trots Hades over to a hitching rack and slides off the saddle to tie the reins to the post. Then, he turns to me and says in a cranky, old man voice, "Get yar' lazy arse in gear, woman. I donna have all damn day ta' wait on ya."

Like most Fae equines, Hades is over six feet tall, a long way to the ground for someone who is barely 5' 4" tall and whose legs have cramped up on the ride down to the valley. The way the disguised Tax Man is standing there with his hands on his hips scowling at me makes it apparent that he's not going to help me down. With more confidence than I feel, I swing my left leg over the pillion and attempt to lower my right leg while sticking my foot into the stirrup hanging from Declan's saddle. I get that foot in position and start to lower myself down when, suddenly, the sole of my muddy boot slips off the leather tread and I fall backwards on my sore ass, hitting the ground with a resounding thump.

I feel my husband cringe and hear him in my head, though in keeping in character, he doesn't offer a hand to help me up. *"Feckin' hell, Rosie! Are ya' alright?"*

"I'm fine. I think my pride is hurt more than anything else."

"I'm sorry, Love. I dinna' think you'd have so much trouble gettin' down."

Folks in the area snicker at my fall in the same way Mundanes often think someone else's misfortune is funny. It makes my response crankier than I intend. *"You're supposed to be my superior officer. Stop trying to coddle me. I don't believe you'd hover over Duncan this way."* I mentally snap at my husband.

"Far' the sake of *Dubnos*, woman, why was I cursed with such a useless daughter? 'Tis no wonder yar' still not mated," my *athair* complains to the listening crowd gathered around us. "Can't even unseat a harse' properly."

I can't keep from turning a deep shade of red, his insults hurting me more than I let on. Standing up, I brush dry dirt from the back of my ill-fitting gown and straighten the awful puce-colored sweater. Somewhere in the crowd, a male Asgardian yells out, "I hope she can cook, old man, lest ya' be stuck with her forever. She ain't no beauty and is pretty long in the tooth for satisfactory beddin'." His comment gets the group around him laughing and immediately I am mentally overwhelmed by Lord *Mac Nuada's* inner cold rage, testament to his brutal experimentation at the hands of the North Koreans. Somewhere in the distance, the glass of a street lamp shatters, and I realize for the first time since leaving *Crann Bethadh* what a risk my coming along on this mission with him truly entails.

TOOTHPICKS 9

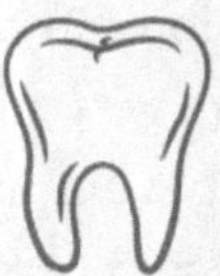

Of Jewels and Juveniles

THE TAX MAN turns away from the laughing crowd and limps off, keeping true to his elderly persona. There's little for me to do but follow behind him, keeping some respectable daughter-like distance between the two of us. However, it's hard to ignore the pulsing vibrations of his hot anger prickling down my spine. If a low-magic tooth fairy, operating in the middle of the day, can feel the vibes of negative energy rolling off my husband's aurora, I have no idea how these *Nordboerne* folk don't seem to notice. *"Whoa there, Cowboy! Maybe you want to rein in some of that fury? It feels like you're sending a live wire up my back!"* I mentally say. *"Someone is sure to notice."*

"I have warded against that, Love. Only you ken' feel the residue of ma' emotions. I am sorry far' putin' ya' through the physical reaction, but the only way ta' prevent it is far' me to close the bond between us, and I will not do that. 'Tis far' too

risky in this situation. Give me a few minutes to get ma' feelins' under control."

"I'm fine, sweetie. Don't worry about me. I was just concerned about the others. You can lay your anger juju on me any time. I can handle it." In response, I get a rather intimate image of an explicit "laying" scenario that leaves me too warm in my ugly sweater. *"I'm holding you to that, Tax Man."*

I hear a low chuckle in my head before the vocal words come out of his mouth. "Sit here, woman, while I attend ta' ma' business," my fake *athair* commands, pointing to a hard wooden bench tucked under a tree across from a row of charming, small shops. "Donna' move yourself from this spot, lest ya' wish ta' test ma' patience and the bite of ma' belt."

"Aye, *Athair Reas* (Respected Father)," I say as I look at my feet, not because I'm a good spy, but rather because I'm pretty sure I'm a bad one. I'm working as hard as I can to keep a straight face. I know some women find calling their lovers "Daddy" super sexy and I'm sure as hell not judging anyone. But calling my Tax Man by that particular pet name, along with the idea of him spanking me, would undoubtedly make me giggle like a crazed hyena. We've just never had that "vibe" and I think his Jr. Lordship would believe I'd gone and lost my mind if I called him 'Daddy," his relationship with his father being what it is. All of those thoughts must transfer from my head to his because he raises that one now-gray eyebrow and gives a questioning, half-assed grimace as he walks away toward a shop advertising the sale of books and parchment.

As ordered, I plop myself on the assigned bench, ignoring the mostly rude stares from passersby. Although I don't regret choosing "ravagin'" instead of lunch, my stomach grumbles over the tantalizing aromas from a street cart selling meat pies a few feet away. I consider purchasing one to eat while I wait, but realize that I've no money on my person and tracking Declan down in the shop to ask for the common gold coinage of the Otherworld is not an option.

Instead, I wile away the time waiting for Declan to come out of the shop by counting the number of people who give me the sign for the Otherworld evil eye as they walk by. At one time, the populations of *I Idir, Avalon,* and *Asgard* shared open borders, and trade between the kingdoms was not only expected, but heavily encouraged. Then, about three or four years ago, several countries in the Mundane world, including the United States, became hell-bent on breaching the Veil between the two dimensions. Each of the countries claimed to have worthwhile and logical reasons for wanting to assimilate Otherworldly culture and tradition into their own, but the actual truth was much darker. Access to the Otherworld and the magic it contained was a jackpot of military and financial opportunities for the Mundanes, and each individual country was using all its available resources to be the first ones to exploit a world other than their own.

From the very beginning, the leadership of *I Idir* and *Asgard* had taken opposite sides over the onslaught of attempted Mundane expansion. The Morrigan had been unbending over her resolute conviction that welcoming the Mundane countries into the Otherworld was an absolute disaster and an end to the magical life that they had known for well over a thousand years. She had vowed to destroy any Otherworld kingdom that even attempted to make Mundane expansion a reality.

The ruling pantheon of *Asgard* sat completely on the other side of the fence, welcoming the idea of Mundanes crossing the Veil into the Otherworld, but not for the reasons the humans naively believed. The *Nordboerne* and their leadership were solidly convinced the Mundanes were a less than intelligent population, one short step up from the apes they descended from, and a race easily conquered and forced into subjugation, giving them unlimited bodies for a massive army and unpaid work-force. Even more horrifying was the concept that because the *Nordboerne* also suffered from the same dwindling population and extremely low birth rates as the Fae, Mundane females could be forced, against their will, into unions with Asgardian males in order to produce larger amounts of offspring.

Through all of this in-fighting, *Avalon* had stayed neutral, though the time was quickly coming when their monarchy would be forced to choose one side or another. Everyone expected the Lady of the Lake, and Robyn Brannigan's great grandmother several times removed, to side with her long-time Raven friend in *I Idir*. However, nothing formal had yet been declared, and until it was, the battle was firmly set between these two larger kingdoms that shared a massive border, with the outlying kingdoms of land and sea, blessed as they were with heavier Veil magic, not yet forced into the discussion.

Even though my loyalty was firmly seated with The

Morrigan, and I found the Asgardian view of humans abhorrent, I still believed it rather sad that the neighboring kingdoms had come to this point in Otherworldly history. For the most part, the Fae and the *Nordboerne* were more similar in appearance, culture, and magical skill than they were different, and until this impasse regarding how to deal with the Mundane world had changed all that, we'd all gotten along peacefully for over eight hundred years.

This was what I was contemplating when the first projectile smacked my head just above my left ear. The hard, green ball bounced off the side of my face and fell into my lap where I recognized it as an unripe, apricot type fruit called *torthai cloiche* (stone fruit) by the Fae folk. Before I could determine where it had come from, another one hit me hard in the back of my head. "Damn it! That really hurt!" I flipped around to look behind me but didn't see anyone within throwing distance. I understand Fae visitors are not entirely welcome in *Asgard*, but I hadn't realized relations had sunk to physical violence. I barely get that thought together when yet another fruit smacks me in the left shoulder. "Sonofabitch!" I mutter. This time when I turn around, I view two young boys, maybe ten or twelve years old, giggling around the corner of a store selling metal work jewelry.

I wag a single digit at them. "*Nil, Nil, Nil* (No, no no)," I say, not even sure if they speak the old Fae language, but figuring they'd still get the general message. In response, the taller of the two makes an obscene gesture and flings another stone fruit directly at me. I duck and it just misses hitting me in the face, making them laugh uproariously.

At this point, I'm one hundred percent pissed, so I stand up and hustle over to where the kids are hiding. Seeing me on the move, they take off down a dark alleyway behind the shops. My original plan is to follow them, but then common sense takes over. The alley looks deserted, however, there are alcoves and doorways up and down the length allowing plenty of places for someone to hide. One would have to be an idiot to wander through there alone and unarmed, so I turn and head back to the bench, hoping my old man *athair* doesn't come out of the book shop and find me not on it. As I round the corner, something in the window of the metal works shop catches my eye so I stop to take a closer look. My attention rests on one specific piece; a heavy, torque-style necklace composed of rose gold and shining platinum. The two metals are worked together in a knot pattern that closely matches designs used in Celtic jewelry, the ends of both sides finished with a sitting wolf, eyes set with round glimmering rubies and their paws joined to hold one single, exceptionally large, oval emerald of such clarity and fire that it takes my breath away.

I've never been the type of girl to gush over sparkly things. I own exactly two pieces of expensive jewelry; my handfasting ring and the garnet and citrine necklace that was a handfasting gift from my Tax Man. I adore both of those items because they are beautifully made and, even more importantly, they were given to me by my beloved Eternal Mate. The torque in this shop window, however, calls to me on a personal "Rosie" level. I can't begin to imagine what something like it costs. I see a tiny tag hanging off the back, most likely revealing the price, and curiosity overwhelms me. I crouch down to try to get a better look at it, forcing me to literally press my nose against the glass. So intent am I on discovering the price that I don't notice when the shop owner comes out the door with a broom in his hand which he uses to swat my behind with more force than is necessary.

"Get away from my window, Fae mongrel," he commands in broken, guttural English.

Red-faced and startled, I stammer, trying hard to not rub my bruised ass. "I was just trying to determine the price of that lovely torque in your window."

"That is a genuine work of art!" the man scolds. "Not meant for the likes of you, you worn-out hag! That necklace belongs on the neck of a regal lady, a high-born woman of nobility and beauty, not some dried-up flop like yourself. Be gone from here, before I call the guards. They're always looking for a free piece. Scat now if you know what's good for ya."

I open my mouth and then close it. The last thing I need is to cause a fuss while Declan and I are undercover. Besides, even if we weren't on a mission, it seems rather greedy on my part to ask for a trinket that probably costs more than my car back in Salem. Despite the Tax Man liking nice things, and even though he's always been extremely generous towards me, I recognize that he's traditionally careful with his money and how it's spent. I can't see him jumping to buy me something this costly simply on a whim without looking more into its quality.

I trudge off, not looking back at the shop or its vitriol owner, embarrassed and not fully understanding why I feel such overwhelming shame. I fully comprehend that

I'm supposed to be playing a role, and that disguised as I am, the shop owner is reacting to the appearance of my low born Fae heritage as well as my abject poverty. Still, his words hit home, reminding me that here in the Otherworld, even as Lady *Mac Nuada,* I'm still just a tooth fairy, low on the Fae social and magical hierarchy and, yet again, pretending to be something I'm not.

And because it's that kind of day, I find my husband standing at the bench, scowling at me as I walk towards it. "Damn it ta' *Dubnos,* woman! Where have ya' wandered off ta'? Ken' you no follow ma' simplest directions?" my fake *athair* grumbles. In my head I hear him add just as angrily, *"Hell, Rosalinda Fitzpatrick! Ya' promised me ya'd sit here and wait. Ma' damn heart almost stopped when I came out and saw this bench empty."* He grabs my upper arm, careful not to grip too tightly, and begins to pull me toward where'd left Hades. "'Tis time for us ta' be on ar' way, woman," he declares in his old man voice.

"We're leaving already?" I mentally ask. *"I thought you wanted to pick up those swords for Dylan and Buaf?"*

"There's no time. It appears ma' questions ta' the bookseller rattled his sensibilities. I fear he will notify those I'd rather not attract the attention of. We need to get out of Gleann Gas. The sooner the better." When we reach the horse, he ignores the old man feebleness of his disguise and lifts me up into the pillion as if I weigh next to nothing. Then, untying the reins from the post, he takes his own place in the saddle and secures the belt around both of our waists before heading toward the city gate. The two guards look up in suspicion, but let us pass without hesitation, an action my

husband takes as a good sign that, as of yet, no one is tracking us.

"*What's the hurry? Did the shopkeeper say something bad? You seem...well...spooked?*"

"*I'll explain later,*" he replies to my mind. "*Right this vera' moment, I need to get us as far away from here as possible.*"

He directs Hades toward an entirely different path than the spiral one we came into town on. This path is far steeper and rockier than the other. "*Aren't you going the wrong way?* I question.

"*I'm going a different way. If we are followed like I believe we will be, they will assume I took the mar' traveled route. The one we're actually takin' would be no one's first choice,*" he explains as the horse struggles up the steep incline. Hades stumbles a bit, and my body tips too far to the right, causing me to nearly slide off despite the belt keeping me attached to my husband. "This isn't gonna' work," he says out loud. "I ken' no have ya' hanging off the pillion."

Declan directs the horse toward a thick grove of trees at the side of the road and unbuckles the belt binding us. He dismounts and reaches up to help me off from my seat behind the saddle. "Ya' will have to sit in front of me so I can keep ya' balanced in the saddle. The ride up is vera steep and we will be movin' at a quicker pace than yar' used ta'."

"I thought you said you didn't want me bouncin on your manly bits? You declared it to be too much of a temptation," I tease, secretly tickled pink to be upfront with my Tax Man and not stuck in the back.

"I guess I will find ma'self takin' one far' the team," he says with a salacious wink. "But I hope ya' will take mercy on yar' par' husband's libido and not wiggle that fine arse of yars' anymar' than is necessary ta' stay on the damn harse'."

"I'll do my best, Tax Man, but sometimes 'ma' fine arse' has a mind of its own," I reply with an equally cheeky wink.

TOOTHPICKS 10

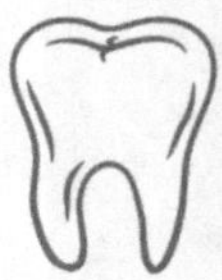

The Travel Unravels

FOR THE NEXT forty-five minutes or so, we don't speak, our concentration duly focused on remaining upright on the stallion's strong back as we make the alternative, more treacherous climb, up from *Gleann Gas* to higher ground. Any sexy thoughts I might have conjured while tucked between my Tax Man muscled thighs evaporate into sheer terror as Hades gingerly trots on a stone path barely as wide as the horse himself, allowing me the opportunity to look down on a drop that would undoubtedly kill all three of us.

I am relieved when we reach the top, but my gratitude is short-lived as Declan declares that we are being followed. He leads us all into a small cavern tucked inside an outcrop of stone and then magically veils it to look as if the open front is solid rock *"We must stay absolutely quiet,"* he says to both the horse and me.

Within our hiding place, I hear the sounds of horses

and men as they search the bush around the cavern. A fearful question pops into my head. *"What about the horse's tracks?"* I ask the Tax Man.

"I've taken care of it, Lass. Just relax and breathe normally," he answers.

I press my back tighter against the rock and do as my husband suggests, but secretly avoid breathing in too deep lest I get an unwelcome whiff of sweaty horse. With Hades between us, I can't see the Tax Man, but I feel his mind entirely focused on keeping the concealing veil solid. The personal energy required to hold a spell as complicated as this for extended periods of time is immense and the vibrations of it run along the nerves beneath the skin of my arm. My sensitivity to my *Mo Shiorghra's* magical energy began the first night we spent together, that new ability transferred along with the ink on my shoulder blade. Up until we added the "eternal" piece to the bond, my mate's magical energy always felt like the gentlest tickle of static electricity. Now, after the addition of the extra bonding, along with the experimentation wrought upon his brain by the North Koreans, it feels as if someone is running a Wartenburg wheel up and down my sensitive flesh, a stinging sensation with a slight burn to it, and something I will hopefully learn to tolerate better.

Eventually, the sounds made by the searchers fade and Declan drops the veil. The three of us step out of the cavern and re-settle ourselves back on Hades. Now that the ground ahead is relatively level, I assumed I'd be relegated back to the pillion at the horse's rear quarters, but the Tax Man lifts me up again to the front end of the saddle and seats himself behind me and I allow myself a grateful sigh for this small gesture of comfortable intimacy.

Since leaving *Gleann Gas,* the sky has darkened, the wind has picked up and I smell the distinct odor of rain in the air. I'm not one of those "nature lovers" who delights in being caught in a downpour, so I hope with all my heart that the bad weather holds off until we reach wherever it is that we are headed. Which reminds me... "Sweetie, can you let me in on where we are headed and why? You still haven't explained why we had to leave *Gleann Gas* in such a hurry. What went on between you and that shopkeeper?"

"We need to travel to the farthest north point of *Asgard,* almost to where the kingdom's border meets the Jade Empire. It's a place the *Nordboerne* call *Dokkr Bygo,* which means 'Dark Settlement' in their old language," my husband explains.

It sounds far, and since I don't really want to know just how long I'll be bouncing along on Hades, I don't ask. Instead, I query, "Why there? Who are we looking for and what do we hope to gain once we get there?"

"Ta' be honest, Love...I'm not really sure. I just know the answers we need require us to go to *Dokkr Bygo.* When I showed the shopkeeper the runes I found in ma' *athair's* ledger, I could instantly feel his fear rise. It took much proddin' on ma' part, along with several fine gems and three magic amulets, to convince him ta' finally share what he knew. It seems that those symbols are part of a long-forgotten form of the old *Futhark* alphabet. They were once used primarily by a sect of *Dokkalfar* practitioners known for the use of *Jotun* magic. When the kingdom was unified under Odin the Youngest, the practice of dark sorcery was officially banned across *Asgard*. History tells that a group of these *Dokkalfar* broke off from the kingdom and moved themselves to this remote location so that they could continue to practice their form of magic in secret. As long as they kept away from the major cities, their king ignored their breaking of the law rather than take on such a powerful group of sorcerers. Most sensible *Nordboerne* folk keep clear of the place."

"And yet here we are," I say, not hiding my irritation, "heading straight for this place with bad 'juju.' You know I trust you with my life, Sweetie, but do you think this is our best option? Maybe it would be better if you went back home to *I Idir* and planned to return to *Asgard* with someone who has stronger magical skills to back you up? I know you love me, but we both know I'm a complete poser when it comes to magical ability."

"In this particular case, Lass, less is more. I am sure the place is strongly warded. If a group of *Sidhe* Fae tried to infiltrate the town, I have no doubt the *Dokkalfar* would feel us coming from miles away and thus plan accordingly. But with it being just you and me, and with me concealing my aura, we may just be able to sneak in under their radar," he reasons.

"And if we do 'sneak in' as you say? Then what?"

"Everything about Marcy Kilcrabtree's murder, as well as *Buaf's* birth, seems to point to *Jotun* magic. If this is the only place in the Otherworld practicing this outlawed sorcery, then the answers are to be found in *Dokkr Bygo*. As to how we will retrieve those answers, I am still without a firm plan. Hell, Love, I am not even sure of the right questions to ask. I only have a magical hunch that I need to proceed there. The pull is strong."

"Will we make it to *Dokkr Bygo* by nightfall?" I ask.

"Nay. 'Tis too far. If I was traveling alone or with Duncan, I would most likely ride through the night and be in the area by dawn. But I would never put ma' Lady through such an arduous adventure. I am hoping to find a local inn where we can shelter and rest for the night. We will leave again at first light."

"I'm not some delicate flower, Tax Man," I protest. "If you think it's best to ride on through the night, I can do it. I want to be a useful member of the team."

He kisses the top of my head. "I have no doubts of yar' fortitude, Love. Ya are surely ma' brave Lass. However, I suggest we leave ar' plans open far' now. We ken' see how well ya' are adaptin' after a multitude of hours in the saddle."

In response, I give him an honorary salute. "Aye, aye, oh fearless 'Capitan.' You'll see. I'm a trooper. I can handle anything that comes our way."

I should have known better than to test the Universe with my words. We'd gone only a mile or two before the dark skies opened up. This was no "spring showers bringing May flowers." This was a frickin' monsoon of cold, pelting rain, only a few degrees away from being hail. In addition, as we continue to trek further north, the temperature drops until it isn't long before I can see my own breath in the air. The Tax Man casts up a veil of sorts, but by the time he adjusts the spell to cover both he and I, along with the horse's head, I'm already soaked to the skin. I consider asking my magically gifted husband for a dry set of clothes, but between holding the veil spell over us, maneuvering the horse through the sticky mud and rough terrain in the blinding rain, and using his third eye to find the exact location of *Dokkr Bygo*, all the while being wet, cold and tired himself, I knew my poor Eternal Mate is stretched to his magical limit. Instead, I keep my suffering to myself, even though the layers of wet clothing are creating a bad case of chafe on my ass and inner thighs.

When darkness eventually falls, it's as if the *Nordboerne* goddess, *Jord* , has taken an Otherworldly paintbrush and coated her sky in thick, black tar. This was 'night' like none I'd ever experienced before; so thick and cloying it almost seemed to press in on one with the intent to suffocate. There was no moon, no stars, not even the tiniest speck of firelight anywhere. I was shivering so hard from the cold, along with a good dose of fear, that my teeth were clicking away in my mouth like a pair of Flamenco castanets.

As a tiny beacon of light suddenly appears further down the road, I initially think that perhaps I am so damn cold and tired that I'm hallucinating. From behind me, Declan announces that he believes the light is coming from a small rural tavern or inn, a place he'd seen a few miles back with his third eye. "I dunno 'bout you, Love, but I'm nearly dead in this saddle. I would hope ma' beloved Lady would not think less of her 'Fearless Capitan' if I decide to stop for the night. I am in need of a hot meal and the opportunity to get out of these wet clothes."

I immediately see this for what it is: Out of love for

me, my darling Tax Man is saving my own sense of pride by claiming that he's the party too tired to go on. Let's look at the facts: Lord *Mac Nuada* is high born, *Sidhe* Fae. Both of his parents can trace their bloodlines back to the *Tuatha De Danann*, and his lineage on both sides boasts kings and warriors. This is the same man who survived six weeks of torture and experimental brain surgery at the hands of the North Koreans. There's no way in *Dubnos* (Celtic Hell) that Declan Fitzpatrick, aka Lord *Mac Nuada*, is too tired or too weak to continue on.

My heart swells with love for this man and I would have immediately kissed him right there and then if only my lips weren't numb from the cold while the physical action of twisting around in the soaked saddle would have put me further into the burning fire of chafing misery. Going for what I can reach, I run my hands over his thighs. "I would never, ever, think less of you, my Lord. You are my Eternal Mate…my One and Only. If you think stopping for the night is the best option, then it most certainly is."

TOOTHPICKS 11

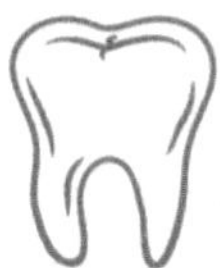

Givin' The Tribe Our Special Vibe

THE FADED SIGN outside the decrepit wooden building welcomed travelers to *Orskots-Helgr*, which Declan explained roughly translated to "a sanctuary near home." Whoever gave this crumbling dump such an auspicious name surely had a different definition of "home" and "sanctuary" than I did. Nothing about the place was inviting, from its filthy, streaked windows, several of which had broken panes, to the noxious odors blowing on the wind from the doorless outhouse set a few feet back.

"I know 'tis not vera' appealin', Love. But it will provide us the barest of necessities; a hot meal and a warm place to dry off," my *Mo Shiorghra* says as he helps me off Hades. "This part of *Asgard* is alive with a type of magic I am not vera' familiar with. I am unwillin' to test its origins or openly use ma' own, lest I give evidence that we are not who we pretend to be. The best scenario is far' us ta' continue ta' play the roles we've built until we are safely back in *I Idir*. My title and ma' connections ta' the Raven Queen will not be of help here."

"I understand, Sweetie. I'll go back to being your homely, dimwit of a daughter," I concede. "But you need to promise me that on our next mission together, I will get a better role to play than this one."

Declan laughs under his breath, but I note that he doesn't actually come out and make that promise. He pushes open the door to the inn, which of course, creeks wide with an eerie groan. Every head in the smoky room turns toward the two of us. It's impossible to miss the wave of general hostility, and for a second, we are both frozen in place. "Either get your *fotrs* (legs) inside or go out the same way you came in," a voice growls. "You're lettin' all the cold air in."

My husband steps further into the room and I follow, pulling the wooden door shut behind me. I try not to gape, but the menagerie of fellow guests is so unusual it's hard not to stare. The only Elven *Nordboerne* people I'd ever met before this mission had been the few who'd taken positions on staff at *Dun Siorai*. These were folks who lived on the borders of *I Idir* and *Asgard* and who had undoubtedly taken mates from the alternate kingdoms. Like the people in *Gleann Gas*, the Elven staff members of *Dun Siorai* didn't look much different from their Fae neighbors, tall, lithe and fair of complexion. Whereas the Fae of *I Idir* usually sported hair in varying shades of red, the *Nordboerne* folk also living there possessed hair colors in multiple shades from blonde to silver and even midnight black.

The Elven folk in the room in front of me were of an

entirely different nature. They were much smaller in stature, so much so, that even at only 5' 4" tall, I looked hideously large next to them, while Declan, at 6' 4" must have appeared to be a giant in their eyes. And speaking of eyes, all of these folks had round, saucer-like peepers in contrasting shades of chilly gray and icy blue, with only the smallest of lids, a striking contrast against their pale, mottled, gray skin. Almost all of the guests had curly dark hair except for those of advanced years whose heads were crowned in wiry, gray corkscrews. The males in the menagerie favored long matching beards with a few braids and silver beads woven into their nest-like facial hair. I guessed these Elven people to be the *Dokkalfar* we were in search of, and in my mind, I tried to find some resemblance to Declan's half-brother, *Buaf*, in the lines of their gray-tone faces.

We were the only non-*Dokkalfar* in the room, and even with my under-whelming magical senses, I could feel the vibrations of powerful energy running under my feet. I followed my "Capitan" to an empty table and took a seat across from him. A very round little man scuttled toward us, his dirty white apron labeling him as the supposed proprietor. "Ya' can pay?" he asked in broken, heavily accented English.

"Aye," my elderly "*athair*" replies, lying two perfectly cut amethysts on the table. "One hot meal with ale, and a bed far' the night. Plus, barn shelter and hay far' ma' harse."

The man greedily examined the fine gemstones with his eyes, then added, "That'll cost ya' three gems. No less. Four if ya' want a bed big enough for a tumble."

As the Tax Man narrows his eyes at the man, a clay dinner bowl rattles on its own. "The woman is ma' daughter. What ya' suggest is disgustin'."

The proprietor shrugs. "What a low born Fae does or doesn't do is no matter to me. We'd heard it tell that the Raven Queen encourages strange mating practices among her peoples. Do as ya' wish, old man. She ain't much to look at anyway. The cost still stands at three gems."

I secretly pray that Declan won't lose his temper and shatter every piece of glass in the room. I can see the strain of holding back in his tightened shoulders as he pulls a third amethyst from a pouch in his pocket. "What manner of meal does three gems buy?" my husband asks, his voice low and strictly controlled.

"Two tankards of ale and your choice of barley soup or mutton stew. Plus, a quarter loaf of brown bread," the man says.

"We'll take the soup," the Tax Man answers. "And I donna' wan' ta' find any mold on the bread."

The man bows in a mocking manner. "As your Royal Jackass desires," he chuckles as he walks away.

I look at Declan whose face is a blank slate. I try to open a channel of mental communication, but find him completely shielded. The nasty old man comes back and dumps two tankards of dark *Nordboerne* ale on the table, along with two bowls of soup and a hunk of bread that he places directly on the wood of the table without the benefit of a plate. The soup is bland and watery, but at least edible, while the bread is mold-free, if not more than a little stale. We eat in silence, aware of a multitude of eyes boring holes into our backs. Given the energy of the room, we don't dawdle over our meal.

Once finished, the inn's owner hands my husband a rusty key and points to a set of stairs. "Last room on the left," he says. "Ya' damage anything ya' pay."

As we pass through the room, me following directly behind Declan, another patron reaches out and pinches me on the ass. Hard. I choke back a response, fully knowing the Tax Man is about ready to explode in rage. The stairs groan under our combined weight and I expect my foot to go through the rotting wood at any given moment. Our room is the last one at the end of the hall which my spy husband dislikes for its far proximity to any type of inside exit. The room's window, however, is centered right over the front entrance's overhang, allowing, he explains, an alternative escape.

There is, naturally, no inside bathroom, just a cracked chamber pot underneath the lopsided platform calling itself a bed. As embarrassing as that scenario is, I consider it a better option than the doorless shack outside. The bed itself is tiny, barely a Mundane twin-sized and obviously built with the slighter *Dokkalfar* people in mind. "Ya' take the bed, Lass. I'll sleep on the floor," Declan lovingly offers. I inspect the stained, filthy linens and hesitate. "I understand it's terrible, Love, and if I could, I'd provide ya' with somethin' better, but I don' dare use ma' magic here. As it already stands, we are objects of heavy suspicion. I don' wish ta' call anymore unwanted attention ta' ourselves." He pulls a small folded blanket from his saddle bag and lays it across the bed. "I always ride with an extra *blaincead* (blanket) in case ma' horse develops pressure sores. It's no feather-down comforter, but 'tis clean."

I throw my arms around his neck and enjoy the comfort of his returned embrace. "Are you sure you don't want to share the bed?" I ask with what I think is a seductive smile. "We can keep each other warm."

"Ya' are a walkin' temptation, Lady *Mac,* and ya' constantly drive me mad with desire. But that would be a vera' bad idea. I don' need that old bastard thinkin' what he's spewin' about the perverted nature of the Fae ta' be true," he says with a grin that doesn't fully reach his eyes.

"I can be quiet as a mouse, Tax Man. I promise. No one will know what erotic things are going on in here," I tease, sticking my hands in the waistband of his breeches.

He gently pulls my hands away and takes them in his own, looking at me with his head in tilted question. "Ya' really don' know, do ya?"

"Know what? I ask, trying not to pout over my refused advances.

My *Mo Shiorghra* tucks a stray hair that's come loose from under my kerchief behind my ear and looks at me. "Because we are now Eternal Fated Mates, when the two of us…'join,' we cast off a certain magical…vibe."

"Wait. What?" I ask, not fully understanding what my husband is trying to tell me. "What kind of…vibe?"

"During intimacy, the two of us together give off a type of magical energy…an aura of sorts that is no aura in the true sense of the word. 'Tis more like a…vibration."

"Are you saying that other people can sense this thing? Like they can tell when we're…doing it?" I ask, now wholly embarrassed.

"Aye. Though it is limited to higher born Fae with more sensitivity to those types of energy patterns," he explains.

"Do you mean Mel and Duncan would know? And *Birgit*? Holy Hotcakes! *Birgit*? She lives with us for Pete's sake! And what happens when Dylan gets older? Are we going to need to wait until he's grown up and out of the house to start having sex again? Oh, hell bells! And now there's *Buaf* too! He's only eight! I'll be a damn dried-up old lady before they both grow up!" I pace the room, a hand to my forehead. "Isn't this something you should have told me sooner?"

"Honestly, Lass, I thought ya' already knew. Ya' said ya' read up on the tenets of the Eternal Bond. I would think that would have been discussed in the writings," he argues.

"Well, apparently, I missed that important part. Feckin' hell, Tax Man, this is so damn embarrassing!" I complain.

"I would not say it's embarrassing at all, Rosie Love. We are Eternal Mates. 'Tis to be expected that we would desire to be intimate. It is part of the magic. I only bring it up now because of our current situation. I do not know if picking up on our bond is within the range of the *Dokkalfar* folk, but their magic seems vera' powerful and I would no want ta' risk having the entire room down-stairs thinkin' the dirty old Fae man was ruttin' his own daughter. That would be more than embarrassin'. 'Twould be disgustin'…and wholly dangerous."

Any trace of wifely libido I might have held goes right out that cracked window along with any heat produced by the small stove in the corner. It's going to take me a long time to work through this unwelcome information. Right now, I'm simply tired of this whole "mission." "Let's shelve this conversation for another time, Declan. I just can't deal with it right now." I shed my wet clothes and drape them across a chair in front of the glowing stove in hopes that they will sufficiently dry overnight. Shivering, I climb on the rickety bed and pull the left-over edge of the horse blanket over myself. I hear his Jr. Lordship undress as well, but instead of taking a spot on the floor like he planned, he squeezes his large frame into the tiny bed next to me, lying on his right side to conserve space. "'Tis a good idea ya' had, Lass. We ken' still keep each other warm, though we will have to work at not lettin' the bond have its way."

There is no scenario I can possibly think of where I would not want my Tax Man next to me, so without a word, I scoot closer and throw the tiny piece of blanket over both of our hips. Being as cold, tired, and worried as I am, the usual swelling lust quiets itself. "Good night, Declan. I love you."

"I love you as well, my Sweet Rosie Lass," he answers. "Try to rest as much as ya' ken. I have no idea what tomorrow will bring."

The stress and physical strain of the day trumps any thoughts my tired brain tries to bring to the forefront. I fall asleep quickly and remain that way until a heavy, hand presses down on my mouth. I wake frantic, pulling at the unknown hand. Now fully awake, I hear Declan's voice in my head. *"'Tis me, Rosie. I need far' ya' to remain absolutely still. There's someone in the room with us. I donna' want him ta' know we're awake."*

I strain my ears trying to hear anything that would indicate the presence of another person in the tiny room, but note nothing but silence. Without any warning, my husband jumps out of bed, completely nude while tussling with a dark form hovering near the room's glowing stove. Lord *Mac Nuada* is obviously much larger than the intruder, and it doesn't take long for my husband to put the wretched scoundrel in a choke hold. He pulls off the man's hooded face covering and gasps, letting the person go as he frantically grabs for his breeches. "Feckin' hell, *Mathair*! I could have hurt ya!"

TOOTHPICKS 12

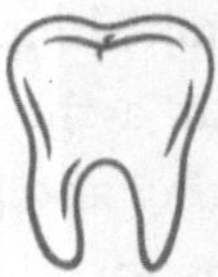

When the Truth Hurts

"MATED life has made you slow, *Deaglan*. You should have never let me get this far into the room," my mother-in-law says, shoving our wet clothes off the chair and taking the seat for her own use. Meanwhile, I tug, pull and tuck, desperate to make the standard-sized saddle blanket fit around my not-standard-sized self.

My husband struggles to pull the wet breeches up over his nudity. "What in *Lugh's* library are ya' doin' here, *Mathair*? And how in *Dubnos* did ya' know where to find us? No one knew exactly where we were headin'. Not even the Black Knight. Feck! Even I wasn't sure myself until yesterday."

Lady *Siobhan* crosses her pant covered legs and steeples her fingertips. "Sometimes you are as stupid as the ass who sired you, *Deaglan*. Surely you have already figured it out?" Her voice echoes in the room, louder than this stealth required situation called for.

"Shhhh," her son warns. "The last thing we need is for the *Dokkalfar* downstairs to hear you and decide to investigate."

"The wee elven critters are of no concern," his mother says. "They are all in a state of deep sleep. As you know, the dark elves are extremely susceptible to lavender and snakeroot. I let the northeasterly wind carry the powder in through the broken windows." Seeing our confused faces, she adds with the usual amount of Lady *Nuada* smugness, "Oh, that's right. You don't know a single thing about the *Dokkalfar*. Rather silly of you to take on a mission like this unaware of basic elven physiology." Sometimes my mother-in-law can be a real bitch. No. Not sometimes. Most of the time.

Declan sits on the end of the bed and scowls at the face that looks so much like his own. "And when did ya' become such an expert on Dark Elves, *Mathair*? I thought all you ever gave thought to was the cut of your next new gown and who is feckin' whom within the Ruling Class circles."

I hate the relationship between my husband and his mother. She always brings out the worst in my Tax Man and their exchanges are incredibly toxic. Granted, since Declan's kidnapping by the North Koreans and the birth of our son, they can now manage to be in the same room together for more than five minutes, but theirs is surely not the relationship I want to emulate with my own child.

"You think that only because that is what your pig of a father has led you to believe. My family might not have had a seat on the Ruling Council, but we had prestige and wealth with more connections at Court and a bigger treasury than House *Nuada* ever had on its own. As a girl, my *athair* had me tutor with practitioners and sorcerers from all over the Otherworld in preparation for becoming the mate of a titled Lord. One of my teachers was a nasty old *Dokkalfar* who lived on a steady diet of fava beans and farted like a pregnant sow. He was, however, full of knowledge, the lot of which he passed on to me." She leaned forward in her chair. "There's a reason why people are careful not to offend your *mathair,* Lord *Mac Nuada.*"

"And all this time I believed it was just yar' viper's tongue they feared," my husband snipes back.

Instead of the anger I've come to expect from Lady *Siobhan,* she claps her hands together and laughs. "There is more of me in you than you think, *a mhic daor* (my dear son). It has irritated the old weasel from the first day it became obvious to him that you would not become his perfect little puppet."

"As much as I always cherish a visit from ya', *mathair mhilis* (sweet mother), ya' still haven't told me why ya' are here or how ya' knew where ta' find me," Lord *Mac* replies with that arrogant lilt that sometimes even grates on my own nerves.

"You still haven't figured it out, have you, foolish boy?" his mother says. She looks directly at me and I try to blush over the fact I'm having a conversation with my husband's mother while I sit here stark naked. "I would bet that your little tooth fairy mate has made the correct deductions, haven't you, girl?"

She's correct. The minute I noticed Lady *Siobhan's* unusual apparel, I'd begun to put two and two together. I have never seen my husband's mother not "dressed to the nines." Whether spending time in the Otherworld or during her infrequent visits to the Mundane plane, her choice of dress is always fashionably chic and outrageously expensive. I assumed that my Tax Man inherited his own exceptional fashion eye from his stylish mother. So, when she popped into our room, I immediately found it strange to see the very vain *Siobhan* Fitzpatrick dressed in severe, black, tactical clothing. Tactical clothing I'd definitely seen on certain other people in the past.

Both Declan and his mother stare at me as they wait on my answer. I address my response to my husband, "I do believe you and your *mathair* are playing for the same team, Sweetie."

Initially, he doesn't get my excellent sports metaphor, then understanding blooms in his startled expression. "Yar' part of the Queen's Intelligence Network?" he asks his mother.

Lady *Nuada* smirks at my Tax Man. "Don't look so shocked, *Deaglan*. The clues were all there. You just missed them because you can't shake all your sire's false assumptions about me."

"When?" he questions, not hiding the anger in his voice. "And how? Does everyone know this but me?"

"Simmer that self-righteous pride of yours down, Lord *Mac*. It's unflattering in someone of your breeding. I was recruited by Herself about five years ago when the Mundane world began pushing hard to cross the Veil. She believed there to be traitorous plotters amongst members of the Ruling Council, those who were actively seeking to make secret deals with the leadership of certain Mundane countries. Her Majesty knew my social influence among the titled Fae is strong and she asked me to be her eyes and ears among the other Lords and their spouses. It made sense for The Morrigan to come to me. As I have said earlier, the Donnelys might not wear a current ruling title, but we are descended from *Niall* of The Nine Hostages fame who ruled in both the Mundane and Otherworld in the 4th and 5th Century. Our Donnely bloodline has been loyal to the goddess of war and destruction for her entire reign. My own mother spent years at *Crann Bethadh* in service to Her Majesty."

"I remember you telling me that," I comment. "But you've always warned me against becoming involved with the Raven Queen."

"Advice which you refused to take, stupid girl. Once you allow yourself to become part of Her inner circle, there is no getting out," *Siobhan* warned. "She will have those Raven claws in you until you take your last breath in the land of the living. I wanted my son's *Mo Shiorghra* to be able to live simply as his spouse and the mother of his children without a Royal burden, but I see that is not to be."

"Have ya' been officially trained by the Black Knight?" Declan asks. I can feel him still wrestling with the unimaginable idea that his own mother was a spy and that he himself had no clue.

"As a young girl, I could already satisfactorily wield a sword and dirk better than most men. My father saw to every facet of my upbringing. But in answer to your question, *Deaglan*, yes, I trained with the Black Knight, though only he and Herself are aware of my involvement in the Network. The less people that know, the less chance that the rat-faced bastard mate of mine will uncover that information and use it against me. There are no boundaries he is unwilling to cross, and I fear for the safety and happiness of my daughters. He is the reason Meghan is the way she is. I hold him personally responsible for her unjust imprisonment."

I don't one hundred percent agree with my mother-in-law's perception regarding Declan's youngest sister. She did try to kill me on three different occasions; however, this isn't a good time to bring that up, especially because another revelation comes to my mind. "Is that why Her Majesty chose you to stay with me before Dylan was born?" I ask.

"She didn't choose me. I asked for the assignment," Dragon Mama says.

"But you acted like you wanted no part of that job," I say. "You were pretty damn convincing."

"Of course, I was convincing. Your life depended on it. There was no telling how low Lord Weasel would stoop to take possession of my grandson. As it was, he planned to imprison you in *I Idir* and marry you off to that pimple-faced *Mac Badh* lad so he could transfer guardianship of House *Nuada's* surviving heir over to himself."

A strange look passes over my *Mo Shiorghra's* face. "But that would mean ma' own *athair* expected me not to return alive from North Korea. How could he be so solidly sure of such a thing?"

His *mathair* looks away and doesn't answer. A sick feeling builds in my gut over the implications of her silence while the same realization comes to my husband. "Are ya' implyin' that ma' sire had somethin' ta' do with ma' capture?" he asks in a low whisper. "If ya' ever once held any maternal affection far' me *Mathair*, than I beg ya' ta' tell me the ugly truth."

The smug sense of confidence slides from Lady *Nuada's* attractive face, replaced with something more akin to grief. "If you are looking for the absolute truth, *Deaglan,* then it is something I cannot give to you. However, there are those in the inner circle that believe the wretched dead tooth fairy woman was manipulated into going to North Korea by her titled lover, which you no doubt know was your abominable sire. It was his belief that as Kilcrabtree's superior officer, you would feel obligated to go into North Korea to rescue her. There's no hiding the consensus that throughout *I Idir,* you are known to be an honorable leader with your loyalty firmly in the Raven Queen's grasp. I can't begin to tell you how much your devotion to The Throne and to The Morrigan's vow of keeping the Mundanes out of the Otherworld sticks in your sire's craw. He's made no secret of the anger he holds over the knowledge that he's lost complete control over you since you've gone from being a mere boy to a grown man. In addition, your physical resemblance to the Donnely bloodline doesn't help matters much. Lord Weasel has always resented the fact that my people had more wealth than he did, all the while with his hand out to grab more of what he himself hadn't earned. Every time he looks at you, and sees the history of my bloodline in your face, he is reminded of that fact."

The air in that small room feels heavier than it had only a few moments before. I guess that it has something to do with all the negative energy that's been released by

Lady *Nuada's* heart-wrenching narrative. I want nothing more than to throw myself into my Tax Man's arms and offer consolation, but two things stop me. #1: From previous experience, I know how prickly Declan Fitzpatrick gets over affection offered with any sense of pity, and I'm not feeling up for his rejection at this awkward moment. And #2: I'm still sitting here embarrassingly bare-assed naked in front of my husband's mother with only a towel-sized blanket to cover myself.

"I appreciate your honesty, *Mathair.* 'Twas not a pleasant tale to tell, and I am sorry for the grief and shame ma' sire has brought upon our House. But what's done is done, and we all must move forward. There is mar' at stake here than ar' personal feelins'. You must have a specific reason far' tracking ma' Lady and I down ta' such a desolate and dangerous spot. I will need to know why so I may proceed with this mission."

My mate's calm, rational response to such a gut-wrenching, awful revelation is odd. With the torturous alterations to his brain by the North Koreans, the Tax Man's emotions have been running full force. At the very least, I would have expected the remaining glass in the window to have shattered in the aftermath of his mother's narrative. This leads me to only one conclusion. Lord *Mac Nuada* was already aware of his sire's treachery well before his mother's visit tonight. I may be new to this whole spy business, but even I know now is not the time to question my husband regarding my suspicions. Instead, I focus on my mother-in-law's answer.

Dragon Mama lets out a dramatic sigh. "Lord *Nuada* is aware that you've left *I Idir* and that you are actively seeking information among the *Dokkalfar* people. There is apparently a mole within *Crann Bethadh,* as well as an abundance of staff at *Dun Siorai* loyal only to your father. He's been keeping track of your every move and knows you've been staying at the Raven's Nest with the supposed 'prisoner.' In light of this, I was concerned for your safety, and that of your mate, so I petitioned Herself to be allowed to come and warn you. She granted that request, but I am forbidden to accompany you both on the rest of your journey. I am to return to *Dun Siorai* before I am missed."

Lord *Mac Nuada* takes his mother's hands in his and bends down to kiss her cheek. "I am grateful for your concern, *Mathair.* And for coming here to warn me. My Lady and I will approach our journey with extra caution."

"You still haven't told me why you are heading so far into *Dokkalfar* territory," Lady *Siobhan* counters.

My husband hesitates, contemplating, I'm sure, of how much he can trust her. Deciding in his *mathair's* favor, he goes ahead and describes my encounter with *Jotun* soul magic and the unexpected death of Rory Dell.

"Do you believe this has something to do with the tooth fairy's death, or do you only seek information about your *athair's* bastard?" she asks with all the bluntness that is *Siobhan* Fitzpatrick *Nuada.*

"So, you know then? About the boy?" he counters.

"I was suspicious from the first day he brought that half-breed *bairn* to *Dun Siorai.* Callum Fitzpatrick is not a man soft of heart and an orphaned infant would be of no use to him. But he kept the child out of my sight and I did my best to ignore him, though I heard the rumors that he resembled the elven folk more than the Fae. When I saw the unwanted infant, now grown to boyhood, *Nuada* blood written in his face, along with his cursed sixth toe, it was as if the Universe's truth bent down and slapped me in the face. And then to have you shelter the bastard under your care was yet an additional blow to your own *Mathair's* feelings. If you had any sense at all, Lord *Mac Nuada*, you would see the boy drowned like the elven mongrel he is."

I can't help but gasp out loud at her comment. Lady *Nuada* is hard to swallow as a person, but I never thought she would be someone who would advocate for child murder. I open my mouth to answer, but Declan beats me to it. "He is an innocent child, and my half-brother. The blood of House *Nuada* runs in his veins. I will not allow any harm coming ta' that lad and those who seek it will answer to me."

She sighs loudly. "I should have expected as much. When you were born, the old House Mage was the one who suggested the name *'Deaglan'* for you. As you are aware, your name means 'full of goodness.' I thought it an odd choice for a child who was the cause of his own twin's death, but back then I was too weak to speak my mind. I often wonder if I had given you a stronger name, would things have turned out differently?"

TOOTHPICKS 13

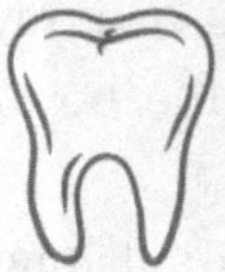

TMI

"A DIFFERENT NAME would have changed nothing, *Mathair*. I am who the Universe created me ta' be…and that be no murderer of children. No one shall lay a hand on the lad as long as I am breathin'," Declan says.

His mother eyes him coolly, and by the red glow of the room's stove, with the light catching the ginger of her hair and eyebrows, she reminds me of the *Nordboerne Valkyries* who walk among dead warriors. "I wonder, *Deaglan,* if this 'goodness' of yours extends to your own *athair*? He is a traitor, you know," she says. "An enemy of the Raven Queen you hold such fierce loyalty towards. Your father has set his sights on the wealth and glory promised to him by the leaders of the Mundane world. He will sacrifice all he has in pursuit of ultimate power he believes will build 'a new Otherworld.' When the time comes, and come it shall, will you be able to take up arms against the man who sired you? The man whose name you share…the very *deamhan* (demon) who gave you your *Nuada* bloodline and then threw you to the Mundane wolves?"

Lady *Siobhan's* question hangs in the space between mother and son. I knew from the first day I met his parents that the Fitzpatrick family dynamics were... complicated. Even dysfunctional. But this goes beyond anything I could ever have imagined. Is my mother-in-law truly implying that my husband should kill his own father? I don't doubt that what Lady *Nuada* claims about his Lordship is true. I've heard him speak treasonous words with my own ears. But saying the words and actually plotting against The Throne are two entirely different things, and I still haven't fully wrapped my head around the idea that Declan's own father was behind his kidnapping in North Korea.

Lord *Mac Nuada* presses his lips together into a thin line. "I don't discount your words, *Mathair*. His Lordship has given us all multiple reasons to question his bad judgment and ill-advised decisions. There are many people in the Raven's inner circle who believe Lord *Nuada* is, without a doubt, a traitor to his people. However, until there is irrefutable proof that he stands with the Mundane world in plotting against Her Majesty, I will not unjustly accuse him. 'Tis one of the reasons I am here in *Asgard*. To gather solid evidence that I believe will answer a multitude of burning questions."

Part of me knows I should stay out of this discussion between mother and son, but I've never been the kind of woman who doesn't say what needs to be said. "Lady *Mathair*," I say, using the more informal title she sometimes finds charming and other times detests, "you seem very sure that his Lordship is guilty of these...crimes. What proof do you base your convictions on?"

Apparently, this is one of those times when my mother-in-law decides she detests my use of the informal title. She narrows those green eyes of hers until they are little slits, reminiscent of the crocodiles I've seen at the Franklin Park Zoo in Boston. "Are you questioning my integrity, tooth fairy?"

"Never, Lady *Nuada*. In fact, I agree with most of what you say. I only seek to clarify things for my beloved mate." It's a lame attempt to smooth things over, but it's the best I got right now.

"You lie almost as well as a high born *Sidhe*, tooth fairy," she smirks. "But I commend your willingness to listen to fact when it is obvious my cotton-headed only son will not. Callum Fitzpatrick *Nuada* has no allegiance to anyone but himself. Your own *mathair*, Rosalinda, should thank the Universe that she wasn't the one mated to this narcissistic villain. There hasn't been one day in all of our years together that he hasn't made me curse the Fates for bonding me to such a vile male. From the moment he was proclaimed Lord of House *Nuada* at the death of his *athair*, he has been plotting to procure a greater position of power for himself. His mate, his children, even the welfare of his own House, mean nothing to him. I have heard whispered conversations about his nefarious dealings in *Asgard* for years. Did you not wonder, *Deaglan*, why your *athair* continues to 'do busi-ness' in the *Nordeboerne* kingdom when the rest of the Ruling Council has all but cut their ties to *Asgard* over their desire to open the Veil?" Declan doesn't respond, so she continues. "Rumors have circulated for years about his disdain for The Morrigan's vow to keep *I Idir* 'stuck in the past,' as he has been known to say."

"Those are just rumors. I donna' hold ta' the prattling of bored aristocrats, *Mathair*, and neither should you," her son says. "He is yar' fated mate. You wear his ink. Should ya' not at least give him the benefit of the doubt?"

My Tax Man's comment draws his mother's anger and she sets her jaw in the same fashion as I've seen her offspring do on a multitude of occasions. "Spoken like a man content in the Universe's match for him, unaware of the misfortune of all others and blindly privileged in his lust-soaked happiness. Not all of us at the mercy of Fate are as fortunate as you, *Mac Nuada*." She doesn't wait for his response and addresses me instead. "You asked how I can be sure, Rosalinda? I will tell you how. The stupid old fool talks in his sleep, more so after we have joined."

My husband jumps in. "Stop there, *Mathair*. I do not desire ta' hear tales regardin' the intimacy of ma' parents. 'Tis…unseemly."

I want to agree with my *Mo Shiorghra*, but my train of thought is running on a completely different track. "Ewwww," I blurt out. "How can you keep…sleeping with him knowing everything that he's done."

Now the Tax Man just looks horrified. If there was a way he could disappear without appearing like a complete coward, I'm sure he would. Which, of course, tickles Dragon Mama's bitchiness, causing her to elaborate on my question. "Surely you've experienced the strength of the physical bond between you and my son, tooth fairy, probably more so since the two of you have become

Eternal Mates, a ceremony, which I might add, I wasn't invited to participate in."

It's my turn in the hot seat. "Yes. That's true. We've experienced this bond. It's quite…intense."

"Did you presume, then, Lady *Mac Nuada*, that the magic of that lust only manifests in couples who have tender feelings for each other?" she says with a marked tone of bitterness.

"I…I guess I did," I stutter, not liking where this discussion is heading and now completely regretting my off the cuff question. I can't help but recall that night after I was arrested; my complete burning hurt and anger when it appeared that Declan had turned his back on me. Despite my grief and the temporary lack of forgiveness toward my mate, I could in no way resist the pull between us. The memory, as well as the topic at hand, make me very uncomfortable.

"How childish of you, tooth fairy. It only reinforces how little you understand the magic that brought you to this point in your life or the history of the Fae people. The Ritual that is demanded of first-born heirs has the singular purpose of providing offspring that will go on to benefit the kingdom and keep the fragile peace among the different Houses. It makes no guarantees regarding the happiness of the partners involved. Yes, it is a special blessing if the union also brings about a deep sense of commitment. Love, if you are silly enough to call it that. But it is by no means a mandated requirement of the magic. That particular casting deals in lust, and lust alone. I can no more resist the weasel's touch than he can deny mine. Our joinings have produced six living children, all born of The Ritual's union, and all meant to serve the future of *I Idir*. Yet, it is no small secret that we absolutely despise each other." She leans forward in her chair. "I long for the day when Callum Fitzpatrick is found out to be the filthy rat that he truly is. And on the day...when his neck feels the vengeance of the Black Knight's *Caladbolg*, I will gladly celebrate finally being free of the curse that has bound me for so many years to such a vile soul."

The only sound in the room comes from the crackling of the fire in the stove and the whistle of the wind through the trees outside the inn. Not once in these past ten months since I met and handfasted the Tax Man had I ever contemplated that a Fated Match, designed by the magic of the Universe, didn't guarantee a love that would last a lifetime. Sure, I knew The Ritual hadn't been a blessing to either of Declan's parents, and it certainly had changed my own mother's view of the world, and not for the better. Even so, I believed their sour relationships had just been a fluke. I hadn't truly understood that the magic of The Ritual was entirely based in physical, biological attraction for the main purpose of reproduction. Had my Tax Man and I been exceptionally lucky in finding true love so quickly, or are we still so madly drawn to each other's bodies that we refused to see anything else as possible? It was a prospect I hated to consider.

I don't dare look at my *Mo Shiorghra*. If his face holds any of the same thoughts, I don't want to see them. Leaning against the window frame, he pulls a slip of paper from the pocket of his breeches and hands it to his mother. "A man can't be condemned on the murmurins' of his pillow talk, Lady *Nuada*. The Ruling Council will demand solid proof of treasonous and illegal behavior. You claimed earlier that you'd studied with a *Dokkalfar* tutor. Do ya' recognize any of these symbols?"

Lady *Siobhan* brought the parchment closer to the fire to get a better look in brighter light. "This first one, 'ᛈ,'" she says, pointing to what looks like a weird letter C to me, "is '*Pethro*.' It's the ancient *Futhark* symbol for 'secrets,' usually dealing with those of an occult nature. And the second one, 'ᛒ,' is *Berkano*. This one was often used to represent fertility or beginnings."

I instantly recall Declan explaining that the second symbol appeared in the ledger around the same time we believed *Buaf* appeared at *Dun Siorai*. I try mentioning that thought to him mentally, but I'm met with a shield that's thicker than a brick wall.

Dragon Mama knits her eyebrows together in concentration. "I'm not sure about this last one. Are you sure you copied it right?" she asks Declan.

"Aye. I traced it directly from the original," he states.

"At first glance it resembles 'ᚾ' which represents 'a new enterprise,' but the lines on the sides seem to come lower than they should," she explains. "With those extending lines, it might be 'ᛗ,' or '*Mannaz*' which is the rune for 'enemy.' It is hard to say without seeing it in the original context. Where did you find these? Very few *Sidhe* would recognize these runes if they came across them."

Lord *Mac Nuada's* face remains a blank slate, but I've spent enough time with him to be able to read some of his body language. He's in the process of trying to decide just how far this new-found trust of his mother actually goes. Eventually, he decides to come clean. "I found these symbols in the margins of House *Nuada's* treasury ledgers. I haven't done enough research ta' be able ta' tell if any deposits or withdrawals are tied ta' them. I planned on doing that once I was sure what the runes meant."

"Is that your purpose for heading toward the Dark Settlement?" Lady *Siobhan* asks.

"Among other things," he says. "I still believe there are more answers to be gained among the *Dokkalfar*. Da' ya' happen ta' recall Master Brendan, the ink mage? He performed my Ritual, as well as ma' *athair's*."

"That old snake? I had heard he left *I Idir* to seek the solitary life. I thought it a ridiculous notion when I heard of his departure, as he never struck me as a very spiritual man. He always seemed too busy lining his pocket and seducing young girls to care about his inner consciousness. Do you believe he has something to do with your sire's treasonous activities?"

"I ken' no say far' sure, but I was told while in *Gleann Gas* that it was believed he'd taken up residence among the *Dokkalfar* of the Dark Settlement. All things considered, it ken'not be a coincidence. I intend to seek him out and bring him back ta' *Crann Bethadh* far' questionin'," my husband says.

Lady *Siobhan* rises from her seat and stretches the kinks out of her back. "I don't guess he'll go willingly, *Mac Nuada*. I hope you are ready for whatever dark magic he will likely throw at you. Or your sire, should you have the misfortune of running into him."

"I ken' handle Master Brendan, Lady *Mathair*. His Lordship as well," Declan says with more confidence than I'm holding onto. "Will you return now ta' *Dun Siorai*?"

"I suppose I should. It wouldn't be prudent for the staff to discover I'm not in my quarters as I should be."

"It's a difficult ride at night, *Mathair.* Perhaps you should wait until dawn to leave?"

"Really, *Deaglan,* you don't honestly believe I traveled all the way here by horseback, do you?" she asks, not bothering to hide her smirk.

"How else? Magical travel is against protocol law in nearly all the Otherworldly countries unless one is jumping from the Mundane world," her son says.

"Exactly," she replies. "I jumped to our estate in Ireland and then here. I'll return the same way, though I do wish I had the time to spend a few days in Ballydonnely. It's been so long since I've visited and I do miss the white pudding from that tiny shop in the center of town. Our Cook never seems to get the seasoning right." She sighs her regret. "I will leave you to your mission. No one hopes more than I that you will find what you need to set Callum Fitzpatrick under the blade."

"I appreciate the warning about his Lordship tracking us, *Mathair.* I will use extra caution."

She draws a circle around her feet to cast her jump, but before she leaves, I take my chances and ask, "Lady *Nuada?* Do you think you can look in on Dylan at *Crann Bethadh* in the morning? I know we plan to be home later tomorrow, but it would make me feel so much better if his *seanmathair* (grandmother) personally checked in on him?"

She gives me a look that waivers between gratitude and wariness. "Aye. I can do that. I haven't seen *mo una beag* (my little lamb) in several days. I will do my best to get permission. The security at the Raven's Nest is especially tight these days." Addressing her son she adds, "And if you intend to continue dragging your mate along with you on these intelligence adventures, *Deaglan*, you will need to get her better trained, the sooner the better. She's virtually useless the way she is." And with that little ray of *Siobhan* sunshine, Dragon Mama disappears.

TOOTHPICKS 14

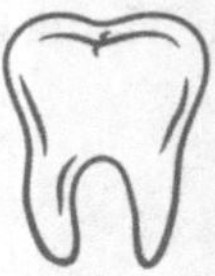

Bad Timing on the Right Road

RETURNING to sleep after our conversation with Declan's mother is impossible. My head is spinning with all the implications her words bring to mind. In addition, both Declan and I find it doubtful that the sleeping *Dokkalfar* will awake from their magic-induced slumber full of warm fuzzies for their suspicious Fae guests. "Are ya' up ta' gettin' back on the road, Lass?" the Tax Man asks, though I'm pretty sure we don't have any other options.

"No worries, Sweetie." I pick up my still damp clothes off the floor next to the chair where Dragon Mama dumped them. "In truth, I can't say I relish the thought of putting these wet clothes back on."

"Given options, I'd rather not risk someone pickin' up on ma' magic," my husband says. "There's always the possibility, however small, of someone openin' the door ta' ma' abilities a bit too wide and peekin' in. But I agree, Love. I donna' want ta' suffer those dank garments ma'self." He crosses two fingers on his left hand and gives them the tiniest of waves. The old apparel disappears, replaced by a fresh set of travel garb. I'd like to say that my new clothes are more attractive than the last collection, but sadly they are not. I still look like an old frump, yet take heart in the fact that these new things are at least dry and made of substantially warmer materials than the old set.

On the other hand, it's hard to miss that his Jr. Lordship's new disguise fits much closer to his body than did his previous ones. The pantaloon style breeches and thin leather boots of the a low-born older Fae male are now replaced with a snugger, form-fitting pair of pants and new sure-heeled boots laced to the knees. Despite the loose-fitting cape of home-spun fabric covering him from head to toe, anyone who bothers to take a closer look underneath could easily spot that the "old amulet maker" has the well-toned body of a younger, trained athlete. Nor would they miss the wickedly sharp, double-edged sword strapped across his back or the hunting knife with the six-inch, serrated blade tucked in the top of his boot.

I whisper softly as he lifts me up into the dreaded pillion seat. The *Dokkalfar* still appear to be soundly sleeping, but there's no good reason to be louder than necessary. "Not that I'm complaining, Tax Man, but your new 'get-up' hardly screams defenseless old man. Oh la la…hot stuff!" I tease

"I have no choice but ta' be ready ta' fight if the situation calls far' it, Lass. I will need ta' have complete freedom of movement the other attire did not provide." My husband places a hand on my thigh and gives it an intimate squeeze. "And if that moment arises, Rosalinda Fitzpatrick, I expect ya' to do exactly as I tell ya'. No second guessin'. No stoppin' ta' questionin' ma' orders. Just straight-out obedience. I say this not only as yar' Lord and superior officer, but as yar' beloved One and Only who would surely die if anythin' bad happened ta' ya'. Do ya' understand what I'm tellin' ya, Love?"

Any plans for a wisecracking quip dies on my lips. My *Mo Shiorghra's* eyes bore directly into mine and there is no light-hearted teasing in them. What he wants is my complete promise, a given vow that that is considered sacred among the Fae folk. I put my hand over his. "You have my word, Declan Fitzpatrick. I will do exactly as you tell me. Immediately and without question."

My promise earns me a beatific Tax Man smile, the kind that always makes me go weak in the knees. "Having yar' word means I am ready ta' face whatever this day will bring, *La Mo Chroi* (Center of my Heart)." The Tax Man lifts my hand up off of his and kisses it, before sliding into Hades' saddle and heading us off into the darkness of the pre-dawn morning.

* * *

It takes only about forty minutes of my ass bouncing on the hard pillion for the after-glow of our romantic "soul moment" to droop like the stem of a spring tulip. Last night's supper is giving me a bad case of acid reflux and I've had to pee since shortly after we left the inn. "Is there any way we can make a pit-stop, Sweetie?" I ask.

"I will stop when we come across some bit of wooded

land where it is safe. As ya' can see, we are completely out in the open. Stoppin' now would make us an easy target," he says.

I grit my teeth and press my forehead against his back thinking in the furthest corner of my mind that if I never "train" properly then perhaps I won't be required to go on any more of these damn "spy missions." It sounds way more glamorous than it actually is. In the dark, banging around in the hard seat with nothing to see while the frigid temperatures give me goosebumps, I look for something to take my mind off my aching bladder. My mind replays our earlier conversation with Lady *Siobhan*. "Do you think it's true?" I ask my husband.

"I'm afraid ya'll have to expound on that a bit, Lass? I am no sure I know what ya' mean."

"What your *mathair* said," I reply, second guessing whether this is actually the best time to bring the topic up.

"She says a lot of things. My Lady *Mathair* likes to hear herself talk," he replies in what sounds like his "cranky Declan" voice. If I could see his face, I'd bet he has that sour puss expression he wears when he's annoyed, all pursed lips and clenched jaw.

In for a penny, in for a pound. One of these days I'll learn to leave well enough alone. Apparently, it's not today. "You know...that stuff she said about The Ritual bond being only a physical connection and having nothing to do with true love."

Even with my forehead alone I can feel the muscles in his back tense. "For the life of Lugh, Rosalinda, I ken no understand why you'd suddenly decide here and now to take what ma' bitter *mathair* says as gospel truth. From ma' experience, ya' never believed her nonsense befar'." There's no missing the anger in his tone. If we weren't in the middle of nowhere, I'm betting anything made of glass would be trash right now. "Unless, of course, ya' are now havin' lingerin' doubts about addin' the Eternal Bond to our match," he adds.

Ouch. That one hurt. I pull myself upright in the pillion. "Of course not! I have no doubts whatsoever about my deep feelings for you. And to have you say such a thing hurts me big time, Bucko! You're being a complete ass, D.P. Fitzpatrick! I'm just trying to work through everything she said in my own mind. It was a lot to take in. And you can't tell me the revelation that, although they despise each other with a burning hatred, your parents still…'do the nasty' isn't a tad weird, even for your dysfunctional mess of a family."

There's a lull of several minutes before my mate answers me. "If I ask ya' to drop this conversation far' the time bein', Lady Wife, would ya' commit ta' that? I am not disregardin' yar' feelings and I understand we will need ta' speak on this topic in the future, but far' now, I need ta' focus ma' energies on what awaits us in *Dokkr Bygo*. There is a vera' good chance I will have ta' take up arms against ma' own sire…ma' sworn Liege Lord. It will not be an easy thing far' me ta' do and I ken' no go into such a task with ma' head and heart centered on the worry that, somehow, I have failed ta' convince ya' of ma' deepest felt devotion."

Now I just feel shitty. Besides the physical aches of the past 24 hours, my heart hurts as well. I wish I had some of that hoity-toity *seior* magic just so I could turn back time and swallow back the whole awful conversation. Not that I don't think I had every right to bring it up, but for the simple truth that my timing of it royally sucked. I can't imagine how I would feel if I found out my own Dad might be a murderous traitor. My eyes burn with unshed tears but I fight them with all my might. If I start weeping, I'll only make matters worse. My boo-hooing never fails to greatly upset my husband, and he's right about one thing; he doesn't need extra distractions.

"I'm sorry, Declan. My choice of timing was very misguided. I agree. Now is not the time to talk about 'us.' Not with the future of your House at risk. I promise not to bring it up again."

"Yar' feelings are valid, ma' Love. And we will talk. At another time."

"I love you, Declan."

"I love you too, *stor mo chroi* (treasure of my heart)."

To keep from crying, I concentrate on the rosy, orange layers of the approaching dawn and the faint outline of wooden houses in the far distance. I want to believe we are close to *Dokkr Bygo* but I know from experience that distances are always a lot further on horseback than they appear to your eyes. We come across the first copse of trees thick enough to hide within and the Tax Man halts Hades in the center of them. "Break time," he says to me as he helps me off the horse. We each wander a bit apart to take care of the call of nature before reluctantly reclimbing aboard the stallion's back. There's no sign of water anywhere and I feel downright nasty in terms of personal hygiene, while I can personally attest to the fact that my One and Only doesn't smell like a bed of roses either. The beginnings of a stubbly beard shadows his jaw and cheeks, which to me looks ruggedly sexy, but is something I know he hates, calling it "itchy and unkept."

"About another eight miles," he says. "I'm vera sorry I dinna' think ta' conjure up a light repast far' ya, Lass. If I wasn't so sure these lands were heavily warded, I would try a quick spell, but any kind of magic is likely ta' sound alarms among these isolated *Dokkalfar* who practice the old ways"

"I'm fine, Tax Man. Let's just do what we need to do here and head home," I reply, not believing for one second that things in this *Nordboerne* outpost will go smoothly.

The first "house" we come to, basically nothing more than a wooden door covering a cave-like opening into a sheer stone cliff, looks long abandoned, with its door hanging off rusted iron hinges. The second door appears much the same. There are pigs in their pen and some mangy looking canine-type animals roaming the property in front of the third door, but when Declan knocks on the entryway, no one answers, though I swear I feel eyes upon us. As he walks back to Hades and me, I notice him rubbing the knuckles of the right hand. "Is something wrong?" I ask when he gets close enough to hear me.

"I dinna' expect the magic to be so negatively charged," he explains. Sticking out his hand, I see the skin that made contact with the door is red and blistered, as if he had been burned.

"Shit! That looks painful!" I mutter. "We need to get some kind of salve on that before it gets infected."

Declan shakes the pain off. "'Tis nothing. I will heal on ma' own in a few minutes. I should have known better than ta' touch the house befar' testin' its magical charge. I will be mar' careful goin' forward." He waves a warning finger at me. "Ya' are not to get off this pillion unless I specifically tell ya' it is okay ta' do so, Rosie."

He stares at me waiting for an answer and I almost begin to argue with him before recalling my earlier promise not to question his authority. I chew down my fierce independence and replace it with, "Yes, Sir. I won't leave this magic horse unless you tell me." I get a smirky smile and a "Good' garl," in return, and then hate myself for getting all warm and tingly over those two words. Damn! That Bond is strong!

We head further up the stone road, passing two other cave dwellings. As far as I can see with my own tooth fairy eyes, the settlement looks abandoned, but Lord *Mac Nuada* insists there are several Elven people in our midst. Eventually, we come across one badly nourished, filthy, pre-teen *Dokkalfar* herding a group of emaciated-looking goats towards a lone dry patch of grass. The boy stops, putting on a false act of bravado, though I can see his spindly legs shaking in his torn, thread-bare breeches.

My husband calls out to the kid in the Elven language. Declan's accent and inflections are harsher and more guttural here than he sounded in *Gleann Gas*. The boy answers him and steps forward, and in return, the Tax Man slides off the horse's back. "*Fanacht curtha* (stay put)," he orders me in the old language of the Fae. He walks to the boy while holding out two amulets made of polished citrine in his right hand and an unusually large sea pearl in his left. I don't understand a word of what they're saying, but by the back and forth of the conversation, I guess a deal of some sorts is being made. I note that the knife in my husband's boot is no longer there, which I assume means he's moved it somewhere easier to reach. The man I know and love would not attack a younger, smaller boy. However, I still mouth a short prayer to all the goddesses that the kid doesn't force the issue and prove me wrong.

Eventually, the lad grabs at the jewels, then stretches out his arm and points down the road. As the kid ambles away, Declan strides back to us, his face locked in determination. "The kid told you something?" I ask.

"Aye. He knows of Master Brendan. Said the goats he was tendin' actually belong ta' the man. My old ink mage goes by the name *Sal Bjofr* these days. It means "Soul Thief." He turns and watches as the boy and the goats continue toward the grass patch. "And Rosie...the goats were all branded with that strange third symbol from the ledger. 'ᛗ'...the one that means either 'new enterprise' or 'enemy.' I have ta' believe we are on the right track."

TOOTHPICKS 15

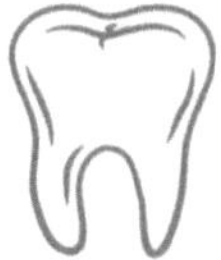

Of Vows and Venom

THE SOUL THIEF'S residence is isolated from the rest of the community, if you could call the coterie of abandoned cave "homes" by such a positive moniker. This particular dwelling was tucked into the side of a cliff that overlooked the *Ruoshui* (Weak River), a body of water that stood as the boundary between *Asgard* and The Jade Empire. It is written within the pages of the ancient history of the Otherworld that the *Ruoshui* flows with water so lacking in specific gravity that even a feather wouldn't float upon it, thus keeping the "unworthy" from entering The Jade Empire. The "unworthy" included pretty much anyone and everyone who wasn't a natural-born citizen of said kingdom.

The two of us halt a moment to take in the majesty of the river that shimmers in dawn's early light like a display of diamonds resting on a pillow of teal green liquid. "Wow," I whisper. "It's so beautiful."

"And just as deadly," the Tax Man says. "A body ken' drown in its depths in a matter of seconds. Even the strongest of Fae magic is no match for the pull of the 'Weak River.'"

"Is this your first time seeing it," I ask.

"Yes and no," he answers cryptically. "When we rode up, I was filled with an overwhelmin' sense of *deja vu*, but as far' as I ken' remember, I don' recall ever bein' this far north of *I Idir*. All ma' missions have been centered in the Mundane world. I have never been called upon to spy amongst the *Dokkalfar* or *Jadeite* peoples. I ken' no explain ma' feelins' about it."

I understand. The energy of this place seeps out of the ground and into one's very consciousness. Even with my extremely limited magical sensibilities, the Fae side of who I am reacts to the call of the sorcery. My head feels as if it could lift off my shoulders and float away.

"Declan...I don't want to worry you...but I feel rather...strange. My head...." The words trail off because I can't seem to make my lips work to form the sounds.

I feel him fumble in front of me, then see his hand holding something near my mouth. "Put this beneath yar' tongue," the Tax Man says.

He's holding it so close to my face I can't tell what's between his fingers. "What is it?"

"It's a piece of polished cat's eye," Declan explains.

"You want me to put a dirty gemstone from your pocket into my mouth?" I question, my face expressing my disgust at the thought.

"Please, Rosie, just do as I say. It will help ya' fight the magic's control and restore yar' personal focus. Once ya' start feelin' better, ya' ken' move it to the bodice of yar' gown."

"Won't it just slip down the front of my dress and fall out the bottom?" I ask before tucking the gemstone underneath my tongue.

My husband snorts. "Not likely. The way ya' are shaped, Lass, ya' could probably carry a generous wedge of cheese in there without it movin' an inch."

"Fa' Fa'…fary' funny, Fax Fan. You're a freal' comedian," I mumble, the awkward gem under my tongue making the words come out all wrong.

He uses the same hand and gives my boobs a gentle pat. "I am in no way complainin', *mo aingeal alainn* (my beautiful angel). Yar' curves bring me ta' ma' knees. Truthfully, the cat's eye will have no trouble stayin' in its most parfect' spot." It's hard to argue with a man who thinks you're lovely no matter how many body flaws you yourself might think you have. My Tax Man always makes me feel sexy and desirable, and if that's all part of the Bond, well, then I'm A-okay with it.

We draw up in front of a cave home that sports a set of heavy wooden doors elaborately covered in carved runes plus a menagerie of frightening beasts, all bugged-out eyes and snarling muzzles. The handles form the shape of two large snakes, their iron fangs poised to strike the hand of anyone inclined to enter, while their rattled tails curl together in an elaborate knot that acts as a pseudo-padlock.

"Futhin' says 'felcome to my fome' more than a fair' of fenomous snakes," I joke, the comment sounding more ridiculous with the obstacle in my mouth.

"I donna' doubt they are just that, Lass. I venture ta' guess the tips of those fangs are coated in some type of deadly magical poison."

Above each side of the entrance hang two ironwork lamps done in the same "mid-century creepy" design; each fixture depicting a fierce gargoyle warrior with arms uplifted to hold a round, glass globe that acted as a shade for the light within. As the morning sun rises higher in the east, the flickering lights inside each of the crystal globes flares and then sputters completely out. The closer we get to the doors, the more I feel the push of negative magical energy fighting against me, though the cat's eye *nazar* (amulet against evil) under my tongue appears to be helping with the majority of the physical symptoms.

Declan slides off the horse's back to get a better look at the snake tail lock on the door, though I note that he doesn't get near enough to it to make physical contact, even accidentally. "Master Brendan...'tis *Mac Nuada!*" he calls out. "I come in the name of Her Majesty, Queen Maeve of *I Idir*, Fae goddess of war and destruction. I need ta' speak with ya."

There is no response so my husband tries again. "Master Ink Mage...Soul Thief...you kenna' no hide from yar' *Sidhe* heritage. The Morrigan is yar' Queen by the blood that runs in yar' veins. She demands answers. If ya' come with me in peace, I will guarantee yar' safe passage and a fair trial."

The only sound comes from the frigid wind whistling between the peaks and hollows of the jagged cliffs and the splash of the *Ruoshui* against the rocks that hold it back. I watch as the Tax Man pulls a piece of yellow chalk from his pocket and draws a circle around himself, placing several pieces of quartz crystal at his feet. With his eyes now closed, I sense his level of extreme focus and concentration as he moves his hands in a series of motions. It takes me a minute or two to figure out what exactly is going on, but then I realize with a sense of amazement that Declan is prying apart the two tails of the door handle snakes using his personal magic instead of his actual hands.

Despite being as connected as we are, my *Mo Shiorghra* has always been shyly reserved about the extent of his magical abilities. I believed this is because he never wants me to feel "less" than he because my own skills are so very limited. I've seen him do various little spells in the course of our short life together; move us back and forth to the Otherworld, clean up a mess around the house, and I've also been witness to his fabulous veiling and disguise talents on a number of occasions. However, he's always kept his spell casting abilities closer to the vest. It's a little disconcerting to watch one's spouse in a role so different from the one you are accustomed to, and the level of magical energy he's using right this minute takes my breath away. It's far stronger than I ever imagined it to be.

After several minutes, the tails of the snakes are completely undone. My husband scuffs out the lines of the circle and picks up the crystals. "Stay put," he says, once again, as he walks closer to the door. "I will see what awaits inside and if it is safe, I will come get ya'. Be forewarned that if I feel ya' are in danger, Hades has direct instruction to flee with ya' on his back. He's perfectly able ta' lead himself and he will take ya' to somewhere safe until Duncan or Beck can retrieve ya'.'"

My stomach falls to my feet. Leave him behind? Not gonna' happen. Not today. Not ever. "Please, Declan. Don't ask that of me. I can't leave you here to fend for yourself. I'll die a hundred times over."

I can tell by the set of his jaw he's unwilling to negotiate and I start to panic. "Ya' made a sacred promise ta' me, Rosie Fitzpatrick, that ya' would do as I asked without question. Ya' are ma' Eternal One and Only. I expect ya' ta' hold ta' yar' word," he says.

I know Declan Phineas Fitzpatrick well enough to know how seriously he takes a promise. Breaking my word to him would be a major breach of trust, and although I know he'd eventually forgive me, my actions would be a rift between us that would linger for a very long time. I can't make myself physically say the words, so I just nod my head in the affirmative. I hear him in my mind. *"I need ya' to say it, Love. I ken' no face what might be inside if I'm worryin' that ya' will break yar' word and disobey me."*

Even mentally, every word stabs me in the heart. *"I will do as you've asked. I will stay right here and if the need arises, I will let Hades carry me off."*

"Thank ya, ma' Love. Hearin' ya say it makes me feel better," my mate replies.

For me, saying it, even mentally, doesn't make me feel the slightest bit better. I can't have another experience like North Korea no matter what Herself says about my "inner strength." If something bad happened to Declan, the only thing that would keep me from immediately joining him in the Afterlife would be our son Dylan, though I know from the bottom of my soul that any sense of real joy or happiness would die with him. I say none of this to my beloved *Mo Shiorghra* as he enters the Soul Thief's residence simply because I know it won't change his mind. Lord *Mac Nuada* is a man full of life-altering questions and he's betting his own life that the answers to them lie inside this desolate cave dwelling.

TOOTHPICKS 16

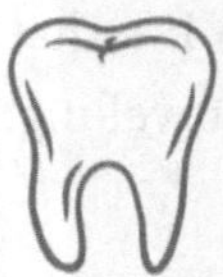

The Dead Don't Speak

TIME MOVES SUBSTANTIALLY SLOWER when your 'everything' is on the line. We've all experienced this frame of mind at one time or another; waiting for that important email, that marriage proposal, those medical test results. Time is not a sympathetic partner to the anxiety of waiting. If anything, it mocks your impatience by creeping by at an incredibly unhurried pace. From the moment Declan walks through those heavy wooden doors, the seconds crawl at a snail's pace while sitting upon Hades's back. I wring my hands and will my stomach not to empty itself of last night's wretched barley soup.

After nearly three hours, which in truth is probably no more than fifteen minutes, my husband exits through the same doors looking grim and pale. "Did you find Master Brendan?" I call out, still honoring the "stay put" mandate and sounding more normal without the gem in my mouth, having moved it to its new location in my bodice.

He doesn't answer immediately, holding off until he reaches me and lifts me from the pillion to the ground. "Aye. He's in there, but in no position ta' answer any questions," the Tax Man answers. I tilt my head in question. "The Soul Thief no longer walks in this world. Someone got ta' him befar' we did."

"Are you saying he's dead?" My tone matches my shock and confusion.

"Dead as dead can be. Brutally murdered, in fact," Declan says.

"Shit!" It's the best I can muster. I'm not very witty under pressure.

"I agree. 'Tis not the outcome I'd planned' far'. Any information the man could have provided died with him. I'm guessin' whoever took him out was lookin' far' information as well. The place has been tossed," he explains.

It's on the tip of my tongue to ask him if he thinks his *athair* is the "whoever" he means, but decide not to go there. Not yet, anyway. "So do you think the murderer found what he or she was looking for?"

"I ken' no say for sure, Love, though my trainin' tells me it would be prudent ta' look for ourselves...just in case. I could use an extra pair of eyes if ya' think ya' could handle viewing such a grisly scene?" Declan asks.

"I'll be fine, Sweetie. I was required to do cadaver dissection during dental school. Plus, I'm an oral surgeon. I've seen more than my share of blood and tissue."

"'Tis quite an...ugly scene, but I am happy for yar' help." Declan takes my hand in his as we walk inside. The gargoyle lamps with their round globe shades look especially hideous when you see them this close up. The inside of the cave dwelling is no better. It's dark and dank, and the odor of decomposing flesh hits me square in the face. I pull my cardigan up around my nose but it doesn't do much to hide the rotting meat smell and I work at not gagging. I must look a bit "green around the gills" because my husband says, "If the smell is too much far ya, Lass, I can do this by ma'self."

Determined not to be a big ass baby, I breathe more shallowly. "Just give me a moment. I'll get used to it," I lie, making a mental note to remember that med school cadavers smell like formaldehyde, which, as unpleasant as that is, doesn't hold a candle to true decomposition.

Declan nods, then begins rummaging through a stack of papers tossed all over the floor near the door, while I try not to gape at what once was a living, breathing person. In the same way people gawk at traffic accidents, I can't seem to pull my eyes away from the murdered ink mage. His throat has been hacked open with his head barely connected to his shoulders by random strands of muscle and tendon. The cornea of his eyes have already clouded over, meaning he's probably been dead for over two or three hours, or perhaps even longer if the sticky, congealed blood pool stands as evidence of the time frame. The whole crime scene area is a mess, which is why the odd symbol, carefully drawn in blood near the victim's right hand, catches my eye.

I bend down to take a closer look, trying not to breathe in as I do. To my eye, it appears to be a round circle with random lines extending outward, ✳. Did the

Soul Thief purposefully leave a clue to his assailant? Or was the strange symbol drawn by the murderer as part of some magical ritual? Another *Futhark* rune, perhaps? "Did you notice this?" I ask my husband.

He stops his searching and looks to where I'm squatting. "Notice what?"

"This symbol next to the body. This circle thingy. It looks like someone used the victim's own blood to draw it," I say.

My husband comes closer and squats down next to me. "I dinna' note it earlier, but ya' could be right, Lass. It does look as if someone purposely drew this."

"Do you think it's another ancient rune?" I question.

"I do not recall there being any circular letters in the *Futhark* alphabet, but I am surely no expert. 'Tis times like these I miss havin' the advantages of Mundane technology at ma' fingertips. I think we should definitely make a point of it in our report. Do ya' think ya' could find some parchment and a pen of sorts and copy this symbol down? I'd like to be able ta' show it to the rest of the team."

"Sure thing, 'Capitan.'" I stand and hunt for a piece of blank parchment and something to write with, the search made more difficult by the lack of light in the cave, as the only source is several lit beeswax candles stuck into a block of wood. I find a scrap of unused paper, but no pen or pencil of any type. Frustrated, I consider using a stick from the hearth and the ink mage's blood, a solution I find too ghoulish. Instead, I poke around the ashes until I find a piece of burned tinder that works in lieu of a pencil. I copy the symbol as best as I can. Holding it up, I comment, "You know...this looks like a sun. Could it represent some goddess or other *Nordboerne* ritual?"

"I ken' not say, Lass. The old ways always included some kind of worship of the sun, but whether it is part of *the dark sorcery* is beyond ma' knowledge." Declan barely gets the words out of his mouth when right before our eyes, Master Brendan's body, along with the blood pooling around him changes into a fine red mist, similar to what happened in the aftermath of the fake Rory Dell's visit. Reflex makes me jump away from the dissolving body, not wanting any of that red, powdery stuff to fall on me. The sigil on the floor that I'd copied only moments before disappears as well.

"This is the second time I've witnessed that happening and it's still mega-creepy. It seems as if the 'Soul Thief' has had his own stolen." I shudder and move further back. "Have you found anything helpful?"

"It doesn't appear so. Ken' ya help me pry these creakin' floorboards up? Maybe somethin' important is beneath them." There's no way my husband can't lift those boards up by himself, so I see the request as his way of making me feel useful while keeping an eye out that I don't handle the wrong things.

The Tax Man is correct in his assumptions. The space below the floor holds a cache of gemstones, gold nuggets, and stacks of money from various countries in the Mundane world. "Holy hotcakes! That's quite a haul. If the mage had this much accessible wealth, why did he live so frugally?" I point to the broken-down bed with its dirty linens. "This place is a dump."

"I guess he didn't want to call attention to his treasure.

When ya' flaunt yar' blessins' in front of others who are not as lucky, ya' make yourself a target far' theft," Declan says.

"I suppose," I reply, not completely convinced that this was the ink mage's intention. "Where would he even get these types of assets, especially out here in the middle of nowhere."

"My guess would be that all of this is payment."

"Payment? For magical work?" I ask.

"Yes…among other things," he answers cryptically.

It takes me a few minutes to process his comment. "You're speaking of hush money, aren't you?"

"Aye. Blackmail is vera' profitable and a common business practice everywhere in the Otherworld. Holdin' other people's secrets is the key ta' bein' successful no matter what kingdom ya' call home."

"Could that have something to do with those *Futhark* symbols in your House's accounting books? Were you able to match the dates up with any deposits or withdrawals?" This is as close as I've come this whole trip to implicating my husband's father.

I can tell I've hit a raw nerve by his refusal to look at me and the silence that hangs between us. Then, he shrugs. "It is possible. As of yet, I haven't been able to make a direct connection, but the amount in the treasury is substantially lower than it should be considering that Herself has called for no new taxes or levies, and we've made no great improvements to the estate for several years. I dinna' have time to do a line by line accountin', but 'tis probably something that needs ta' be done when I return home." Declan pulls a burlap sack from the back of a chair and begins to deposit the items under the floor into it. "I will bring these treasures back to *I Idir* and let the Black Knight decide what to do with it." He points to a large chest stuck into a niche in the cavern wall. "While I do that, could ya' go through there and see if ya' find anything of interest. I'm hopin' to locate the mage's Grimoire. If he was castin' ritual magic on a regular basis, he would surely have kept a log of what worked and what dinna.' That information would be useful to have if we are required to do battle with *Jotun* magic."

Glad to be kept busy, I do as my Tax Man asks. I struggle a bit with the heavy lid and then start the chore of going through it, piece by piece. "What does a Grimoire look like? I don't want to miss it among all this other junk," I say, as I pull old clothes, empty jars and unpolished stones from its interior.

"It will most likely be a book or journal of some kind. It varies from practitioner to practitioner, but they all lean toward usin' natural materials. If ya' come across somethin' like that let me know, but do not open it. Most Grimoires are magically booby-trapped by their owners."

We spend the next hour searching every nook and cranny in the dwelling, but find no sign of any spell book. I'm beyond tired and hungry so when he announces his intention to give-up the search, I secretly cheer. "I'm sorry, Sweetie. I realize you were hoping for answers."

" 'Tis always the chance a mission won't go as planned, but I had hoped to at least get a lead on the lad's *mathair*. I truly dinna expect the community to be as deserted as it is. I ken' not imagine where they all went. There have been *Dokkalfar* in this part of *Asgard* for hundreds of years."

I think about Master Brendan's title of "Soul Thief" and develop my own theories about what might have happened to the dark elves, but what I'm postulating is too gruesome to share. "What's our next move?"

"At this point, I think it is best if we return to *I Idir*. They are expecting us to meet this evening and I would like to get another look at those account books before speaking with the rest of the team. In addition, I do not want ya' to be away from our wee boy any longer than ya' have to. Master Dylan is no fan of the rubber nipple."

Hope springs in my heart that his Jr. Lordship won't insist on traveling ten hours by horse. "Does this mean we're jumping home?" I ask.

"I would prefer ta' get away from the wards that guard this place before attemptin' travel magic. Maybe twelve or thirteen miles south. Once we are on ward-free land, we'll take ma' *mathair's* suggestion and jump to her home in Ireland, and then ta' *Crann Bethadh*. We should be home by late afternoon."

"What about Hades?" I question.

"As ya' are aware, animals, even gifted ones, are unable ta' cross the Veil. Before we go ta' Ballydonnely, I will instruct him ta' return on his own to his Mistress. He can move twice as fast without the burden of riders. He'll be fine."

Inside, I'm doing the happy dance. I can put up with another dozen miles on that horse if it means we're going back to *I Idir*. Thinking about my son, I don't pay attention to where I'm going, and as I pass through the wooden door, I bang my head on the low hanging gargoyle lamp, hard enough to make the glass globe wobble and fall. Natural reaction causes me to grab it as it falls out of the metal goblin's upraised hands. "Damn, that hurt," I say, but my husband is ignoring me and staring at the item I'm holding. I look at it carefully. It's not at all hollow inside like a lamp shade should be. In fact, it's a perfectly solid, round sphere. A ball. A crystal ball.

TOOTHPCKS 17

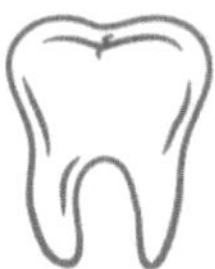

When The Past Meets the Future

"Is this what I think it is?" I ask, holding the globe out in front of me.

Declan stares wide-eyed at the sphere. "I've read about these, but I've never seen one in person. It requires a great deal of top-level, magical skill ta' create such a thing."

"Create what, exactly? Is this some crystal fortune telling device? The kind used for scrying? I thought those devices were usually fake, mostly used by charlatans and scammers."

"From the beginnin' of time, sorcerers have used reflective surfaces to center their focus and magical energy for the purpose of divining. I've seen our own Queen use pools of water and mirrors to see into the past and future. But if this orb is truly what I believe it to be, then it may contain all we need ta' know."

"You're talking in circles, Declan," I complain.

He puts both his hands on top of the sphere. "I ken'

feel the vibrations of contained magic, but I don't have a single clue as to how I can access it."

"Access what, damn it?" I say, my frustration getting the better of me. Sometimes the Tax Man can be obtusely long-winded.

"I believe this crystal ball, for lack of a better name, is a reservoir for information and knowledge."

"Like a computer's hard drive?" I ask.

"Aye. But magical in nature and actin' the likes of a Grimoire. A sphere of this size could hold a phenomenal amount of data," my husband explains.

"Then why put such a resource out in the open where anyone could find it?" I counter. "It doesn't make a whole lot of sense. Plus, I'm one hundred percent sure that when we first arrived, the sun hadn't fully risen and both lamps were lit and glowing."

"That's exactly it, Lass. The sphere was hidden in plain sight because no one would expect it to be in such an obvious place, unhidden and unguarded. To the eye, it looks like nothing more than a glass lamp shade."

The revelation crosses my mind like a solitary flash of lightning. "Shit and shovels!" I exclaim, shoving the crystal ball toward him. "Hold this for a second," shoving the sphere into his hands. I rummage in the pocket of my cardigan and pull out the piece of parchment with the drawing I made of the mysterious crime scene sigil before it disappeared. I stare at it and then at the glass orb. "Well, I'll be damned! Look at this symbol again, Sweetie," I say, pointing a finger at the ∗. "What if this isn't a sun after all, but an orb with rays coming from it? Which is exactly how the lamp looked when we first rode up! I bet Master Brendan wanted someone to find this orb.

That's why he drew this with his last bit of life."

"I think ya' are very clever, Lady *Mac Nuada*," my Eternal Mate grins. "Ya' will make an excellent spy once we get ya' properly trained. But for now, we need ta' get this orb back ta' *Crann Bethadh*. No doubt Herself and the Merlin will know how to access the data contained within. I have not a single doubt that the answers ta' our many questions are locked away in this sphere." He kisses me with the exuberance of the moment as we walk back towards Hades.

I'm excited and relieved that we are heading home with some type of reward for all our trouble. There's a hopeful bounce in the Tax Man's step for the first time on this trip and I'm secretly pleased that, in my own way, I helped put it there. In the same vein of gratitude, I try to feel some outrage and empathy for the violent murder of the ink mage, but something in my soul tells me the Soul Thief got exactly what he deserved for all his crimes against the will of the Universe. *"Live by the sword, die by the sword,"* I think to myself, as the cliche fits this particular situation perfectly.

Declan carefully tucks the sphere into one of the saddle bags, and prepares to lift me up on the horse when I hear a piercing wail cut across the wind. It goes straight to my brain and my body suddenly stops any type of motion. The sound is most definitely a baby's cry. One I know very well. I strain to listen more closely and recognize the familiar pitch and the tone, which, in turn, instantly causes a natural physical reaction. In response to the wailing, the front of my gown shows the beginnings of a large wet stain from my leaking breasts. There's no doubt at all in my head. The baby crying so pitifully is mine. Ours. Dylan. I grab my mate's arm. "Do you hear that?" I say, panic filling my entire soul.

"Hear what, Love?"

"It's Dylan! He's here. He's crying for me!"

Concern washes across the Tax Man's face and he leans in to hug me. "I don' hear anythin', Rosie. Perhaps you are just over tired. Once we get to Ballydonnely, I think maybe ya' should have a rest and somethin' ta' eat befar' we head back ta' *I Idir*."

I shimmy out of his arms. "I'm not crazy, Declan! Dylan's here! I can hear him crying to be fed!" The sound rises up again, coming from a grouping of scraggly trees. I push out of my husband's reach and begin to run towards where I hear the sounds coming from.

Startled, my husband stops short for a second and then comes after me. "Rosie! Stop, Lass! It could be a trick!"

All my thoughts are focused on reaching my son. I ignore my mate's warning and plunge directly into the wooded out-crop, frantically searching for my baby boy. Dylan is nowhere to be found, but I suddenly find myself face to face with my husband's father. Lord Callum Fitzpatrick *Nuada* pulls me roughly towards him and hangs a thick forearm across my throat, a long, sharpened dirk in his other hand. Declan enters the space a few seconds later and stops dead in his tracks over the sight that meets his eyes. "Hello, *Mac Nuada*. As ya' ken' plainly see, yar' precious tooth fairy has found har'self in quite the perilous predicament. I strongly suggest ya' take a few steps back and keep yar' hands where I ken' see them," his Lordship says.

"Don't do this, *Athair*. It does not have ta' be this way."

"What way, *Deaglan*? With me havin' the upper hand? Of course, this is the way it all would end. Ya' had ta' have known that when ya' turned yar' heir's loyalty over to that Raven sorceress. 'Tis no great surprise that ya'd turn out ta' be no better than the bitch that whelped ya'. 'Tis her bloodline in the face ya' wear. I was mad ta' think otherwise…weak of mind ta' imagine I could change the hand of Fate. The wrong *bairn* died on that awful day in August. Surely ma' other son, yar' poor dead twin, would have been the better heir. I have been cheated by some wickedness borne of Donnely magic.

The words coming out his Lordship's mouth are so vile it dampens my fear of the situation. I twist and fight in the man's hold, but make little progress. His grip is like a vice around my neck. "You're an evil man, Lord *Nuada*. I hope the Universe delivers just punishment," I say. *Nuada's* reaction to my curse is to press the blade into the flesh of my throat. I feel the burning pain and then the tickle of something wet dripping down the front of my chest. Bright red.

I am overwhelmed by the magical push of being sandwiched between Declan's fear and grief and Lord *Nuada'a* hatred and rage, and the *nazar* inside my bodice is no match for ancient *Tuatha da Danann* power. The magical energy surrounding me is so encompassing, I fight to remain in an upright position. My *Mo Shiogrhra's* emotions shift towards fury and vibrate deep inside of me. "I swear I will kill ya' in the most painful of ways if ya' harm her, *Athair!* Even if I must spend the rest of my days in this world, and the Mundane one as well, trackin' ya' down ta' do so. I will kill ya' and take ma' time doin' it without a single drop of mercy. In that way, you are correct...I am indeed ma' *mathair's* son," my Eternal Mate vows. "You will never draw my *Mo Shiorghra* and I apart. Not in this life or any other."

His father laughs with a bitterness that extends outside of his physical body. "I had heard you'd both taken the Eternal Bond. So foolish. No woman is worth that kind of trouble, *Deaglan.* Surely ya' had already figured that out far' yar'self in those many years ya' waited far' the Universe ta' make its choice known. Females, in any world, all deliver the same fleeting pleasure. 'Tis nothing more special than that, though the females often believe that breeding your offspring is beneficial when, frankly, 'tis not so. The idea that siring a child is your sacred duty is propaganda forced upon we males by that Raven bitch. Children are just another useless burden, a drain of a man's intellect, wealth and ambition."

"Is that why you murdered those women, Lord *Nuada?* Because they conceived yar' children." his son asks. "Marcy Kilcrabtree and ma' half-brother's *mathair* as well?"

"Females always want more than their due. That is their fatal flaw," he says, as he pulls his forearm even tighter against my windpipe. It was now getting more and more difficult for me to take complete breaths. "I realize ya' will not accept ma' sound advice, *Deaglan.* Instead, I recommend ya' hand over that crystal sphere and perhaps we can pretend this unpleasantness never happened."

Either the old man is completely out of his mind, or he is simply bluffing. There was no way he or his son could move unchanged from what was happening here in this forlorn land. As sure as I knew anything, this moment in time would end badly, but who would come out as the supposed 'victor' was still anyone's guess.

"I'm afraid I can't do that, your Lordship. Herself's stallion is already on his way back to his royal mistress with the sphere safely in his possession. No matter what happens here, the truth will be revealed to the people of *I Idir*," my *Mo Shiorghra* says, his face void of any emotion visible to the eye.

It's impossible to miss Callum *Nuada's* anger and fear over Declan's revelation. I can literally smell it oozing from every one of his pores, providing proof that whatever information the crystal container holds, it's damning to Lord *Nuada*. "You will regret this day, *Deaglan* Phineas Fitzpatrick," he growled.

"Perhaps so, *Athair*. But if this is to be our last stand, you and I, then I prefer ta' do it via the sacred ways of ar' people. Ya' demean yar'self hindin' behind a woman and makin' silly threats. Come take on yar' heir, Lord *Nuada*… *Sidhe* ta' *Sidhe*…*fear go fear* (man to man)."

The older man weighs the offer for a moment, then pushes me aside with such force that I fall hard into the dry dirt at his feet. "Come ta' me, Rosalinda," my husband orders. I wobble up from the ground, brush the dirt off my dress, and then walk calmly to Declan's side. He wipes the trickle of blood off my neck with the back of his hand, kisses my cheek, and then begins to draw a chalk circle around me. It takes only a mere second to recognize what he's attempting to do.

"Don't do this, Tax Man!" I plead. "Don't send me away to die of worry and grief without you. I am your One and Only. Eternally. My place is with you...whatever happens."

"Ya' gave me yar' word, Lass. Ya' promised to obey without question," he reminds me.

I can't help my emotions and tears fall of their own accord. "Please, Declan. Oh please! Don't send me away. Not this time! I can't do it again. I can't! Let me stay here with you."

A flood of his emotions runs through my head and I sense a slight wavering of his initial commitment. "Feckin' hell, woman, there is nothin' I can deny ya', even when I know what ya' ask is wrong on all measures." He presses the piece of chalk into my hand. "I will set up the spell but leave the circle unfinished. If there comes a time when I believe all is lost, I will let ya' know. Ya' must promise me, on the sacredness of our bond, that if this comes ta' pass, ya' will close the circle on yar' own, Rosalinda, and return ta' *Crann Bethadh*. Without hesitation. Ma' wee son needs his *mathair*. I will not orphan him to the whims of others. Give me yar' word."

"I promise," I blubber, wondering how in the hell we all came to this moment. Is this the way it was always meant to go? With the Universe showing me what true love can be like and then snatching it away like some big joke? Nothing about this is fair. My Beloved Tax Man and I shouldn't be here on this foreign soil. Not even here in the Otherworld. We should be at home, in Salem, loving our new baby and building a happy, normal family life. I want to curse the Fates that brought us to this twisted chain of events, but my rage won't change what has become our only path forward. Instead of raining down useless curses, I wipe away my tears and watch the love of my life attempt to take the life of his own father.

TOOTHPICKS 18

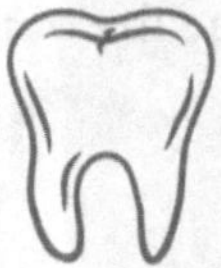

The Cruelty of Curses

I HAVE no idea what to expect next. When Declan tells his *athair* they should "face each other in the old ways of their people," does he mean that they should use *Sidhe* and *Jotun* magic? Or does my husband plan on going after his own flesh and blood using that bad-ass sword strapped to his back? I've never seen the Tax Man wield his ancient weapons in anything other than training exercises while sparring with Duncan. I've heard rumors that he is 'deadly precise,' but with the limited context of my own personal experience, I'm having a hard time understanding what that means in a situation as awful as this one.

The concept of working out one's family differences using medieval style weaponry is foreign to me. I am the product of the Mundane world. While I was spending my summer vacations working minimum wage jobs, fighting acne, and flirting with cute boys, Declan was studying Otherworldly history, Fae philosophy, and the extent of his personal magic. He also spent his afternoons in the training arenas of *Dun Siorai,* learning hand-to-hand combat and swordsmanship from the best of the best, all in anticipation of one day being House's *Nuada's* Lord and a seated member of *I Idir's* Ruling Council. There is nothing in my personal experience that can aid me in watching my beloved spouse fight for his very life.

Granted, the Mundane world itself is no stranger to horrifying violence. The daily news reports are full of senseless brutality brought upon by family members and strangers alike. However, I can't remember a single time I ever witnessed someone running a body through with a 40-inch sword. There's absolutely no doubt in my mind that I will be horrified by what I see here in *Asgard.* I consider calling out to The Morrigan for help, but somehow, I know sure as anything, that she will not interfere in this particular situation. For all the compassion she showed me when my *Mo Shiorghra* was kidnapped by the North Koreans, there's little doubt in my mind that she will let the Universe decide this outcome. Instead, I speak to her as the Goddess of War and Destruction and not as my Queen, asking not for intercession, but to steady my husband's mind as well as his hand, and to give him strength when his own is failing. The way I see it, those gifts should be an asset in whatever the choice of weapon might be.

I don't wait long for an answer to the style of the battle. Lord *Mac Nuada* pulls his sword from its sheath at his back and takes a position. His feet are shoulder width apart with his left foot facing forward and the right at a

45-degree angle. I can tell that he is balancing his weight between both feet and his back is rigid straight.

Declan's father stares back at him, as if trying to determine if his only son and heir will really use that deadly weapon against him. A snarl forms at the corner of his mouth and with a wave of his hand, Lord *Nuada* is holding a sword of his own, though his is several inches longer than my husband's blade. "Still usin' a broadsword, I see," the older man says. "Apparently I have taught ya' nothin' regardin' a warrior's choice of steel. The claymore is undoubtedly the better weapon."

"I prefer the agility of the broadsword. In the right hands 'tis just as deadly," the Tax Man counters in a voice so cold I hardly recognize the sound of it.

"I suppose we will see if that statement holds true," his Lordship replies.

The two men advance on each other while I can hardly bear to look. I close my eyes as the first clang of metal meeting metal echoes through the open space, eventually deciding I'd rather see what's coming next. My husband is extremely light on his feet, quick with precise movements that suggest years of repetitive training, and able to parry every one of my father-in-law's blows. Neither of them is using a shield of any type, so when Declan misses deflecting an underhanded thrust that catches him across the arm and draws blood, I have to put a hand over my mouth to keep from squeaking my alarm out loud, lest I become a distraction.

The wound to the arm doesn't seem to rattle my husband, but I can tell his *athair* isn't moving quite as quickly as he originally did. Plus, there is a sheen of sweat on the older man's forehead despite the chilly temperatures. Between the weight of the sword and the constant aerobic exercise, a Mundane man of Callum Fitzpatrick's age, even one in excellent shape, would be in trouble right now. Because both men are *Sidhe* with a *Tuatha de Danann* bloodline, and because they are so closely matched in skill, there's no doubt this back and forth advancing and retreating could go on for an indefinite period of time, leaving the victory to whoever holds out with the most stamina.

His Lordship must come to the same conclusion. In a battle of fortitude, Callum's son, being twenty-three years younger and in his Fae physical prime, definitely has the upper hand. Declan's *athair* suddenly yells, "*Go Leor* (Enough!)," as he pulls his weapon to the side and throws it to the ground. "We are no longer in *I Idir* and the Raven Queen's laws have no meaning to the *Dokkalfar*. By ma' vera' seed, I brought life ta' ya' in this world, *Deaglan* Phineas Fitzpatrick, and as yar' sire, it be ma' given' right ta' take it from ya." Then with two obscure hand movements, a sizzling ball of fiery energy is directed towards my husband's head. Declan quickly pivots on his left foot causing the racing power to barely miss him. It crashes into a leave-less oak tree twenty feet behind him, where it bursts into red and yellow flames.

In response, the Tax Man puts both hands up, palms toward his father, and a shimmering wall of white light blocks his body. "I am grateful far' the gift of life, Lord *Nuada*, but ya' have perverted the very essence of *Sidhe* magic with yar' foraging into *Seior* black sorcery." Declan takes several steps toward his father, holding the shield of white light in front of him. In response, Callum Fitz-patrick aims a second ball of light at his son. It hits the shield and rolls off, the flames making a path on either side of Declan's body.

My father-in-law begins to look unwell, his skin a grayish-greenish color, and his lips nearly bloodless. He takes several steps back in the direction of the cliff's edge and in that instant, I see the tragedy of where this will all end. My beloved Lord *Mac Nuada* must see it as well. He stops moving. "I do not relish yar' demise, ma' Lord. Come back with me ta' *I Idir* and face the charges against you. I swear on the life of ma' son that I will see ya' receive a fair and just trial."

His father's response is to hurl a third ball of *Seior Jotun* magic at his oldest child, while continuing his subtle maneuvering to the cliff's edge. What he hopes to achieve is anyone's guess. If the fall doesn't break his neck, there'll be no surviving the waters of the *Ruoshui*. The older man's face is the color of wet cement and I swear I see it contorting into an entirely different shape right before my eyes, something from the landscape of the Underworld.

"Dunna' do this, *Athair*," my husband calls. "Do not choose the coward's way out. Face yar' accusers like the man I know ya' once were."

"My actions are mine alone, *oidhre fealltach* (traitorous heir). I answer to no one. How dare any of you pass judgment on me when you all follow The Raven so blindly! She will lead you all into destruction, *Mac Nuada*. The Mundanes will cross the Veil no matter how hard the Queen of *I Idir* tries to prevent it from happening. And when they do, they will roll over that mean-spirited, conniving *soith* (bitch) with their superior technological weapons and the Fae will lose everything they hold dear. Magic is a tool of the past. It has no place in modern history. Our only way out of this tragic end was to negotiate a treaty. Now that door has closed as well." He took a step closer to the edge. "What comes of this day is on you, *Mac Nuada*. I lay this curse on yar soul; that one day in the future yar' own son will turn against ya'. I promise he will spit in yar' face the way ma' own has done to me." Then, the Lord of House *Nuada,* put his arms out to his sides and fell backwards, carrying the sound of my mother's name, *Aine,* over the wind of his least breath.

TOOTHPICKS 19

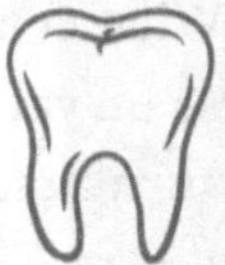

In Need of Solace

IN THAT VERY SECOND THAT Lord Callum Fitzpatrick *Nuada* threw himself off the cliffs of *Dokkr Bygo,* time stood still. I'm not speaking in the metaphorical sense, as if this was no more than my experiencing an emotional response to the awful scene I'd just witnessed. No. Time, in the way we commonly measure it, seemed to suspend itself on that desolate scrap of *Nordboerne* soil. It felt akin to a vacuum of sorts, a void empty of sound or movement, and when I went to open my mouth to call to my husband, I found myself unable to make the lips on my face obey the messages from my brain.

I can't say, with any type of accuracy, how long we remained in that strange stasis. However, I knew exactly when the vacuum fell apart. It ended with a loud tearing sound, similar to the ripping of tightly woven fabric, and all at once I could again hear the sound of the wind through the tree branches and the waves of the *Ruoshui* crashing against the craggy cliffs. "Declan," I called out. "What just happened?"

He ignored me as he walked to the point on the cliff where his father had just fallen off, the broadsword still gripped in his left hand. Going down on one knee, he bent over to look closer at what I assumed was the river below.

"Don't leave me trapped in this circle," I beg.

He turns to me with a face marked in confusion and grief. "Take the heel of yar' foot and disturb ma' chalk line. The spell should break down without any resistance."

I do as he asks and find myself able to step away from the make-shift "safe-room." "Is it okay if I come join you?"

"Aye, Love. I would welcome both yar' company and yar' insight," the Tax Man says.

I meet him at the cliff's edge and look downward, grateful that I've never suffered from a fear of heights. The drop to the bottom is treacherous. "Do you think he went into the water?"

"In all truth, I no ken' say far' sure. His body is obviously not crushed against the rocks. If he pushed his body outward, 'tis possible he missed the cliff edges altogether and fell directly inta' the *Ruoshui*. But I was not able to watch him go over, held like we were in some kind of magical void. I have never experienced a spell like that. 'Twas not born of white magic, of that I am sure. Even the most gifted Fae ken' no alter time. A castin' like that requires complicated ritual."

I ask the million-dollar question. "Do you think his Lordship is dead?"

He shrugs. "I am unsure." He looks at me with such pain in his green eyes that it pulls hard at my heart. "Is it wrong of me ta' wish him forever gone from the land of the livin'?"

It's a loaded question and I carefully tiptoe around my answer. "Your father was a troubled soul, Declan. I'm not sure whether it was his personal demons that brought him to this point, or if the *Jotun* dark magic he was obviously practicing finally corrupted his mind. But his Lordship made the choices he did on his own. You're not at all responsible for his misguided actions...or his decision to take his own life." I hope I sound sincere and that my mental shield is holding tight, because from my personal point of view, I hope the evil bastard got what he deserved.

We both stare at the water below. "I wish I knew far' sure that he went inta' the water and was dead. It would make things so much easier far' the future of ma' House."

"Will the Black Knight order a dredge of the river? Or perhaps his body will wash up somewhere downstream?" I suggest.

The Tax Man shakes his head in the negative. "Neither scenario is likely. The Jade Empire would not allow any trespassin' onto their lands, especially since they believe the *Ruoshui* is sacred. And if my *athair* went into its waves, his body is gone far'ever. The 'Weak River' never gives up its dead,' especially not a soul belongin' ta' the *Tuatha De Danann*. The river spirits would consider his Lordship's soul quite a prize."

I give a shudder over the thought of vengeful water sprites stealing one's soul...their entire essence. "If all of that is true, then proving his death is going to be difficult."

My husband sighs. "More than difficult. It will put ma'

House's standin' and wealth at risk of bein' gobbled up by other Rulin' Council members, and that's only if The Raven doesn't decide to claim ownership of it Herself under the laws regardin' treasonous acts. It all will depend on what information is found on that crystal sphere."

I throw my arms around his neck to hug him. "Oh Declan, I'm so sorry. I know how important your House is to you. I'm sure Her Majesty will understand that you personally had nothing to do with any of this," I say, doing my best to offer comfort in a situation I know nothing about.

"'Tis you I feel sorry for, ma' Love. And our son. I wonder how ya' both will feel knowin' ya' tied yar'self ta' a House dissolved in shame."

I want to tell the love of my life that I don't give a rat's ass about any of that Fae hierarchy shit. I'd be more than happy if the five of us could return to Salem and live our average, boring suburban life in the Mundane world. I also understand with my whole heart that saying just that would be like kicking my One and Only straight in the gut. I absolutely know without any doubt how much his Otherworld heritage means to my mate. Even though his genetic make-up contains elements of human DNA, Declan Phineas Fitzpatrick, Lord *Mac Nuada*, holds a *Sidhe* soul. He puts on a good front as the Mundane Tax Man, but in so many ways, that personae is simply an act. Part of him is always in *I Idir* and my new role as his Eternal Mate won't change that. I swallow my anti-Fae prejudice. "I would never measure my feelings for you against the mistakes of your father, Declan. And if Dylan could talk, he'd say the same thing. You are an amazing husband and father, Sweetie, and we love you more than I can put in words." As I mention our son's name, I recall Callum Fitzpatrick's vile last words. I don't understand enough about the magic behind Fae curses, but its weight is something I'll have to research for the future.

The Tax Man draws me into an embrace and kisses me. "I am forever grateful far' yar' deep love of me, *mian mo chroi* (desire of my heart), though I surely don' know what I did in ma' par' life ta' deserve such a loyal and loving Eternal Mate. We will face whatever the future brings together." He takes me by the arm away from the cliff's edge and draws another large circle, this time around the both of us. "We need ta' get back to *Crann Bethadh* via Ballydonnely in the Mundane world. There is much we need ta' explain ta' the Powers That Be. I ken' only hope that the secrets contained in the ink mage's sphere aren't seditious enough ta' bring down ma' House in its entirety."

* * *

The jump to Lady *Siobhan's* ancestral home in Ballydonnelly, Ireland, is quick and uneventful, making me ponder why the hell my husband insisted on traveling to *Asgard* by horse. The Tudor Revival structure is smaller than *Dun Siorai,* but infinitely more beautiful, its furnishing and decor a blend of antiques and expensive modern pieces. The staff, all with Fae roots, are thrilled to see their Mistress's only son home for a visit with his new bride and seem genuinely disappointed we aren't staying the night. They insist we at least let them provide us with a luxurious soak in the over-sized marble tub and a spot of Otherworldly-style Afternoon Tea. The Tax Man is anxious to return to *I Idir* and begin his crusade to save his House, but apparently, I look bedraggled and weary enough for him to take them up on the generous offer. Besides, inborn vanity won't allow him to return to *Crann Bethadh* looking the mess he's become.

We spend a good long hour soaking together in an over-sized tub full of bubbles and then take some personal time for ourselves, damning any "vibes" the staff might be able to "pick up." This interlude isn't about passion or lust. Our lovemaking in one of the estate's huge canopied beds is centered around providing comfort and solace in the aftermath of tragedy and is more of a joining for our wounded souls than for the pleasuring of bodies.

As for the tea, the staff goes above and beyond with an array of scones, pastries, tiny sandwiches, along with an array of fresh shellfish, and by the time we were ready to make our final jump back through the Veil, clothed in fresh appropriate apparel, we almost feel like we could begin to face whatever fallout awaited us in *I Idir*. Almost.

* * *

We return magically to our quarters at *Crann Bethadh* only to be met by an abundance of unexpected guests anxiously awaiting our arrival. Granted, we are a few hours later than anyone expected, but their level of concern is more than likely fueled by Hades own return nearly three hours earlier. "Good to see you and your Lady back, Fitz. We were beginning to worry," the Black Knight says, his usual grim expression in play.

"We jumped via Ballydonnelly, as I had sent Hades in advance of us," my husband explains. "I expect that ya' found the unusual sphere in his saddlebags?"

"We did," the Knight said. "Quite an unusual method of storing information. The Lord Merlin and Her Majesty are working on unlocking it as we speak. We're also hoping you can bring us up to date on any intelligence you may have gathered during your mission to the north-lands of *Asgard*. Apparently, Her Majesty's favorite stallion has related to her some rather disturbing news."

I ignore the absurd idea that the horse can speak directly to its mistress and instead take a quick headcount of the people crammed into the small parlor. I recognize most of them. Nearly all of Declan's team members are in attendance; his cousin, Duncan, Connor Dell, who is the deceased Rory Dell's uncle, Mac O'Kelly and Sean Callighan. Only Dennis Flagherty seems to be missing. Across the room, sitting next to the Black Knight, is a tall, pleasant-looking man who resembles the *Banphrionsa*. We've never met, but I guess him to be the Lady Dear Heart's brother, Lord *Caohmin*. Strangely enough, The Morrigan's grandson, many times removed, serves as a Catholic priest in the Mundane world, an odd twist of Fate I can't begin to fathom. He smiles at me warmly, and I feel, without even being introduced, that he's a Fae with an especially compassionate soul.

"I am glad Hades returned safely to *Crann Bethadh*, and as ya' might expect," my husband offers, "I have a lengthy report ta' give. But I ask far' yar' patience as ma' Lady and I check in on the *leanai* (children). We have been gone far' a day and a half and we wish ta' see ta' their welfare."

"I understand completely, Fitz. Take all the time you need. In the meantime, perhaps Herself and my father will have made some headway into accessing that sphere. I have a feeling all the answers we seek are hidden in that glass ball."

TOOTHPICKS 20

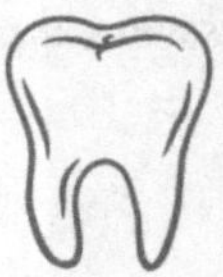

Games People Play

EVERYONE in the make-shift nursery is happy to have us home, even the little dog who prances around on his two back legs while *Buaf* sends out a piercing series of notes on a small wooden flute. I clap in exaggerated enthusiasm before sticking a finger in my right ear as the high-pitched sound cuts right through me. "Goddess help us! Where the hell did the kid get that damn flute?" I murmur to *Birgit*.

"'Twas yet another gift from the Black Knight. Himself said he felt bad the lad's toy sword had burned up in that awful Rory Dell incident. He told the boy he hoped he'd play many a fine tune for his Lord and Lady on it," the *scathach* explained, hiding an obvious giggle behind her hand.

"He did, did he?" I answer with more than a little sarcasm. "How lovely of him. Perhaps I should return the favor by offering the youngest *Banphrionsa* a gift in return? Do you think Princess Maeve would like a set of especially thunderous bongos?" I ask.

The nanny laughed again but added "I do na' know that I would have the courage ta' start a prankin' game of one upmanship with the *Ridre Dubh* (Black Knight), ma' Lady. I have a feelin' the man no likes to lose."

"Hmmm," I mutter. "I don't especially like to lose either, *Birgit.*"

My husband, who until now has pretended not to hear us, smirks, "I must agree, Lass. I would no suggest startin' any such game with Beck. 'Tis likely ya' will not appreciate the outcome."

"You all tip-toe around the man like he's…Superman untouchable," I grumble, though I secretly decide to shelve any plans regarding sending bongo drums to the Black Knight's daughter. At least for now. With all that went on in *Dokkr Bygo,* House *Nuada* is probably already in the Black Knight's line of fire.

While I nurse Dylan, Declan shows his half-brother how to hold the flute correctly and instructs him on where his fingers should be placed over the holes to produce different notes. Even with the expert tutorial, the instrument in the boy's hands produces nothing but a racket and I wonder how long it might be before that flute goes…uhmm…"missing?" Knowing that we have a room full of people waiting on us, we try not to dawdle, promising to check in again before bedtime.

As we return to the parlor, I am startled to find that additional guests have joined the group. VIP level guests. For someone of such small physical stature, the Queen of *I Idir* always manages to command the most demanding…

presence. It's not just her apparel, though she is absolutely stunning in a gown of midnight black velvet covered in silver threaded Celtic sigils. It's more than just the clothes. The natural magical energy of the goddess of war and destruction surrounds her like a transparent shadow of shimmering power, as if her petite body is unable to hold it all inside. I've said it before, and I'll say it again: The Morrigan scares the living daylights out of me.

She's joined by the Lord Merlin, who holds the crystal sphere in his hands. I consider offering her Majesty some type of refreshment as protocol requires, but then remember that we are the actual "guests" in her home, so now I'm left unsure over what's the correct thing to do. I hear the tinkling of bells in my head that signals the goddess's laughter over my awkward moment, as a fluted glass of some type of amber colored liquid appears in her hand. "Lord *Mac Nuada* and Lady Rosalinda…'tis nice to see you returned to the safety of *Crann Bethadh*. According to Hades, you've had quite an adventure," she says as she takes a delicate sip from her glass.

Declan bows and I drop a full curtsy. "Thank you for the gracious welcome, Your Majesty," my husband says. "It has been a trip bringing on the most shocking turn of events."

The Queen waves a hand towards a chair across from her. "Please make yourself comfortable, Lady *Mac Nuada*. I am sure you are most weary after such a taxing endeavor."

I do as I'm told, although all the men in the room remain standing, making me feel singled out. "I'm most appreciative of the rest, Your Majesty. I am being truthful when I say I am not accustomed to long rides in a pillion."

Before the Queen can respond to my statement there comes the sound of angry confrontation behind the entrance to the suite. The heavy wooden door swings open as two burly guards escort an obviously disgruntled Lord *Mac Badh* into the room. He appears not to realize that Her Majesty is in attendance and thus lets loose with a string of obscenities and threats. "I'll have yar' pitifal' balls far `draggin' me around in such a disrespectful manner," he tells the guards. "Her Majesty will hear about this and ya'll find yar'selves out on yar' asses before ya' can even whistle a farewell tune."

"Watch your words, Cillian *Mac Badh*" the Queen says. "'Tis I who summoned you here."

Startled, the young Lord's face goes two shades paler as he bows stiffly. "Your Majesty. I did not realize you were here."

"That's more than obvious, *Mac Badh*, but still, I would expect better from someone of your position. There is never a reason to be so vulgar."

"I am sorry, Your Majesty. 'Twas rude of me. I shall make it a common practice ta' think before I speak," *Mac Badh* mumbles, his cheeks and ears now tinged pink with embarrassment."

"I should hope so." The Morrigan points to an empty chair next to mine. "Sit," she orders.

He does as she asks, but not without noting, like myself, that all the other men in the room are standing. I sense his alarm by the tentative way he settles himself down and looks straight ahead. He's very uncomfortable in this position, and as much as I dislike the pompous ass for his nasty treatment of Declan and me, I can't help but feel a twinge of pity. The Raven is that intimidating.

"I assume you know why you are here, *Cillian*," Herself says, using his first name rather than his given title.

"I'm afraid I do not, Your Majesty. The guards told me nothing except that my presence was demanded at *Crann Bethadh*. I must confess ta' being vera'...confused," the young Lord says.

"You are aware of the death of a certain female tooth fairy? One Marcy Kilcrabtree?" The Queen asks, her right hand resting on her cheek.

The man tenses in his chair, and I note the slightest jiggle in his left leg. He puts a palm on it to stop the shaking. "I have had word of it, Your Majesty. It is always tragic when violence comes ta' *I Idir*."

"'Tis more here than tragedy, *Cillian*. Her death 'tis only a small part of evil plans leading to seditious attempts against the Throne of *I Idir*."

Mac Badh goes still and his face drains of all remaining color. I'm not sure where Herself is heading with this line of questioning. After all we have uncovered in *Dokkr Bygo*, it's more than likely Lord *Nuada* killed Marcy Kilcrabtree. I would go as far as to say that whatever was uncovered on the sphere will stand testimony to that. If *Cillian Mac Badh* is part of the treason against the Queen, a relative of his, it would be shocking information. Across the room, I see Declan slightly knit his brows together, a sign that he's also unsure of the nature of The Morrigan's questioning.

"I know nothing of that, my Sovereign Queen," he stammers. "She never expressed a word of that ta' me."

"Did you not have carnal joinings with this woman, *Mac Badh*? I was told that you did."

Cillian seems to physically shrink in his chair. Having his dirty laundry aired in front of some of the kingdom's most influential men has to be a blow to his gigantic ego. "What you heard was true, Your Majesty. But I knew nothing of any sedition."

"Come now. You expect me to believe that you and the dead tooth fairy never shared 'pillow talk' common to devoted lovers?" the Raven asks. "Surely she whispered her deepest thoughts to her beloved, especially after you gifted her that pair of stunning emerald earrings pilfered from your House's treasury?"

Embarrassed as he is, the younger Lord must sense an "out" in the framework of her question, because he sits up in the chair and squares his shoulders. "I donna' deny your words, most gracious Queen. I did, in fact, spend some intimate time with the woman. But 'twas no type of deep connection. Just a young lord's physical needs bein' met, which I believe is no against *I Idir* law or Ruling Council protocol. And the token ya' speak of was more in line with...payment than affection. As ya' are certainly aware, my Queen, I underwent The Ritual at age fourteen. I am incapable of such a deep emotional relationship until I find ma' *Mo Shiorghra*." He rolls up his right sleeve to reveal the ink marking his bicep. It depicts a band of Celtic knotwork similar to Declan's, but the center piece, a sharp-beaked raven, is still clearly part of the tattoo. "As you can all see, I have yet ta' find ma' Fated Mate."

"Just because she is not your One and Only doesn't mean the girl didn't have feelings for you, *Mac Badh*.

Perhaps she offered you this treasonous information as a way to win your heart? Or perhaps you killed her to hide the fact that she was pregnant with your offspring." The Morrigan insinuates, knowing full well that the DNA testing proves Lord *Nuada* fathered the child. And naturally, no one in the room contradicts her. She coolly examines her painted nails as if she's completely bored with the conversation, seemingly ignoring the awful truth that *Cillian Mac Badh's* very life depends on it. The Raven Queen obviously has a cruel game in play here, but I can't fathom what it might be.

The Lord's eyes open wide with shock over these comments. "Your Majesty, there is no possibility of me producing a child with any woman who is not my Fated Mate, nor could she ever hope to wring that kind of affection from me, Your Majesty. Not when my arm is covered with the ink magic of The Ritual. Surely a gifted sorceress as yourself is aware of the parameters of the spell?" When the Queen doesn't answer, *Mac Badh* begins to panic. He looks at the other men in the room staring at him with cold suspicion. His terrified eyes rest on my husband. "Tell her, *Mac Nuada*! Explain to everyone here how life is under The Ritual! You of all people understand the burden of it," he pleads.

I find the whole situation highly ironic: *Cillian Mac Badh,* who has done his very best to make a fool of my husband every chance he gets, is now reduced to begging my Tax Man to save the young Lord's sorry ass for him. And the thing is, I understand my mate well enough to know that it's exactly what he'll do. My beloved *Mo Shiorghra,* a man "full of goodness," will come to the younger man's aid simply because it is the right thing to do.

"Lord *Mac Badh* speaks the truth," Declan says. "Within the boundaries of the spell, a man under The Ritual ken' be intimate with a woman and feel not the slightest regard far' her feelins'. 'Tis the cold hard truth and one which I ma'self have experienced before the Universe gifted me with ma' One and Only. It is also known ta' be impossible ta' father a child with anyone other than one's Fated Mate. 'Twas the whole reason The Ritual was instituted for all House heirs; ta' prevent the killin' of Fae against Fae over the love of a woman or the question of rightful inheritance."

There's not even the slightest chance The Morrigan doesn't already know all of this. I'm not sure how brutally embarrassing *Cillian Mac Badh*, a member of the Queen's own family line, helps us get to the bottom of Lord *Nuada's* crimes. If this is nothing more than some kind of silly ploy, it seems unnecessarily cruel, even for the Raven Queen. This thought earns me a sharp poke inside my head. *"Tis not your place to second guess me, little tooth fairy mama. I do what needs to be done for the good of I Idir,"* says the familiar voice. *"You'd be wise to remember that."* I must subconsciously flinch over the Queen's words, because Declan looks over to me with a questioning look. I ignore him and tighten my mental shield.

Relief floods *Cillian's* face. "As you can see, Your Majesty, Lord *Mac Nuada* backs my claims. I may have had a physical relationship with that tooth fairy, but as misguided as my actions were, I did not sire that woman's child, nor did I kill her. I had no purpose to do either. She was just a way to fill the call of spring ruttin'. She never revealed to me any words of treason. Her only desire was to further her own value at Court. All I did was escort her to a few events and introduce her to other influential *Sidhe*. The idea that you believe me to be disloyal to the Throne of *I Idir* wounds me greatly, my Beloved Queen. We are of the same bloodline. I am yar' kin. I could never do such a thing."

"Betrayal is not uncommon among families, and to think so is naive, *Mac Badh*. Blood relatives have more reason to turn on each other than most strangers," she says, looking pointedly at my husband. "But if *Mac Nuada* is willing to speak in your defense despite your childish jealousy of him, then it can only mean he speaks the honest truth." She waved an impatient hand at him. "In the future, I hope you will remember *Mac Nuada's* gracious support of you, *Cillian*. You may go now. I have no further use of you."

The young man rose and gave a low bow. "Thank you, Your Majesty."

"And Lord *Mac Badh*...may I also suggest that in the future you select your rutting partners with more discretion and taste?" she adds.

His face turns beet red. "Of course, Your Majesty. I appreciate your wise counsel. I will do just that."

As he exited the suite, The Raven Queen smiled and addressed her Black Knight. "Well, that went rather well, did it not?" She put her hand out so the Lord Merlin could place the crystal ball in her hands. "Now, shall we discuss the mystery of this amazing piece of *Dokkalfar* black magic and what it means to the kingdom of *I Idir?*"

TOOTHPICKS 21

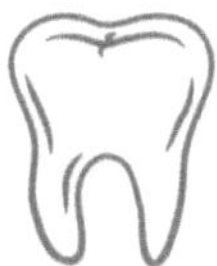

The Young Deer

"So, I assume that means you were able to access it," the Black Knight asked his wizard father.

"Aye, though it was more difficult than I expected. The sphere was fraught with spell-casted 'land mines' that were meant to destroy the data if not accessed correctly," the Lord Merlin explained. "Much like encryption codes in technology. But Her Majesty was able to detect and defuse all of them using a combination of white and ritual magic."

"I am amazed Master Brendan was able to create such magical genius. I hadn't realized he'd advanced so much in skill. 'Tis a shame he wasted his grand potential on a people who could never begin to appreciate it," the Queen said. "Once we broke through the locks, gaining access to his Grimoire, as well as his personal journal, was easy enough. For the sake of brevity and security, I will only reveal information relevant to the most serious issues at hand; mainly the attempt to overthrow *I Idir's* monarchy in hopes of thinning the Veil between the two worlds. The man's Grimoire notes, those regarding his castings and spells, will remain available to only Lord Merlin and myself, lest this dark magic find its way into unsavory hands, Furthermore, I believe some of the secrets contained in his journal are best left to the dark space of ignorance. They are revelations that could only lead to chaos and the temptation to thwart the will of the Universe."

I could see a huge level of disappointment settle on the faces of some of the men in the room. Several of them had their own differing reasons for needing information they felt might be on the sphere. Only Connor Dell had the courage to say it. "With complete respect, Your Majesty, if that sphere contains information on who killed ma' nephew, Rory, I believe 'tis ma' right accordin' ta' the laws of *I Idir* ta' have the name of his murderer as well as the first privilege of huntin' him or her down and endin' their sorry life."

In return, the pub owner and part-time spy received a frosty glare from his Queen, one from which he did not shrink. "I understand your need for retribution, Master Dell. And be assured you will receive whatever just bene-fits are within your rights." She let her words hang in the air. "As long as you understand that I will allow nothing to come before the goal of keeping the Mundanes out of the Otherworld. That must be the central focus of all we do going forward. To allow human access to the Otherworld means the end of life here as we know it. No amount of extra wealth or promises of increased power can match what we will lose in the end game. As long as I still breathe the air of this world into my lungs, I will do battle against anyone who works toward the breakdown of the Veil."

Connor Dell gave a bow. "I understand completely, my Queen. I hold true to the same goal. I only want ta' see justice done far' ma' brother's only son."

"You shall have it, Master Dell, with my blessings…in due time," the Queen replied.

"Before we proceed, Your Majesty, perhaps Lord *Mac Nuada* should report on what he and his Lady discovered in *Asgard*," the Black Knight interjected.

"I agree, as I have no doubt that the information on this sphere will bear witness to *Mac Nuada's* tale. Proceed with your report, young Lord," the Queen ordered.

Declan stepped forward and began to tell our story in precise detail, beginning with the hostile treatment we received from the people of *Gleann Glas* and *Orskots-Helgr*, a sign, my husband explained, stood as a testament to just how tense the relationship had become between the Fae and the *Nordboerne* people. He described how void of residents the village of *Dokkr Bygo* seemed, as if the very essence of their life energy has been sucked completely from it, and discussed the murder of Master Brendan, the "Soul Thief," in graphic, blunt detail. It is only when he related the confrontation that occurred between him and his father that I sensed any cracks in my *Mo Shiorghra's* emotionless facade. There was a slight change to the pitch of his voice and I noticed that he tucked his left hand in the pocket of his breeches to hide what I am sure was a mild tremor. When he finally came to Lord *Nuada's* backward fall off the cliff and into the "Weak River" of the Jade Empire, his voice became breathy in an attempt to get the statement out in one very long sentence without a break. "I examined the sides and bottom of the rocks, but found no sign of his Lordship's body. I ken' not say far' sure if he went inta' the *Ruoshui,* nor could I determine one hundred percent that he has forever left the world of the livin'. For that I am deeply sorry, Your Majesty."

"There is nothing to apologize for *Mac Nuada.* Callum Fitzpatrick has been hiding behind a wall of deceit for a long time. The information on this sphere will bear this out. You have been a most loyal subject to this Throne and I regret that you will undoubtedly be forced to wear the dark mantle of your sire's actions," the Queen replied, "but it cannot be helped. Moving on, our Lord Merlin will now relate to us the sequence of events that has brought us to these perilous times."

The wizard gave a nod and stepped forward. "I also regret that what I say here today will surely be difficult for Lord and Lady *Mac Nuada* to hear and I apologize in advance for the hurt I will unwittingly cause you both. I invite you all to take a seat as the details are rather lengthy."

Panic begins to crawl over me like an army of stinging red ants. It's one thing to know there are skeletons in your closet, and something completely different when you realize they're about to come out and dance with you. My Tax Man takes a seat next to me on the settee and I feel the pent-up energy roll off him and onto me, giving my "red ants of anxiety" a tingly zap of magical electricity.

Once everyone is settled, Lord Merlin proceeds.

"According to the earliest of Master Brendan's journal entries, dated some forty plus years ago, the beginning of this tale centers around Callum Fitzpatrick's feelings of affection for a young tooth fairy by the name of *Aine*, a member of House *Fiacail*."

I grimace at the sound of my mother's name. Somehow, I'd naively believed her memory wouldn't be dragged into this sordid tale. The wizard notices my reaction. "I am sorry, Lady *Mac Nuada*, for the need to air your family history in such a public forum, but there is no way to avoid it. Your mother is truly at the heart of this matter through no fault of her own. By Fate, she had the misfortune to meet and fall in love with a man destined for someone else."

I prickle at the idea that my mother was just "unlucky." There's a lot more to it than that. "I'm well aware of this story, Lord Merlin. I've heard it from a few different sources, one of which was Lord *Nuada* himself. But I feel, for clarification sakes, that I need to add that when my mother first met his Lordship, he was disguised as a common laborer. A low-born, village farm hand. He didn't actually tell her who he really was until their relationship had...well...progressed and she had fallen in love with him. I'm sure if she'd known in advance that he was House *Nuada*'s heir and bound to the decisions of The Ritual, she would have never ventured to give him her heart," I say, chin up, daring anyone in the room to contradict me.

"I don't disagree, dear Lady," the wizard replied. "The journal is full of the Lord's falsehoods. The ink mage doesn't explain how Lord *Nuada* met the girl, only that he was madly in love with her, and she with him, but we all appreciate your input. There are many victims in this story."

His statement makes me feel more placated than justified, but I hold my tongue. If my Beloved can handle what will be said regarding his father, how can I do any less?

"Because of the border skirmishes with the Fomorians, Callum's father was away in battle and his mother made the poor decision to hold off The Ritual until her husband's return. By that time, his young Lordship was already two years past the year marking manhood and solidly in love with *Aine*. He fought bitterly with his parents about going through with the magic intended to mate him, but as it was sacred tradition, it was an argument he would not win, with his *athair* threatening to shackle him to a chair for the entire proceedings. In desperation, the boy stole a piece of expensive jewelry from his *mathair*'s possessions and bribed the ink mage to intentionally leave parts of the spell unfinished so that he could claim *Aine* as his *Mo Shiorghra*. and proceed with their handfast. The ink mage admits in his writings that he knew it was unlikely leaving only a few words out of the spell would entirely cancel the power of the magic behind it, and he was unwilling to risk major adjustments, lest his actions be noticed by the House mages. However, young Callum was insistent, and Master Brendan, seeing a recurring source of income in the boy's misguided hopes, took the jewelry and did as he was asked."

While the Merlin tells this sordid tale, no one in the group looks at me. No one except The Morrigan, who watches me like a bug in a jar, pondering her next move.

Suddenly all of Lady *Siobhan's* warnings about tying oneself to the Raven Queen creep into my head, and in response, I hear the familiar tinkling of those awful bells.

The wizard stops for a moment and fills a glass with water, taking several sips before continuing. "Callum Fitzpatrick sat for his Ritual thinking all would work toward his end game, and for several months it did, as no other *Mo Shiorghra* appeared. But despite Master Brendan's magical 'attempts' to force the ink to transfer to *Aine's* body, it did not. In frustration and misery, the tooth fairy broke things off and disappeared into the Mundane world. Callum was beside himself, sinking into a deep depression while Master Brendan continued to defraud him of more and more stolen jewels, promising to find the missing tooth fairy, but never actually venturing into the Mundane world to do so."

"This makes me wonder if those ink charlatans all be nothin' but liars and cheats," Mac O'Kelly mumbles.

"Offerin' magic far' a fee surely lends itself to such dealins'. It steals the purity of the castin'," adds Duncan.

Both men receive a death stare aimed their way by Herself, and they quickly rein in their opinionated chit chat. The Lord Merlin goes on. "When Callum became Lord of House *Nuada* at the death of his father, he ordered the ink mage to make *Aine* appear or threatened the money would immediately stop. It's here that Master Brendan changed tactics, switching from fraud to blackmail, threatening to reveal how the new Lord had attempted to thwart the magic of his Ritual with jewels stolen from his own mother, and how he had paid the ink mage to locate a woman who wasn't his *Mo Shiorghra*. Not wishing to lose his seat on the Ruling Council, Callum had no choice but to pay, though now he could pilfer from the House's treasury rather than from his mother's jewelry box. The ink mage marked every payment with a little symbol in his journal, so it's easy to gather how long these payments went on."

Declan and I look at each other. "Did this symbol resemble an ancient *Futhark* rune?" my husband asks.

"As a matter of fact, it did. I believe it appeared as the symbol for *Pethro*. It would make sense, as the rune sometimes refers to 'secrets,' often the magical kind," the sorcerer said.

"I have seen the matching symbol in the House account books, but as of yet, I haven't had time to figure the amounts," the Tax Man adds, "though the symbol eventually stops after about twelve years."

"I believe I can explain that as well," the Merlin says. "It would seem Lord Callum *Nuada* built up enough influence and power in the Ruling Council to run Master Brendan out of town. His leaving had nothing to do with seeking solitude and everything to do with saving his neck."

"That would have been shortly after the ink mage completed ma' own Ritual," Declan says with a shudder.

Duncan risks the Queen's annoyance by adding his two cents. "No one with a pair of eyes and a lick of Fae magical sense could miss the true bond that ya' share with yar' Lady, ma' Lord. It is like none I have ever seen befar' or since." He gets up and bows toward the Queen. "I am sorry far' interruptin' the Lord Merlin, Your Majesty, but

I felt it needed ta' be said on behalf of ma' Liege Lord and his Lady."

She tisked at Declan's cousin. "Sit down, *gancanagh*, so we can get on with this. I appreciate your desire to come to your Liege Lord's aid, and though I agree that their bond is extremely strong, this is becoming a very drawn-out story." She rolled her hand in an impatient motion. "Please continue, Ambrose. I am growing bored with all this familial drama. Get to the part about the man's sedi-tious actions against my Throne. And," she added with a lethal glare, "I shall expect no further interruptions."

As if the ears of Fate had been listening in and willing to call The Morrigan's bluff, *Buaf* suddenly skipped into the parlor wearing his little boy nightshirt, his copper-colored hair, a match to my husband's, still wet from his evening bath. His eyes widen when he takes in the large gathering of guests, but upon viewing the Queen of *I Idir*, instantly drops to his knees and buries his face in the carpet. *Birgit* is two steps behind him, Dylan howling in her arms. She drops a quick curtsy. "I am so sorry, Your Majesty. I turned ma' back far' only a second and the boy scooted away from the nursery. He moves like the wind, swift and silent."

I pray to every other goddess in the pantheon that the one sitting here in front of me doesn't threaten either of my children because then I'd be forced to make a spec-tacle of myself. Instead, she gives me a withering stare and says, "Are you not a believer of proper bedtime schedules for your wee *bairns*, Lady *Mac Nuada?*"

If she wants to scold me, so be it. Just leave my kids out of it. "I do try to adhere to proper meal and bedtime routines, Your Majesty, but unfortunately our lives have been rather…upended in the past few weeks, through no fault of the children, of course." I try to keep the sarcasm out of my voice, but apparently that's a complete "fail" if the frantic looks I'm getting from my husband and his cousin are any indication.

"Get up off the floor, boy, before you soil your night clothes," The Morrigan orders *Buaf.* The child picks his head up high enough to peek at the Queen, and seeing no immediate danger, hesitantly stands up. "Come closer so I can get a good look at you," the Raven commands.

Buaf obeys, taking tiny, timid steps, his little body shaking so much I just want to scoop him up and carry him back to the nursery. Sensing this, Declan puts his arm through mine, which I suppose is meant to keep me from doing just that. When the boy gets close enough, the Queen takes his chin in her hand and turns his head from one side to another. "Thank the Universe your *Sidhe* bloodline is stronger than your Elven one. I am told you are a child of House *Nuada.*"

"That is what ma' Lord told me, Lady Queen. He is ma' half-brother," he says softly, but not without a look of pride on his small face.

"And this makes you happy?" The Raven Queen asks.

"Oh, vera' much, Your Majesty! Lord *Mac Nuada* is the best Lord in all of *I Idir*! He is kind and smart and vera' brave. I hope to be like him when I reach manhood so that I can best serve him as ma' Liege Lord." Realizing his faux pas, he adds quickly, "And you too, Lady Queen. And *I Idir.*" I catch Duncan and several of the men on my husband's team hiding grins at the boy's blatant hero worship of Declan.

"Those are high goals, child. What do they call you?" The Morrigan asks.

"Ma' name be *Buaf,* Your Majesty."

The Raven frowned. "You are called "Toad?" Why are you named after a squat, ugly river dweller? You look nothing like that creature, though the transformation behind its spirit does make it an appropriate moniker." She pauses a moment as if thinking, then says, "'Tis time you had a more fitting name, boy. A new name for a new beginning. Hence forward, per my decree, you shall be known as *Oisin* Fitzpatrick *Nuada.*"

"Thank you for gifting me with such a fine soundin' title, Lady Queen. 'Tis more than I expect I deserve, bein' a bastard and all. May I ask a question, if it pleases your Majesty?"

"Ask your question, *Oisin,* the Queen replied.

"Why name me "young deer," ma' Lady Queen? I am neither fleet of foot nor cautious by ma' nature. Seems a vera' grand title far' a boy with such humble beginnins'."

"The deer is your spirit animal, *Oisin.* As time passes and you grow in knowledge, you will understand your place in time. Until then, be loyal to your brother and walk your path with confidence."

TOOTHPICKS 22

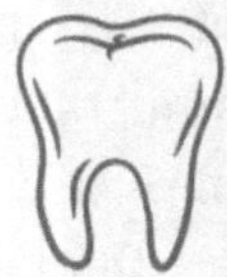

Little Deer and Pressing Fears

THE EIGHT-YEAR-OLD STANDS there shyly beaming. I confess that my emotions are conflicted concerning this turn of events. I'm glad to know that, despite the wicked actions of his sire, the boy will carry the *Nuada* name and whatever benefits the title comes with. However, Declan and I have formed a parental bond with the child and have made him a part of our family. Should not the decision regarding his name, or the changing of it, have rested with us and not the Throne? The response to my thoughts comes quickly enough. *"Rein in your pettiness, little tooth fairy. Although I am well pleased that you have generously taken on the role of mathair to the boy, his path is far different from yours,"* says the terse voice in my head. *"You will find enough twists in your own journey to focus on."*

Because nothing is simple in my life, the blasted dog has now joined the party, taking a respectful pose next to *Birgit* as if he understands the required protocol. The

Raven Queen acknowledges the dog with a nod of her head, then addresses the nanny, sending them off with a shooing motion. "Lady *Scathach*, it is time to take your young charges back to the nursery. Be sure to keep them there this time."

Birgit gives a final curtsy and then nudges *Buaf*...I mean *Oisin*...who bows grandly from the waist. The little group turns and heads to their room at the far end of the suite, the lad walking as if he is every bit the title afforded him, while *Seamus* follows behind him, wagging his tail in celebration. It's an adorable sight, and everyone in the group, except The Morrigan, cracks a grin, even the Black Knight who always reminds me of a shark when he does it.

"If we are done wasting my time, I'd like for Ambrose to continue," says Herself in a tone so icy the water in the Merlin's glass freezes.

"Seriously, Grandmother, how can you not find the kid and the dog worth a smile? You have to admit they're pretty darn cute," the Prince of *I Idir* comments with more informality than the rest of us would ever dare.

"If it is 'cute' you want, *Caoimhin*, then run off and join a traveling minstrel show. We are here to discuss the future of *I Idir*," she snaps. "I find nothing humorous about that."

"A little levity never hurt anything, Grandmother," he answers.

"Spoken like the fool you are, *Caoimhin*," she replies. "Proceed, Lord Merlin."

The wizard clears his throat, while I note the definite smirk the Black Knight gives his brother-in-law as they exchange the look of a shared joke. "It's actually quite ironic that the boy made his appearance when he did, as the next part of the ink mage's diary concerns him." The Morrigan's grandson opens his mouth to speak, but suddenly closes it as if he's been mentally warned off from expressing an opinion. The Merlin continues his tale. "Once he was forced out of *I Idir*, Master Brendan wandered through *Asgard* before finally settling in the north lands among the *Dokkalfar* people. His entries here are mostly rambling threats against Lord *Nuada*, but this also appears to be the same time he becomes fascinated with the goddess *Freyja* and the study of *Seior* magic. He mentions studying the ancient *Nordboerne* texts and eventually taking in an apprentice, but there's really no useful mention of House *Nuada* until twelve years later when his Lordship reaches out to Master Brendan, again asking for help to erase the Mate Bond between he and Lady *Siobhan* lest he go mad and end her life."

There's an awkward silence in the room that my husband ends. "'Tis no secret that ma' parents have despised each other for as long as I ken' remember. Their venom was a regular part of our daily lives. Every time my *mathair* would announce the impending birth of another sibling, I was always…well…shocked."

"That is the irony of The Ritual, or with most magic for that matter. It is produced on the whim of the Universe and even when wrought by the most skilled of practitioners, the intended outcome is never guaranteed." Ambrose sighed. "In the case of Lord and Lady *Nuada*, the Mate Bond produced six living offspring, a boon to the future of the House, but at a high price. It was Lord

Nuada's desperation to free himself from that magical pull of physical desire that ultimately led to the point we find ourselves today. Master Brendan saw the Lord's torment as a way to pad his wealth while testing his new found magical prowess. He convinced Callum that if he came to *Dokkr Bygo*, the ink mage could use the newly learned dark sorcery of *Jotun* magic to unravel The Ritual casting. Despite the ink mage's earlier deceptions, Callum immediately left for the northlands of *Asgard.*"

"I recall when he left," Declan adds. "My *athair* told me he was setting up some lucrative business contacts in Asgard. When I went home for Meghan's birthday, he was gone and my Lady *Mathair* was actually pleasant." There are nods of understanding and sympathy from the other guests. Considering how intensely private this information is, my Tax Man is putting on a good front.

"From the ink mage's notes, it appears Lord *Nuada* stayed in *Dokkr Bygo* for nearly four months during which time he met and began an intimate relationship with Master Brendan's apprentice, a young woman of both *Ljosalfar* and *Dokkalfar* heritage, something that would have undoubtedly made her an outcast of both peoples, as the two groups never mix. Through his alliance with the woman, his Lordship took a keen interest in the ancient practice of early *Nordboerne* sorcery and within the parameters of *Jotun,* the three of them were able to undo some aspects of the original Ritual while not completely unraveling the entire spell. As a result, despite the basic framework of The Ritual to prevent offspring outside the Bond, Callum Fitzpatrick eventually conceived a child with his Elven mistress."

"And the wee lad we just met is that child?" asks Connor Dell.

"Yes," the Black Knight adds. "Robyn ran a DNA profile. We're sure."

"Why do I have a bad feelin' about this?" Declan's team member murmurs. "How did the boy get ta' *I Idir*? And where is his *mathair*?"

"Your bad feelings have merit, Master Dell," the Merlin says. "From the journal entries, Lord *Nuada* left *Asgard* to return home a week after the apprentice shared the news of her pregnancy with him. He promised to send for her when he could make all the 'proper arrangements' along with monthly stipends, which he apparently did send, though how much she saw of the funds and how much went into Master Brendan's coffers is hard to say."

"Let me guess," Declan says, "he marked the payments he received from my *athair* with the *Futhark* rune *Berkano*?"

"Correct," the wizard confirms. "I gather the House accounts also list it."

"Aye. I guessed it had somethin' to do with the lad based on the dates those symbols start ta' appear' along with the perceived age of the boy," Declan says. "Are ya' able ta' tell us something about the woman apprentice, Lord Merlin? Her name? What became of her?"

The Black Knight's father looks pointedly at Herself, who answers instead. "The woman's name is not important. The boy has a new life and a new name here in *I Idir*. There is no need for his future to be clouded with his past."

The Queen's caginess regarding information about

Oisin's mother sets off all kinds of warning bells in my head. Before I can say anything, my husband squeezes my hand twice, a signal we've developed to use when we can't trust our mental communication is entirely private. I double down on my shields, but against The Morrigan, I don't stand much of a chance of keeping her out of my head, even after tooth fairy sundown.

"What I can tell you," the Merlin explains, "is that after waiting eight months for Lord *Nuada* to send for her and hearing nothing, the woman finally set off on her own for *Dun Siorai*, carrying the child and all of the wealth Callum had sent her, or at least that is the story Master Brendan tells in his journal. He claims that she never arrived in *I Idir* and assumes she was killed by brigands along the way. We know the child ended up here at *Dun Siorai* so we can assume that parts of his story are untrue. What actually happened to the woman is a mystery."

Connor Dell mumbles something under his breath that sounds suspiciously like an obscenity. "Beggin' yar' pardon, Lord Merlin, we all have sense enough in ar' heads ta' realize that there is no mystery here. That wretched bastard *Nuada* murdered that par' woman, just like he did ma' nephew. And if none of ya' have the guts to say it, then…"

The man suddenly disappeared into thin air. One minute Connor Dell was sitting on the chair across from me, and the next he isn't. I see several hands reach for weapons when the Raven Queen says, "Reconsider your actions, gentlemen, with cooler heads. Your comrade is safe and equally unharmed. There is no need to make more of this than is necessary. Master Dell has been given a chance to privately cool down his temper and to remember to whom he owes his fealty. I suggest you do the same. I understand that emotions are running high, but as I said earlier, my solitary goal is focused on the safety of *I Idir* and I will not tolerate any deviance from it."

The tension in the room is a living, breathing entity and for the first time in a long time I am truly afraid for the safety of my family. I can't imagine how I ever thought I could move in the same circle as the goddess of war and destruction. I grossly underestimated what that would mean to my life going forward and I realize with growing horror that I truly traded any shot at "Mundane normalcy" for the safe return of my husband from North Korea.

The Prince of *I Idir* seems to be the only calm person in the room. The only one not ready to take up arms. He smiles serenely. "All this hostility isn't going to solve anything, gentlemen. Let's take it down a notch, shall we. I don't know about the rest of you, but I could really use a shot of *"Uisce Beatha* (Water of Life-whiskey) 'bout now." A tray appears on the round table in the center of the room with several crystal rock glasses and an exquisite decanter filled with a golden-brown liquid. All I can do is hope that the fancy glassware doesn't end up in itty, bitty, tiny pieces because my Tax Man is definitely not a happy camper over Connor's disappearance. Anger trickles through his fingertips and runs up the hand of mine he's gripping.

Lord *Caoihmin* pours a heft finger of whiskey in each glass. "Top rate stuff, fellows. Courtesy of the Black

Knight's Special Reserve," he says as he flashes his brother-in-law a grin. Picking up the tray, he offers everyone a glass, beginning with the Queen, who surprisingly accepts. Not wanting to call attention to myself, I take a glass as well, figuring I had already nursed the baby and was only planning to wet my lips anyways. The Raven's great grandson lifts his own tumbler. "A toast to Her Majesty, Queen Maeve of *I Idir*. Long reign the Queen! *Slante!*" Everyone answers the toasts and swallows their whiskey in one gulp, all except me, who takes a polite little slip then puts the mostly full glass back on the tray behind the decanter where I hope no one will notice it.

Fat chance of that happening. I feel the Black Knight's smirk rest on me. "Too much 'bite' for you, Lady Rosalinda?" he asks, nodding toward my unfinished glass.

"Oh no, it's very good, Lord Knight. Extremely smooth. It just has...well...a lot of alcohol...and I'm a nursing mother," I say.

"Of course," he says in such a condescending tone that I want to reach out and sock him in the arm. It dawns on me that the Lady Dear Heart is also nursing their own daughter, and her husband, no doubt, is aware that I just finished feeding Dylan and that this single shot of whiskey won't do me any harm.

I've always been the kind of girl who stands her ground, and if I can't control any of what will happen regarding my damn father-in-law, I can at least make a point here and now, in front of everyone, that we Fitzpatricks are a tough bunch and not to be taken lightly. "Though it does seem a shame to leave such fine whiskey in the glass, your Lordship. Why not enjoy it after all," I say, as I toss the contents down my throat in a single swallow. The whiskey might be called the "Water of Life," but it's "water" that burns like scalding lava all the way down to my gut. It's all I can do to keep from sputtering and coughing the stuff right back up. My entire head feels as if it's on fire and when I speak it comes out in squeaky pants. "Yup…that's the real stuff," I choke out.

Everyone laughs and *I Idir's* Hand of Justice gives me what I think is a genuine smile and the "thumbs up" signal. "Nicely done, Rosie," he says. "I'm impressed." And in that moment, I realize that I've just played a key role in an attempt to de-escalate a volatile situation that could have gotten completely out of hand. For the first time since agreeing to sign on as a "spy," I feel like I'm actually a member of the team. Declan squeezes my hand, and I squeeze back.

"Now, if everyone can still think straight, I need to get to information that directly affects the safety of the Veil," the Lord Merlin says.

"I wish you would, Ambrose. I could have raised an entire army in the time it has taken you to tell this tale," The Morrigan complains, although her body language seems more relaxed than it had been a few minutes ago.

"I apologize for the time I've taken, Your Majesty. I don't wish to leave anything of importance out of this conversation. The ramifications of this sphere have wide ranging implications." In response she rolls a hand at him indicating that he should continue. "I would like to say that Lord Callum *Nuada's* poor decisions ended with the disappearance of his mistress. Unfortunately, that's not the case. While in *Asgard*, his Lordship also made some connections with a group of men and women from various kingdoms, who were tired of *I Idir*'s role as major "gatekeeper" to the Veil separating the Mundane world from the Otherworld. They felt our monarch's firm promise to keep humans out of the Otherworld prevented the rest of them from expanding their own wealth and power. This was despite the fact that most of the leadership of these fellow kingdoms had already signed a treaty pledging their support of *I Idir's* policies. We are still currently unaware if this rebel group has the secret backing of any of the other kingdom's rulers, or if they working 'under the radar,' so to speak.

This band of 'freedom fighters,' as Master Brendan refers to them in his journal, met in secret in the northlands of *Asgard* to amass money, which they then invested in science, technology, and genetic programs in Mundane countries that held a primary goal of equipping humans with the ability to not only cross the Veil, but to also spend extended periods of time here." The wizard turns specifically to me and Declan, and I can see the sadness in his eyes. "I'm sorry to say that there is direct evidence linking Lord *Nuada* to the government-backed terrorist group that abducted you, Fitz. Seeing it on this sphere made me physically ill. It also explains Marcy Kilcrabtree's involvement in all of this. Lord *Nuada* used her in the same manner he did Master Brendan's Elven apprentice, though the tooth fairy did seem to hold a personal vendetta against the two of you that made her lover's job easier. But it was Callum himself who sent her to North Korea, knowing full well his son would insist on rescuing her, and thus offering the

North Koreans his own flesh and blood to experiment on. It made the government of that country feel that they could absolutely trust him to further their plans."

Declan is so still beside me I feel as if I need to check if he's even still actually breathing. He has his shield up so tight that I have to push like hell to feel anything from him, and when I do, his grief and pain is like ice in my veins, so cold it burns. The empty glasses on the tray rattle, then explode, but no one says a word. "When did my *athair* begin to hate me so much?" he asks no one in particular.

"Look at me, *Mac Nuada*," The Morrigan says, her tone demanding obedience. When he does, she says, "I realize your heart will never fully believe what I tell you, so I am ordering you to let go of your emotions and use only pure, magical logic." My husband's eyes seem to glaze over as he stares into those of the goddess. "This has nothing to do with you and everything to do with effects of *Freyja's* evil magic. It is a corrupt use of energy and thus it corrupts everything it touches. It relies on the Universe-given life force of stolen souls to work its awful deeds. The man you knew as your sire has long been gone from you. He fell off a cliff long before today when he gave over his heart and mind to this ancient black magic. That is why the practice of it has been forbidden for centuries. Nothing good ever comes of it."

The Raven breaks the intense gaze between them, and my husband shakes his head as he turns to me. His pupils are still dilated and he seems out of it. I guess she somehow spell-drugged him, which to my mind crosses all kinds of boundaries. However, the energy rolling off of him is less intense, less entrenched in turmoil and grief, and if Herself saved my *Mo Shiorghra* from at least a shred of painful thoughts, I guess I'm down with her intrusive hocus-pocus. Perhaps even grateful for it.

"He cared far' me at one time, Lass. I swear it," my *Mo Shiorghra* mumbles.

"I know, Sweetie. People get…sick. They change. Drugs, alcohol…magic. All of it has the potential to take over your life," I offer. It sounds lame, but I can't tell my Tax Man what I'm truly feeling. I hate Callum Fitzpatrick with a fire I didn't even know I possessed. What he's done is inexcusable. Unforgivable. Unpardonable. And if the Universe makes any sense at all, Lord *Nuada* will receive the afterlife karma he deserves.

"So do you think he is dead?" the Black Knight asks, directing his question towards The Morrigan and his father.

"He most certainly is not," the Queen says.

"I concur," Lord Merlin adds.

"So where is he now and what do we do about him?" Beck questions, a man more comfortable with concrete plans than spiritual philosophies.

"No doubt he's gone into hiding like cowards often do," Herself says. "He will bury himself in the buzzing humanity of the Mundane world where he believes he can stay well hidden. If I had to guess, I'd say he's gone back to his cronies in North Korea."

"Shall I send a team in? Retrieve him and bring him back here to stand trial?" the Knight asks.

"I should be the one to go after him," Declan says. "He is ma' House's responsibility."

I'm about to leap out of my seat over that insane suggestion but The Morrigan beats me to it. "Absolutely not *Mac Nuada*. I strictly forbid it. If it even appears that you have tracked your sire down to kill him, it will break one of the most sacred of laws against patricide. It will seem that you seek to end his life only to steal his title."

"But surely in these circumstances..." my husband protests.

"There are no circumstances that the other members of the Ruling Council will find acceptable. Keep in mind that they are all fathers as well. They must be secure in the knowledge that their own heirs do not seek a quicker path to power. No. You are not to avenge your *athair's* crimes, no matter how loudly your soul calls for you to do it."

"I respect your wise words, Your Majesty, but the man ken' not be left ta' continue his path of destruction. There is no reason to believe he will stop his quest to help the Mundanes cross the Veil," Declan says.

"I agree," said The Morrigan. "I will offer a universal bounty on his head, a reward that is meant to entice a wide range of mixed-blood mercenaries from all over both worlds. It will, at the very least, keep *Nuada* busy looking over his shoulder at every turn."

"What about my family, Your Majesty? Here and in the Mundane world? My sister, her husband and my nephews? My father?" I ask with more boldness than usual, courtesy, I believe, of the whiskey.

"I will guarantee their safety, Lady *Mac Nuada*, though I do not think Callum so stupid as to take such risks. Still, 'tis best not to take any chances. The Black Knight will personally see to their security."

The man in question nods to me. "Rest assured, Rosie. I will treat their safety in the same manner I protect my own."

I suppose I can't ask for more. The man does have a reputation for ruthlessness. "Thank you, Lord Knight. I appreciate your dedication."

He ignores my gratitude and instead asks. "So, what's our next move, my Queen?"

The Raven sighs, and for the first time this evening, I sense an aura of weariness cross her demeanor. "We need to track down any members of that rebel group who are taking up residence in *I Idir*. Arrest them and bring them to *Crann Bethadh* for trial and sentencing. Unfortunately, we cannot pull them out of *Asgard*, Avalon, or the Jade Empire should there be any there, not without causing additional problems with neighboring kingdoms. We do not need to fight multiple battles on multiple fronts, not with the Mundanes breathing down our necks. But word of the arrests and sentencing will keep the others from becoming bolder."

"How do we determine who the rebels might be?" asked the Black Knight. "Did the sphere have any intel? Lists of names?"

"No. Unfortunately, Master Brendan was too smart to note specific names. But he did give us a clue on how to detect them. The ink mage marked each member with a small tattooed symbol behind their left ear." The Merlin glances over to my husband. "Can you guess what the symbol is, Fitz."

The Tax Man frowns. "I venture it is the bastardized rendition of two joined *Futhark* runes; 'ᛞ,' *Dagaz*, the symbol for 'new enterprise,' and *Mannaz*, meaning enemy."

"Correct. I presume you also found that symbol in your House's account books as well?" the wizard questions.

"Aye. In the most recent pages going back a few years. I assume my sire was sending money to the cause."

"Likely," the Merlin replied. "But those tattoos will go a long way in helping identify the traitors."

"Excellent. Start sending security out tomorrow to round up as many of these *fealltoiri* (traitors) as you can," the Raven Queen ordered. "Use my trolls if you require additional forces," The Morrigan says as she rises from her chair and we all follow suit. "The most pressing issue at hand is to contain this damaging information that will certainly circulate in gossip around *I Idir* before it poisons the Ruling Council. 'Tis too dangerous to have an open seat in times like these." She turns and specifically addresses my husband and I. "I cannot personally save you from your deceptive sire's actions, *Mac Nuada*, lest it seem I am playing favorites in stacking the deck according to my needs. You must defend your House before the rest of the Ruling Committee. As the law is written, your father's seditious activities are cause enough to take your seat from you, as well as the assets of your House. There has been a *Nuada* on the Ruling Council since its inception eight hundred years ago. I would be very disappointed to see that cycle end, but there is little I can do to stop it. You must argue your way against it, *Deaglan* Fitzpatrick *Nuada.*

Thus, tomorrow you and your kin will return to *Dun Siorai* as its heir and build the best case you can. I will lend my Black Knight and Lord *Caoihmin* to aid you. My Knight is the foremost authority on the sacred law of *I Idir,* and my grandson has a special knack for clear thinking and clever persuasive speaking. If anyone can help you, they can."

I glance over and see the Black Knight and the Prince of *I Idir* give each other a fist bump which earns them both a scathing look from Herself. "I take my leave now. May the Universe give you fortitude to see this through. I fear our future depends on it."

TOOTHPICKS 23

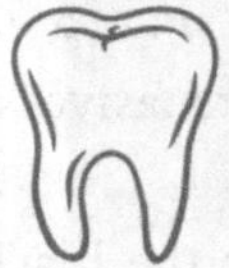

Hope Floats...

IT FEELS good to be home even if I have my fingers crossed that his particular home is only a temporary one. Being surrounded by some of my familiar treasures from Salem is a definite mood lifter. It wasn't that the suite at *Crann Bethadh* was in any way lacking. Far from it. It was lavish and comfortable, and considering that I had expected a dank and dark prison cell, the hospitality of The Morrigan, shared with my nearest and dearest, was above and beyond generous. The truth is, these rooms at *Dun Siorai* are "home" to my Tax Man, a place where he's spent a lot of time and loves more than any other place he's ever called "his" in the Mundane world. I feel his spirit in every corner; in the carefully chosen decor, the well-loved furniture, and the plethora of thriller crime novels tucked between the business tomes on the shelves of his bookcase. Our *Dun Siorai* space screams "Declan" from every nook and crevice, making it a place I can find solace.

The staff is quiet and subdued when we return, obviously aware of the rumors surrounding the status of House *Nuada* and the gravity of the situation. Many of them have spent their entire lives at *Dun Siorai,* with an abundance of them being distant relatives of both Lord and Lady *Nuada.* If Declan were to lose this ancestral home as payment for his father's crimes, a reality *I Idir* law condones, there would be a large group of folks who would suddenly find themselves homeless, a thought that surely keeps both Declan and I up at night. Not just with worry, as one might expect, but with guilt as well.

I mention feeling guilty because as much as I know that *Dun Siorai* means the world to my husband and the people living here, I'd be a cold-blooded liar if I pretended not to have considered the alternative. If the designation of Fate decides that House *Nuada* will no longer would have a seat on the Ruling Council, and if the estate is required to be sold off as restitution for its treasonous Lord's crimes, then the decision allowing us to permanently return to the Mundane world, once it is safe to do so, would become far less complicated. Thus, I'd get my true heart's wish for a "normal" life in Salem.

Granted, it sounds selfish on my part. But is it really wrong for a wife and mother to desire what she feels is best for her family? Currently, as an infant, Dylan doesn't know the difference between life in the Otherworld vs that of the Mundane. However, as he grows older, switching lifestyles will undoubtedly cause him more than a little confusion, not to mention the anxiety I assume he'll have over that ridiculous Ritual forced upon him come his fourteenth birthday, along with the expectations that will undoubtedly be put on him as my husband's heir.

In the case of *Oisin,* because he's only eight years old, he's still young enough to adapt to a new name and a new way of life among the Mundanes. My childhood was a happy, normal one, and frankly, I can't say I ever felt deprived over not exploring more of my Fae heritage. I never even paid it much mind until I met Declan and learned who he really was. Although little *Oisin* is a quick learner and seems to be catching on to my lessons, the educational opportunities that would be available to him in Salem far exceed the ones here, including that so-called "magic academy" everyone here is in such a hurry to enroll him in. Most importantly, a fresh start away from the wagging tongues and Elven prejudices of *I Idir* could mean the difference between a happy childhood and a miserable one.

Every maternal instinct pulls at me to want the best; not only for my own beloved child, but for this other one that has been gifted to my care. With all that considered, there's a part of me that secretly hopes the Ruling Council's decision will go against House *Nuada,* and because of that, I hold on to a secret heart divided. However, as Declan's *Mo Shiorghra,* his Eternal Mate, I don't have a single shred of doubt that being cut off from his Fae heritage and his ancestral home would damage the Tax Man's soul forever. I would die before willfully hurting my husband. Thus, I vow to do everything in my limited power to keep that from happening.

While we are glad our return to *Dun Siorai* is without much fanfare, the fact that we are met only by the Estate Manager wringing his hands does not bode well. He is an older man with a braided goatee who goes by the single name of Tuck, and his grave expression as we enter the heavy main door hints at the bad news to come. It appears that somewhere in the past twelve hours, the bulk of House *Nuada's* treasury has gone missing, along with a sizable portion of Lady *Nuada's* personal funds that were being held for her youngest daughter's handfasting expenses. In addition, the House's accounting book, the one going back seven centuries and which was supposed to be a key piece of evidence against Callum Fitzpatrick, is also nowhere to be found.

I'm surprised that the Tax Man takes the news as calmly as he does, and though the crystal bowls of the chandelier sway and rattle, none of them break. Instead, Declan matter-of-factly sets up a time later that afternoon to meet the Manager in the Treasury room to do a complete inventory of what's missing and what still remains. I, on the other hand, am treated to a passionate litany of every Gaelic obscenity in the privacy of my head, many of which I am sure are physically impossible.

It's easy to fall back into our old *Dun Siorai* routine, only this time it is under the distinct shadow of uncertainty. The Morrigan has called for a special gathering of the Ruling Council in four days, claiming that to wait any further is to invite chaos and mistrust to consume the natural order of the kingdom. Without knowing anything about *I Idirian* law, I have to assume this gives my *Mo Shiorghra* insufficient time to prepare any viable defense against his father's deeds, and although we all try to keep optimistic attitudes, the magnitude of that upcoming meeting weighs on all five of us in different ways.

True to her word, Her Majesty sends the Black Knight and Lord *Caoimhin* to help my husband construct the arguments he'll use when he's allowed to present his case. Much to my annoyance, I'm not invited to sit in on any of their closed-door sessions. I am told my exclusion has nothing to do with my being female or a low-born tooth fairy and everything to do with the fact that I am not a member of the Ruling Council and thus not privy to what is discussed.

I get the little bit of information I do from Declan each night over our evening meal. To allow us this precious private time, we wait until both children are settled in for the night so that we can talk freely. It's my only opportunity to speak openly about our future and what these laws all mean as the Tax Man has forbidden any mention of our troubles in the sanctuary of our bedroom and the nursery. "We need ta' have these 'safe spaces,' Rosie Love, to forget about the hounds snappin' at our heels. Otherwise, I donna' think I could get up the next mornin' and give ma' best effort knowin' you and the *bairns* are consumed with worry."

Because of that dictate, I squeeze all my queries in between bites of supper in the small dining area of our quarters. "I don't understand, Sweetie. If your *athair* is guilty of these terrible crimes, including treason, why is he still a member of the Ruling Council? Shouldn't that automatically negate his privilege of serving the people of *I Idir*?" I ask, stabbing a piece of roast chicken.

"The laws were written ta' prevent one House from gatherin' too much power by riddin' the Council of members who did no' agree with them. Removin' a House Lord from his seat on the Council is no small deed. The law states that the Lord is entitled ta' his own in-person defense. Since ma' sire is not here ta' defend himself, that ken' not be done," my husband explains.

"That just means we're stuck in a Catch-22 until he's captured and returned. And who knows when that will be. Callum Fitzpatrick is obviously quite the criminal mastermind. And if your father can't be removed from his seat on the Council, why are you in danger of losing *Dun Siorai*? It doesn't seem fair." I argue.

"That part of the law was written to appease the members who felt that the Lord in question 'owed' the Ruling Council far' the time and trouble this 'uncertainty' caused them," Lord *Mac Nuada* explains. "This clause was only added to keep a small group of naysayers willin' to accept it, knowin' that they could perhaps gain from this 'Catch-22,' as ya' call it. The loss of his land and property would surely make the Lord in question less likely to fight vera' hard ta' retain his seat on the Council if he had no property to go with it."

"That sounds like a no-win situation, Declan. Even if House *Nuada* retains its seat on the Council, you still lose everything else. What are you even hoping to gain from your defense?"

"I fight ta' keep the title ta' pass on ta' ma' son," my husband says, clenched jaw and thin-lipped. "The *Nuada* name is an ancient one. We carry the blood of Fae kings and warriors. It deserves its continued existence despite the doins' of one mentally unstable man. Plus, there is a loop-hole ta' ma' havin' ta' give up the entire estate. The Black Knight has found a clause buried in some old fine print. In lieu of dissolving *Dun Siorai*, I can ask that the property remain in ma' name with the promise that in ten years I will pay each House on the Council a generous stipend for their trust in me."

Sounded more like blackmail to me than anything else, but I keep that thought to myself. However, I do add a serious quandary to the discussion. "Uhmmm…according to Master Tuck, the House is broke, Sweetie. Your father took it all, even your mother's money. How do you expect to even run this place with no capital?"

It's the first time I see him smile all day. "Ya' forget that I handled all of ma' sire's Mundane business investments, Lass. It's what I do and what I've proven ta' be vera' good at. There are several safety deposit boxes in Boston, Washington, D.C., and New York that contain things of great value that only I have access to. Plus, Fitzpatrick Capital, ma' House's Mundane conglomerate, has investments of its own, and as its CFO, I have exclusive say over that money. Ma' father never wanted to deal with any of the Mundane tax and business law, so he never gave much interest to it, trustin' me to make the money and then hand it over to him when he decided he needed it. Aye, it's true we've taken a tremendous hit with the theft of the treasury, but we are not completely 'broke' as you suggest."

I sometimes forget that my Tax Man is…well…the Tax Man. Numbers are in his soul. "That's good to know. And you're also aware that I have some investments as well, so

I think we're good enough to withstand your *athair's* treachery no matter how this shakes out." Out of seemingly nowhere, a troubling thought comes to mind. "There's no chance that the Ruling Council will make you Lord of House *Nuada*, is there?"

My number's guy shakes his head in the negative. "There's no chance of that happening, Love. Accordin' to *Idiarian* law, the full title of 'Lord,' along with its seat on the Council, can only be passed on from father to heir upon the honorable death of the Lord. Even if ma' sire would be caught and brought to trial, 'tis more than likely with all the evidence the Throne has collected that he would be found guilty of treason and...executed. And even if he were to somehow be killed in an attempt to bring him to justice, it would also not be considered an 'honorable' death accordin' to sacred law. At this point, it is vera' unlikely that I will ever inherit his seat on the Ruling Council," he says, his voice catching with emotion, "but I would still like to retain the legacy of the title for Dylan, along with our ancestral home."

The swell of guilt grows inside of me, this overwhelming sense of relief that comes with the knowledge that my family won't somehow be pushed into a role I don't want for any of us. "I'm sorry, Declan," I expertly lie, a sure sign I've spent far too much time among the Fae. "I know you've been raised with the possibility of being House *Nuada's* Lord someday. It's crazy hard when you're forced to let go of a dream. But whether you're Lord or not, you are the center of my heart. My *Mo Shiorghra*, My Eternal Love, and the solid foundation of our family. Whatever life brings to us, we'll handle it together."

He leans over the table and kisses me. "That's all that's keepin' me together, Sweet Rosie Lass, the knowin' that ya' are walkin' this path with me and that ya' will always have ma' back. With ya' as my mate, I know I ken' handle anythin' the Universe throws ma' way."

In any other situation, these are undoubtedly the most beautiful words a woman can hear, but somehow, feeling the way I do, wracked with both guilt and fear, each one spoken stabs at my very conflicted heart

TOOTHPICKS 24

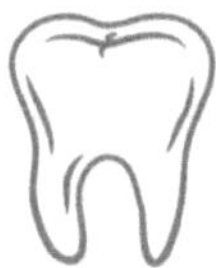

...and Reality Sinks

THE NEXT FOUR days amble on, one sliding into another. I see very little of my mate, his hours spent hidden in his study with *Crann Bethadh's* "Dream Team," all of them in pursuit of the best argument to use in front of *I Idir's* self-serving Ruling Council. I've gotten used to one or the other of the two men popping into our quarters with little to no warning, almost always still wearing the apparel of their Mundane occupations. It does give me pause to suddenly see Lord *Caoihmin,* who prefers to be called just "Kevin," standing in my foyer dressed in his pastoral black suit and Roman collar. Truthfully, though I'm not a follower of the Judeo-Christian belief system, there's something about the man's calm, peaceful demeanor that sets him apart from his magical Fae counterparts. It's more than just the clothes or the title of "Father." It's the vibe of positive energy and goodwill that simply surrounds his presence. What does cause me to shake my head is the knowledge that he is a direct descendent of The Morrigan, who, frankly, exudes none of those things.

On the morning of the anticipated Council meeting, at the request of my husband, we gather as a family in the estate's main dining room for breakfast. I'm not sure of the reasoning behind Declan's thinking. I, myself, have zero fond memories of any meals I've eaten here. Still, understanding the level of my mate's anxiety, I cheerfully comply with the odd proposal. Six- week-old Dylan has no reaction to this change of scenery except to be quite content in his father's arms. On the other hand, because this is *Oisin's* first visit to *Dun Siorai's* formal dining room, the opulent setting draws the boy's attention away from both his breakfast and the conversation around the table.

"What do ya' have planned for the day, Love?" the Tax Man asks, as if this were just any old day and not the single one that will, perhaps, direct our entire future.

"I think the best thing is for the rest of us to keep busy," I say. "If the rain holds out until later this afternoon, I thought we might pack up the carriage and go for a little picnic."

"Truly, ma' Lady? We ken' forgo our lessons far' today?" *Oisin* asks with the unabashed hope of a small child. "I would like ta' bring a *liathroid* (ball) along ta' play fetch with *Seamus*. Ma' par' boy has been cooped up far' a long time. He sorely needs a good run."

"I suppose we can bend the rules a bit about staying close to our quarters. Don't you agree, ma' Lord," I ask Declan, working to keep the conversation away from the events taking place at *Crann Bethadh*.

"I do," he says. "The poor doggo could use a day under the sun and wind. I think ya'll all could."

"Then it's settled," I add. "I'll have Cook prepare us a nice hamper to take along."

Eventually breakfast ends and the Tax Man goes off to change into appropriate Court attire while *Birgit* and I finish up our tea and a discussion about changing Dylan's feeding schedule. As we linger in the dining room, I see Declan's mother step into the doorway. "Good Morn, Lady *Mathair*. Would you care to join us for a cup of tea?"

She gives me a disgruntled look. "Not in the least. I am looking for my son, but it appears I have missed him."

"Yes. He's gone back to our quarters to change for his meeting. I'm sure you can catch him there."

She makes a sour face and stomps off without a polite farewell. *Birgit* shakes her head at the woman's abruptly rude departure. "I know," I concede. "Under normal circumstances she can be very...difficult. With everything that's underway, I'm sure she's a force to be reckoned with."

"I am aware it's no ma' place ta' comment, Lady Rosie," the *scathach* says, "but I thought she was just beginnin' ta' warm up a bit over her delight in wee Dylan. Yet, she hasn't been in ta' see him since ya' both went to *Asgard* and she checked in on us at *Crann Bethadh*. I thought far' sure once we returned to *Dun Siorai* she'd come to yar' quarters ta' see the *bairn*. Or at the vera' least, request that I bring him far' a visit."

"I believe she's just having trouble dealing with... things," I say, not wanting to mention *Oisin* by name. "Plus, Lord *Nuada's* disappearance does put her in an unusual spot. As long as he's still alive, he remains her *Mo Shiorghra*."

"In this particular case, I am sure The Crown would consent to some type of dissolution of their bond. Her Majesty is known to be sympathetic to the female plight," *Birgit* replies.

"Lady *Nuada* would never ask for it. If their bond was dissolved, all rights and privileges to the *Nuada* name would also be forfeited. She would never do that, mostly in deference to her children. Even in the midst of all this trouble with Callum Fitzpatrick, the *Nuada* bloodline traces back to key ancestors of the *Tuatha De Danann*, the original "Shining Ones. Lady *Siobhan* would never give up that part of her children's lineage."

"I suppose I can understand that," the nanny says. "Mothers go to great lengths for their children."

"Aye. That they do," I agree, my thoughts set on a life in Salem where I truly believe my family group will be the happiest.

* * *

The picnic plan is a smart one. The Universe grants us a glorious day with the bluest of skies and only the slightest of breezes to remind us that the warmer months are not far off. By the time we return to our rooms, both children are sated with fresh air and showing signs of an early bedtime. Even the dog yawns, exhausted after several hours of exuberant ball chasing.

I would have expected to find Declan returned from

his Council meeting, but discover our quarters empty. The rest of us enjoy Afternoon Tea, and begin the evening ritual of bath time and stories with a night time nursing for Dylan. *Brigit* and I settle both of the boys down in their beds, and when my Tax Man still hadn't returned, I begin to fret.

The Ruling Council meeting was set to begin at 1:00 PM. The clock on our mantle now chimes eight times. Seven hours have passed. Can the discussion still be going on this long? I mentally reach out to try to send a message but am stopped by a very solid wall of Declan's shielding. This doesn't surprise me. My *Mo Shiorghra* warned me that he needed no distractions on this of all days, and that I wasn't to try maneuvering around his shield unless I was faced with a life-or-death situation. I suppose my high level of impatient anxiety doesn't count as such.

Birgit offers her companionship, but I really don't feel like chatting, so she politely retires to the nursery and I curl up on the sofa with one of my husband's detective novels. The abundance of fresh air and the small print eventually does me in and I apparently doze off there on the sofa until I feel someone shaking my shoulder and speaking softly, "Rosie, Love. I'm home. 'Tis finally over."

I jump awake to find the Tax Man sitting next to me on the sofa. He seems tired to the point of exhaustion and his expression gives nothing away, but the energy rolling off of him is not necessarily negative. In fact, there's a genuine feeling of accomplishment. I hug him first, then ask, "So…how did it go? Did the Ruling Council come to a decision?" He starts to open his mouth, but I stop him and jump in. "Wait. Before you tell me, I want you to know that wherever it was that was decided today, I'm one hundred percent behind you. We'll face it together." Years later, I would laugh and wonder if I had any kind of inkling of what he was going to tell me, would I have been so naively agreeable. The answer is probably not, so I suppose it's best I didn't have a clue.

Declan shyly kisses my cheek. "I thank you for that, *mo ghra amhain* (my only love). I could have not borne the weight of this day without ya' in ma' heart."

"So...tell me! I can handle it."

"This is an outcome I could have never foreseen," he says, taking my hands in his.

"Stop teasing and tell me."

The Tax Man sighs, then says, "Blessed be, ma' love. I am ta' be Lord of House *Nuada*, Rosie. You are ta' be its Lady."

I hear the words but they don't register in my brain. "Wait. What?"

"The Ruling Council has declared that I am ta' replace ma' sire as Lord of my House," he repeats a second time slower, so I can fully take in the words.

"How...how is that possible?" I stammer. "You said yourself the law forbids it. That the Lord of a House had to die an 'honorable' death for you to inherit the title. You told me that very thing in those exact words just a few days ago," I say, as Salem and a life there begins to slip through my mental fingers.

"They changed the law, Love. For me. Right then and there. Key figures in the Council said 'twas better ta' fill the empty seat with a rightful heir than far' the position ta' remain empty and somehow fall inta' the wrong hands. The more they search, the more the Crown is finding traitors wearing the rebel ink. The treachery runs much deeper than first imagined. I am to be sworn in on Beltane. In front of the whole kingdom before the formal celebrations begin."

I sit stunned, not having the remotest idea of what I should say and worried the honest truth will fall unhindered from my lips. "Say something, Lass. I know this was not what we expected, but 'tis a miracle in ma' eyes. I have been generously gifted yet another boon from the Universe. First ya' appear as ma' wonderful, beautiful, loving mate, then I am given the gift of a son, an heir, and now, out of the blue, I am granted the monumental opportunity to lead ma' people. It is surely too much treasure far' one man."

Raining on other people's parade is not my usual vibe. I'm more of a "rah rah," kinda' girl. Still, the words leave my mouth of their own accord. "That's awesome they have such deep faith in your ability, Declan. It truly is, and my heart is so happy for you." I stop and take a breath. "But what about our life in Salem? My father and my sister? My dental practice and your accounting firm?" The last words leave my lips as a strangled sob. "Our little house?"

My *Mo Shiorghra* gathers me in his arms and squeezes tight. "I swear to ya', Rosie Fitzpatrick, on everything I hold dear, that we will make this work. We'll find a path that is good far' us both, here in *I Idir* and in the Mundane world. Ya' said so yourself...together there's nothing the two of us can't do."

And as much as I love this man, and as much as I want to desperately believe the words he's speaking, the last hope I'd hung on to of having a "normal" Mundane life, free of Fae treachery and intrigue, floats away and sinks like a paper boat on the "Weak Waters."

TOOTHPICKS 25

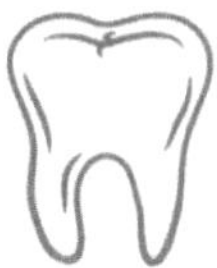

When You Assume the Wrong Doom

WHEN ONE IS DROWNING in a sea of self-pity, nothing pulls you out of it faster than good ole' fashioned indignation over someone else's injustice, especially if that someone just happens to be your very best friend.

I'll be the first to admit that I was doing a bang-up job of hosting a private pity party over the recent turn of events. In hindsight, I should have been better prepared for the realization that, at some point in our lives together, my Eternal Mate might be required to take on the mantle of House *Nuada's* Lord. It was no secret that this was the reality he was born into. Yet, from the beginning of our relationship, I had naively assumed the two of us would have plenty of time to grow as a couple and a family before we were thrust into those undesired Otherworld roles.

That was the whole trouble with "assumptions." They

are almost always based on the facts you have on hand and never include the sneaky ways the Universe has of turning everything you thought you knew on its head. As a teenager, I had "assumed" my mother would live a very long and healthy life, thus saving me from having to take on her role as a member of the Tooth Fairy Corps until I was old and gray. I had also assumed that my dad would always be around to help me through the ups and downs of adulthood. I never figured that an unexpected stroke and subsequent dementia would change that future. So, I suppose it's no surprise that I was just as wrong over the supposition that Declan's bloodline responsibilities wouldn't show up on our doorstep much sooner in our lives than we'd ever anticipated. As these things go, before I could even finish wrapping my head around my own ill-fated misconceptions, a newer, unproven postulation, one that had the possibility of wrecking additional innocent lives, was shockingly dumped on our doorstep.

It was a few weeks after the Ruling Council's decision to make Declan Lord of House *Nuada,* but before his official installation during the Beltane festival, that Mel and Duncan appeared, unannounced, at *Dun Siorai,* late in the evening. I could immediately tell by Duncan's grim expression and my BFF's red eyes and runny nose that whatever was the cause of their night time visit, it wasn't good.

"Heartfelt apologies, ma' Lord and Lady, far' intrudin' on yar' peace so deep inta' the eventide, but we have news that we ken' no longer bear on our own. Nor do we have anywhere else ta' turn," Duncan said.

I look at Mel and she falls into my arms sobbing. "Oh Rosie...it's all a mess!"

I let her cry it out a bit while the two men watch in uncomfortable silence. When her sobs finally subside into whimpers and hiccups I ask, "What's 'all a mess,' Melly? Tell us what's wrong so Declan and I can help you."

My BFF pulls away from my embrace and blows her nose in the burp cloth still on my shoulder from Dylan's feeding. She shakes her head in disgust. "I can't say the words out loud, Rosie. It's just so...awful and mean-spirited. Let Duncan tell you," Mel says among her sniffles.

We all turn toward Duncan who looks down-right miserable himself. He reaches out and takes Mel's hand before explaining. "As ya' are both aware, ma' Lady and I have pledged ta' handfast. In keepin' with tradition, we went ta' ar' parents to receive thar' blessings on ar' union. The meetin' did no go...favorable," the *gancanagh* adds, unable to look any of us in the eye.

And because Rosie Parker Fitzpatrick never seems to learn her lesson regarding making random assumptions, I blurt out, "Oh Mel, I'm so sorry. Truth is, I was a bit concerned that despite your parent's modern-day thinking, they might hold some prejudice against Duncan's... *gancanagh* heritage. Old beliefs die hard. Maybe if I were to sit down and just ...."

Mel puts a hand on my arm, "Stop Rose...it wasn't my parents who objected. It was Duncan's."

Everyone goes instantly silent and I can feel my face getting warm. It is the Tax Man who breaks the embarrassing hold my dumb-ass, *faux pas* has on the room. His

Lordship invites the group to his study, and closes the door before warding it against outside prying ears and eyes. Once everyone is seated, Declan pours each of us a few fingers of the whiskey-like libation, "*Uisce Beatha* (Water of Life), that the Fae can't seem to live without. I can't ignore that Duncan seems to be avoiding looking at me, and I sure as hell don't need high-level *Sidhe* aura magic to understand that I've gone and deeply wounded my BFF's Intended.

A toast is raised to the Throne of *I Idir* and everyone tosses down their whiskey in anticipation, I suppose, of the uncomfortable discussion I've gone ahead and made ten times worse. Before I can choke out a lame apology, the Tax Man takes over. "It might be beneficial, Cousin, if ya' bring us up ta' speed on what has transpired."

Duncan pauses, then reaches over to take Mel's hand in his own. "As my Lady has already stated, ma' Lord, both of ma' parents have refused their blessings to this match. It is the first time I have ever seen them so strongly united over a cause. 'Tis no secret that as ma' parents have added years to their life, they rarely agree on anythin', but they are both beyond adamant that a handfast between my Lady Love and I is…'unacceptable.' Their exact words, ma Lord."

"I understand that the blessin' of one's parents is greatly desired when joinin' two families, Cousin, but 'tis only a polite tradition, albeit a long held one. In truth, the approval of yar' *athair* and *mathair* is a heartfelt boon, but not required by sacred law if both intended parties have reached the age of adulthood. In the case of my Lady and I, ma' own *mathair* was dead set against the union, but she has eventually come to accept it. 'Tis usually the word of our House Mages that holds the most weight. Have ya' spoken to them yet?"

At this question, Mel begins to cry, silent tears running down her cheeks. I move to attempt to try to console her, but stop at the Tax Man's words in my head. *I would hold off from yar' offer of sympathy, Love. I dunna' think it would be much appreciated in this moment.*

My husband's words cut like a knife, mainly because I know he's right. I already have "shown my cards," so to speak, regarding my true feelings about Duncan and Mel's plans to handfast. I feel an ache in my own throat while wishing I could turn back the hands of time and think before opening my damn big mouth

Duncan's handsome face is grim and pale, and I can tell he's squeezing Mel's hand tight by the bloodless color of her skin. "We have done just that, ma' Lord. After ma' parent's negative reaction, we sought a readin' by House *Nuada's* Mages." He stops, as if the words are caught in his throat, and I get a very bad feeling about what he's about to say. "The Mages have concluded that though a union between the Lady Sparks and I would give us personal happiness, they could no guarantee the match would be... fruitful. As I am my sire's only son, and the future of furtherin' our family bloodline rests in me, ma' *tuismitheoiri* (parents) have found the Mages' pronouncements to be a reason enough ta' withhold their blessins'. There be no changin' their minds. We have tried ta' no avail."

It takes me a second or two to comprehend what's being said, and outrage fills every part of me. Before I can express my thoughts with an especially graphic string of obscenities, I once again hear Declan in my head. *"Please, Rosie Lass...befar' ya' make things worse with yar rage-induced words, I beg ya' ta' let me handle this. Your righteous indignation and sympathy will not make our dear friends and family feel any better. They did not come here far' pity, but far' a solution."*

I open my mouth and then close it. *"Solution? You heard Duncan! They've got their mind made up and you of all people understand how friggin' stubborn and pig-headed the high-born Sidhe can be when they think they're right."* I don't mention that in certain situations, my own beloved *Mo Shiorghra* can be one of these obstinate Fae types.

The Tax Man ignores me and leans forward in his chair, addressing both Mel and Duncan "I assume, Cousin, that despite the predictions of our House Mages, ya' both wish ta' go forward with yar' plans ta' handfast?"

Mel vigorously nods her head in the affirmative, too emotional to speak. Duncan's voice sounds high and strained to my ears. "Aye, ma Lord. That is why ma' Lady and I have intruded on yar peace this evening. 'Tis our hope that ya'd be willin' to stand for us and declare *Riail an Tiarna* (The Lord's Rule) and bless our union over the refusal of ma' parents. We understand that the timin' is far from perfect, as yar' confirmation as House *Nuada's* Lord is only a few weeks away. Ma' lady and I are vera' much aware that the support of our family elders is key ta' a smooth transition into yar' new role within the Rulin' Council and I have no doubt that ma' sire will be mar' than a little disgruntled over yar' interference in family business. The Lady Sparks and I will completely understand and hold no ill will if ya' decide ya' ken no take this risk ta' support our determination ta' tie our lives together. She and I will be satisfied with a civil ceremony in the Mundane world if we are forced ta' do so. But as believers in the Old Way, we greatly desire ta' profess our vows in the sanctity of the *Nuada* Sacred Grove."

I am well aware of the ancient tradition of *Riail an Tiarna*. My father-in-law, Callum Fitzpatrick, tried to invoke the very same thing regarding his treacherous plan to whisk my pregnant self off to *Dun Siorai* against my will while Declan was missing in North Korea. And the old goat might have gotten away with it if The Morrigan hadn't interceded on my behalf. According to the sacred laws of *I Idir*, a Lord of a Ruling Council House has the power to override personal and family decisions at will. Only the Queen of *I Idir*, The Morrigan, Herself, has the power to rule against any decisions made by a Lord with Ruling Class standing, as she had done in my case.

One didn't have to be a political genius to understand that, as a Lord, having this power was a mixed bag of opportunities. On one hand, the ability to rend personal favors for influential cronies was an asset, and a good way to curry favor with the House's movers and shakers; on the other, there was also the possibility of making long-term enemies who often let their need for retribution burn slowly over a number of years, waiting in secret anticipation for proper payback. Worse yet, there was always the chance that the Lord might have his ruling turned over by his Queen, a complete embarrassment to the House's leadership. If they had even half a brain in their heads, seasoned Ruling Class Lords, even those with years of political confidence and clout, refused petitions for *Riail an Tiarna*. This was, however, Duncan doing the asking. A man my *Mo Shiorghra* loved like a brother. I had little doubt what Declan's answer would be, consequences be damned.

TOOTHPICKS 26

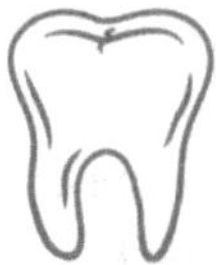

The Weight of Loyalty

WHEN IT COMES to matters of personal loyalty, my Tax Man is stalwartly predictable. As I had forecasted, the newly appointed Lord of House *Nuada* solemnly promises the use of the ancient law of *Riail an Tiarna* in regards to the "blessing" of Duncan and Mel's handfasting. My husband's guarantee that the supposedly "doomed" couple would, without a doubt, exchange vows in *Dun Siorai's* Sacred Grove is met with heartfelt gratitude but little celebration. Our somber friends leave our home shortly after Declan's pledge to help them, and it was obvious by their stiff body language and staid expressions that I was still *personae non gratae*.

As the hour is late, we check in on the children before the Tax Man and I retired to our own bedroom for the night, the events of the evening still weighing heavy on our minds. "I feel awful that I hurt Duncan's feelings," I sheepishly admit.

The response to that statement is met with what I call "the husband sigh." You know the one I mean; that breathy noise meant to represent long-suffering patience, but is really a cover up to hide plain, old annoyance. "I hate when you do that," I comment.

"Do what?" he asks as he obsessively folds clothes that I know he's just leaving for the staff to launder.

"When you don't reply to my comment, but instead make that 'Rosie is driving me crazy' noise."

He starts to sigh again, but then catches himself and grunts instead, which to my mind, is just as maddening. "'Tis late, Love, and I am vera' tired. I have an early mornin' meetin' with some candidates applyin' ta' take over Rory Dell's position that I am no lookin' forward to. The last thing I want is ta' argue with ma' One and Only in the wee hours of the night over what sounds may have escaped ma' par', unfortunate mouth," the Tax Man replies, not bothering to hide his exasperation.

"Whatever," I toss back as I head to the bathroom to take care of my nightly routine. When I return, Declan is in bed, eyes closed but not sleeping. It's an easy tell because he's not snoring like a wood chipper. I slide in on my side and pull the covers to my chin determined not to say a single word. That conviction lasts all of two minutes. "I truly am sorry, you know. Mel and Duncan are like family to me. I didn't mean to hurt his feelings."

My *Mo Shiorghra* reaches across the bed and takes my hand in his. I feel that crazy tingle of lustful energy, but fight off the urge to roll over and give in to it. My mate does the same, determined not to let the magic of the Bond rule our life. "I understand ya' didna' intend to share yar' private feelins' about ma' cousin's heritage, Lass. Ya' have the gentlest of hearts, but sometimes yar' beautiful mouth has a mind of its own."

I want to be insulted by that comment, but my husband's not wrong. I'm not sure if it's a result of my Mundane upbringing, or I just have some neurodivergent issues with boundaries when it comes to expressing my opinion. There's been far too many times in my life that I've blurted out things I later wished I'd kept to myself. "I was just so…shocked! I never imagined that it would be Duncan's parents who would put the kibosh on the two of them handfasting."

"Because he is *gancanagh*?" My husband asks. I hear the edge of sarcasm in his voice. It's no secret that he finds my lingering Fae prejudices frustrating.

"Don't say it like that, Declan. It's common knowledge that *gancanach* men do not make the best long-term, faithful mates. Duncan's *athair* is a perfect example. You yourself told me that the man has made a life-long game of seducing women, even cheating on Duncan's *mathair* the entire time she was pregnant with him. Then, when Duncan was born, his father just…well…moved on to do his own thing. No permanent commitment to either the mother or the child. Do you think that's what I want for Mel? The best friend I ever had?"

"So, you reason that because my cousin's sire was a *Sidhe gancanagh* male with no honor, Duncan will be the same? I hope that is not the weight of yar' argument, Lass, as that thinking ken' be applied to me and ma' own sire's murderous leanings?"

"Hells Bells, Declan! Don't make this about you!" I

definitely didn't like the way this discussion was going. "What's going on with your *athair* is an entirely different kettle of fish. Callum Fitzpatrick's bad decisions are products of his own compromised moral and ethical compass. A *gancanagh's* psyche is written in his DNA, just like your wowza *Tuatha de Danann* magical abilities are written in yours. For Pete's sake…I'm a tooth fairy only because my mother was one. It sure as hell wasn't a choice I made on my own. And as much as Duncan loves Mel, and wants to be a good and faithful mate, his heritage won't, in the end, allow for it. The pull of his bloodline is too strong."

The Love of My Life grunts again in response. It's in no way a sound that implies support of my reasoning. "You disagree?" I ask.

"I do not find yar' logic wrong, Rosie Lass, though I find it a mite ironic coming from someone who fought against her own bloodline for nearly her entire life."

That one hurt. I pull my hand out of his, not because it's a false statement but because my husband's is bluntly spot-on, regardless of my feelings. "Ouch, Tax Man. You go right for the jugular, don't you. You're gonna' fit right in that jungle pit of the Ruling Council."

The Lord of House *Nuada* rolls from his back to his side to face me. "I love ya' enough, *Stor Mo Chroi* (Treasure of my Heart), to speak only the truth. 'Tis yar' love far' me, and mine far' you, that allowed our hearts to accept who we both truly were, takin' the good along with the bad. Do ya' not think our dearest friends are capable of the same level of bondin'? I, ma' self, would like ta' give them the benefit of the doubt. They are entitled to the full 366 days to put their love ta' the test. I do not feel that decision should rest with anyone but the two of them." He smiles at me and, even in the dark, I can see the intensity of his emotions in his aura. "Not every couple is so blessed in the complete knowledge of their everlastin' love that they are willin' ta' take the Eternal Bond before their original handfast is up, *A Stor* (Darling). Can we not share a little of our belief in the power of such grand devotion with our dearest friends?"

Okay. Even though my ego sometimes hates it when the Tax Man is right, I'm the kind of girl who calls it like she sees it. I stick out my hand and once again grab his across the expanse of the mattress, letting the familiar live-wire feeling run through me. "You're right, Declan. Mel and Duncan deserve the opportunity to find their own 'Happily Ever After,' no matter how that might end up looking." I pause, contemplating my next words. "Do you think the House Mages are right? You know…about their union not being…fruitful."

Declan is silent, weighing my question with what I assume is his life-long Otherworldly spirituality. When he answers his tone is wrapped in sad resolve. "They are usually not wrong, ma' Love. A House's Mages are chosen for their ability to read the future as it pertains to the fullness of time and the effects it will have on the House they serve. In addition, 'tis no secret that each *Sidhe* generation produces less and less offspring. Many Otherworldly couples face a life with no children. My sisters are prime examples; as of yet none of their unions have produced a child. We are beyond blessed with our Dylan. I almost fear speakin' this out loud, less the Universe hear ma' words and change its bounty."

I shiver at my mate's words: One can't live daily in the Otherworld and not pick up some of their superstitious nature. "That makes me sad for Mel and Duncan, Tax Man," I find myself subconsciously whispering, lest the Powers That Be hear me.

"Aye," he replies. "It is not the future I would have desired for them. Still, it is their decision ta' make, and I will support them as they ask."

"I'm going to take a wild guess that Duncan's parents aren't going to be happy with you for going against their wishes. Will this make your installation as Lord of House *Nuada* at the Beltane celebration more difficult?"

"I have already been unanimously and officially voted in by the members themselves, so barring any acts of outright treason or the breaking of sacred law, the installation at Beltane is simply a ceremonial public display. I am, for all intents and purposes, already the named Lord of House *Nuada*. Still, push-back from members of my own House and them holdin' mean-spirited grudges will certainly make life mar' difficult. It is, however, part and parcel of what it means to be Lord of any great House. 'Tis ma' path and walk it I must."

House *Nuada's* newest Lord yawns loudly and returns to a position on his back. "Perhaps we ken' continue this discussion over breakfast, Love. *Ta cos amhain i mo bhrion-gloidi agam* (I have one foot in my dreams)."

My own mind is now wide awake and I know sleep won't come easily to me. I let the magic attached to our bond trickle downwards and consider moving closer to the Tax Man for some artful seduction of my own. However, the equally-spaced whistling and gurgling broadcasting from across the bed suggests that My Beloved has already gone from drowsy dozing to full-on sleep mode. Although the Tax Man is always game for me taking the lead in our amorous adventures, he's far less enthusiastic about being woken up so soon after falling asleep, especially if he's relaxed and in his own bed. I decide not to risk cranky Declan. Instead, I lay staring up at the ceiling, running through the events of the last hour and fretting about it all until sleep finally overtakes me... just in time for Dylan's 3:00 A.M. feeding.

TOOTHPICKS 27

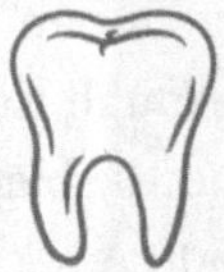

When You Mean Well

DESPITE MY HURTFUL VERBAL BLUNDER, Mel still asks me to stand as witness to her and Duncan's handfast. I am so relieved over her forgiveness and understanding that I want nothing more than to go overboard in my new role as "Matron of Honor" by hosting loads of joyous pre-handfasting parties, helping her select her gown, and sharing the anticipation of her special day with laughs and female teasing. Sadly, the truth of the situation doesn't allow for most of that. My BFF and her Intended are adamant that they desire to handfast as soon as possible, in advance of Declan's installation as Lord of House *Nuada* during the Beltane celebration. This decision leaves very little time to plan detailed festivities, plus the general mood of the couple's situation puts a damper on the usual exuberance associated with a handfasting.

Neither set of parents is happy with Declan's "interference" in "personal, family business." Their vitriol centers on completely opposing arguments: Mel's parents, highly educated, successful people living mostly in the Mundane world, find the outdated prejudices of Duncan's entirely Fae parents ridiculous and insulting. Despite their own efforts over the years at keeping their Otherworldly heritage alive for their only daughter, Rhianna and Michael Sparks apparently draw the line at anyone insinuating their precious only child is anything less than a "perfect treasure." To their mind, Mel's decision to proceed with the traditional Otherworldly ceremony while knowing her future in-laws have determined her worth solely on her ability to produce children, "reeks of dominating patriarchal prejudice against the Universe-given rights of females." Their exact words. Both of them want Mel and Duncan to return home to Salem to marry in a generic, Mundane civil ceremony, making a political statement by thumbing their noses at the Fae archaic notions regarding "bloodlines and male dominated ceremonies."

Duncan's folks, on the other hand, are mostly in an uproar over House *Nuada's* newest Lord's "blatant disregard for the future of their familial bloodline," and Declan's "obvious mocking of the sacred predictions of the House Mages." Rumor has it they'd even petitioned Her Majesty to intercede and were bluntly told by Herself to "handle their own family drama," as "she had enough to worry about with traitors seeking to undermine her Kingdom to get involved in a silly parental temper tantrum." Duncan's *athair* and *mathair*, as well as several of his older second cousins, have publicly stated that they would not attend any handfasting ceremony that "went against sacred, ancient traditions and the dire warnings of the mages."

All this puts a damper on what should be the happiest of days for our two dearest friends. I'm personally more angry than sad. Why any parent would wish such unhappiness on a child they claim to love is beyond me. I will admit that I still have misgivings on whether this joining won't cause the parties involved some future trauma, but I've come to realize that the Tax Man is right; Mel and Duncan's path is not mine to walk.

Despite all these negative vibes surrounding the handfast commitment, Declan and I still try to make our dear friends feel special. His Lordship hosts an extravagant House stag hunt in Duncan's honor, complete with a very large, solid gold, loving cup as first prize. Because of the in-bred competitive nature of *Sidhe* males, and the Fae cultural predilection for chasing wild things down with a bow and arrow, the response to his invitation is robust. Even those who secretly believe that my Tax Man has crossed the boundaries of House leadership by using *Riail an Tiarna* in this particular instance, don't pass on a day of male bonding excitement and the chance to corral a valuable prize.

On my end, I play hostess to a lady's spa day for Mel and some of her closest Fae friends. The afternoon includes opportunities for feminine pampering complete with facials, manicures, pedicures, massages, and even waxing, which of course, I take a hard pass on. Mimosas flow like water using Mundane French champagne brought through the Veil at great expense, and Cook provides an ever changing array of delicious finger foods. It's a lovely, cozy "girls only affair" made into a "social coup" when the *Banphrionsa* of *I Idir*, the down-to-earth, fun-loving Maureen Beckett, who also happens to be the Queen's own great granddaughter and Lady to the Black Knight, attends my little soiree. As a member of the royal family, the princess's presence here at *Dun Siorai* for a celebration in honor of Mel's handfasting is a subtle way of expressing her support for my BFF's choice and my husband's decision even if The Throne won't officially comment on the controversy surrounding it.

The late April day of Mel and Duncan's handfast dawns cloudy and cool, and by lunchtime the sky opens up as the Universe sends a spring storm of monumental fury. The wind is strong enough to rattle the windows of the estate and it's so dark outside that lights are required in the middle of the afternoon. All of this makes my best friend, a thoroughly modern Mundane but with Fae blood still running in her veins, take to her bed in a torrent of tears, superstitiously convinced that her hand-fasting is, without a doubt, doomed.

It takes every bit of my persistent coaxing to convince her to allow the staff to dress her hair and attend to her makeup even while I keep to myself the news that there's a whole discussion going on about whether to go ahead and move the ceremony indoors because of the foul weather. It has been Duncan's only wish that he and Mel should take their vows within the space of House *Nuada's* Sacred Grove, out in the open under a canopy of oak boughs, with the stars glittering above their head, and I spend most of the day mouthing invocations to most of the Fae's ancient pantheon of gods and goddesses to allow them this tiny slice of happiness.

Mel has chosen to wear her mother's handfast gown as her own, and because they are similar in build, the dress needs little alteration. Her mom is a beautiful woman and I have no doubt that the gown looked stunning on her, but Mel...well...she looks simply ethereal, which is saying a lot since we're here in the Otherworld surrounded by a population of magical entities. The fabric is a silk chiffon that seems to come alive on my best friend's perfectly toned body, and the soft teal color brings out the blue-green of her cat-like eyes. The fabric is scattered with tiny silver flecks that catch the light when she moves, while teal-colored gemstones are woven within the strands of her complicated braids. She looks so "unearthly" she takes my breath away and I can only imagine Duncan's face when he sees her for the first time.

"Oh, Mellie..." It's all the syllables I can push out.

"Do you think I look okay, Rosie? You don't think the style is too outdated or anything, do you?"

That's my Mel. Always worried about being trendy. "Absolutely not, Girlfriend! Buttons to banjos," I add, using one of my bestie's favorite phrases, "I'm seriously starting to worry that one of the goddesses is going to take issue with you outshining them in that dress! Girl, you look more at home in *Bru na Boinne* than *Dun Siorai*. That gown moves on you like the sacred river itself."

This makes my BFF laugh, which in turn makes my heart swell. She deserves so much more happiness than this day is bringing to her. I am glad her parents have swallowed their righteous indignation over the Fitzpatrick's prejudices and are planning to attend the ceremony despite their personal feelings. I wish I could say the same thing about Duncan's folks. Nothing Declan says to them makes any difference and they promise my husband, with shaking fists and colorful curses, that they will never forgive his "black-hearted display of disloyalty to his flesh and blood kin." When it comes to threats like that, I guess Duncan's parents will just have to stand in line behind my Tax Man's own father, who has basically said the very same thing to him.

Miraculously, sometime after sundown, the rain lets up, the sky clears a bit, and we all breathe a sigh of relief. From the windows in our parlor, I watch the staff head out to the grove to set up for the ceremony. Mel is spending some private time with her mother in our suite's guest room, and I find myself antsy over what might happen if Duncan's parents show up to cause a fuss. His Lordship thinks the scenario unlikely; no matter how disgruntled his extended family might be over his decision in their son's favor, the Fitzpatricks are thoroughly Otherworldly, schooled in the ways of Court politics, and not stupid enough to go against a House Lord of the Ruling Council. To so boldly ignore traditional protocol would cast them in a bad light, both socially and politically, and even though The Morrigan works hard not to show favoritism, it's no secret around *I Idir* that the Raven Queen looks fondly on my mate.

My fingers are crossed that Declan is right in his reasoning, but before I can contemplate the "what-ifs," Declan's valet comes to announce that Master Duncan is at the door and wishes admittance. "Duncan?" I question.

"He shouldn't be here. Not when his Lady is in residence and already dressed for the ceremony. If he's looking for his Lordship, tell Master Duncan that he's dressed and gone to the Grove."

"He wishes ta' speak with you, ma' Lady. He says it is quite important that he meets with ya befar' the ceremony," the valet explains.

I try not to let my angst show. The first thing that pops into my head is that Duncan is here to tell me he's got cold feet and doesn't want to go through with the handfast. As I have mentioned before, Rosie Parker Fitzpatrick is always on board for wrong assumptions. There's no way of avoiding my husband's cousin so I dismiss the valet and go to greet Duncan myself, anxious to lead him away from anywhere within Mel's sight or hearing.

When I see Mel's Intended in the suite's entrance foyer, I stop dead in my tracks. Not for the first time do I think that he's one of the prettiest men I've ever met. In truth, most high-born *Sidhe* males are physically attractive. It comes as part of the whole Otherworldly, ancient bloodline package. My own husband is no slouch in the "wowza handsome category," and the Black Knight should have his very own "dangerously hot, bad-boy" bracket. But Declan's cousin is outrightly beautiful, with his perfectly symmetrical, chiseled features, his midnight-colored locks, and deep blue eyes framed by the lushest, black lashes, a picture that any sane person could lose their soul over. Dressed in House *Nuada's* maroon and gold, he looks every bit the fairytale prince to Mel's princess. Still, he shouldn't be here in our family quarters when he knows Mel is here as well. "Jumping Jelly Beans,

Duncan!" I scold. "You know you're not supposed to see your Intended before you meet in the Sacred Grove. What in *Dubnos* are you doing here? Shouldn't you be with Declan?"

His pensive expression does little to lessen my anxiety and I try not to jump the gun and think the worst. "I am aware that I break all rules of tradition, dear Lady, showin' up here so close ta' the time of the ceremony. But I ken' no go ahead and make ma' vows ta' ma' Beloved without sayin' the words of my heart ta' ya' and ya' alone."

TOOTHPICKS 28

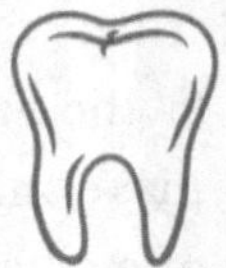

Called to Task

THERE ARE FAR TOO many staff members milling around our quarters to have a private conversation standing here in the foyer. I consider meeting with Duncan in Declan's study, but decide against being anywhere in the suite where Mel could come upon us. I take the bridegroom's arm and lead him into the hallway. "Let's talk in the library. I would expect it to be empty today," I counsel.

Even if I had enough magical skill to read Duncan's thoughts or aura, my husband's cousin is shielding so tight it's as if he's had an iron gate installed in his head. I try not to let my imagination run away with me. If the worst happens, I can't imagine how I will tell my best friend since childhood that her Beloved is leaving her at the altar. And, as I have been so many times before, my half-assed assumptions bowl me over like a runaway train.

The two of us enter the empty library, and I shut the

door behind me. With a higher than normally pitched voice, I ask, "What's so important that you needed to speak to me now, Duncan? The ceremony is set to start in an hour."

Although his thoughts are locked up, his body language registers every bit of his apprehension in the way his eyes dart to the floor and back up again, and the way he sets his shoulders, as if he is physically preparing himself for whatever terrible words I might throw at him. If only I had prepared myself in the same way.

"Lady Cousin, what I have to say ta' ya' is harder than ya' ken ever imagine. But say it I must. I know ma' Beloved Lady holds ya' in the highest regard. You are like a sister of the heart ta' her, and there is no one she wants more at her side when she commits to me than you. Therefore, what I ask of you is surely…difficult."

"I feel the same way about Mel, Duncan. She is my dearest friend in the whole world. Both of them. You can ask me to do anything for her," I say, not truly understanding where this is all going.

"That is good ta' know, dear Cousin. I owe ya' my life and the last thing I would ever want to do is cause ya' pain, but the needs of My Intended mate must come first," Duncan says, adding fuel to my growing anxiety. "I know that the Lady Sparks has asked ya' to stand witness for her. I am asking that if you have any doubts at all about the commitment the two of us are about ta' make, that ya' step down from this role. The last thing we need is for the Universe to hear yar' doubts and work to see them through."

I am one hundred percent stunned. This particular

request was totally off my radar. I open my mouth to argue against it when Duncan cuts me off. "Please, sweet Lady. Let me finish. 'Tis no secret that ya' find ma' heritage…questionable. Ya' are not wrong in thinkin' such thoughts. The *gancanagh* have a sordid history, and ma' own sire is no role model when it comes ta' the sanctity of vows and faithfulness. I will no lie ta' ya'. Going against my Universe given urges has been mar' than a mite difficult. But I swear ta' ya', there's been no one in ma' life since the two of us became a couple. And if the Universe does no see fit ta' gift us with children, then my Love and I will work through that life together. 'Tis no one's business but ar' own. I love that woman with the heat of a thousand burnin' suns, and if ya' can't see that in me, then I respectfully ask that ya' do not stand as if ya' do."

Nothing the man says is wrong. I've never been all that supportive of a serious relationship between the two of them. Not from the very beginning, with Duncan's *gancanagh* heritage as the reasoning behind my prejudicial attitude. Shame and embarrassment crawl all over me in the knowledge that I am as closed minded and judgemental as the people I claim to abhor. It's a very humbling moment. Suddenly, the bridegroom lowers his mental shield and I see and feel all of his emotions roll over me like a head-on-collision. His reactions are brutally honest and the absolute truth. He loves Mel above everything else, even to the point of risking my displeasure, and subsequently, that of his Liege Lord, by stating the truth and asking me to step down as his Intended' witness. Duncan has always been a sincere believer in the Old Ways, and he just isn't willing to take a chance that my heart isn't in the right place to be Mel's Matron, lest somehow I call down the bad luck of the Universe down upon their commitment. For a few seconds, I say nothing, so shocked by the realization that, deep down, I've been nothing more than the kind of person I've always thrown my disdain towards. I scramble for the right words to say. Then, either by the grace of the Universe, or perhaps just by good old fashioned Mundane common sense, a Universal certainty suddenly becomes very clear to me.

It's not just a worn out cliche: Love DOES conquer all. Real love, that is. Not the heady, lustful draw of passion, or the teasing infatuation dance of new lovers as they explore each other's mind and body. Nope. Real love is the armor that protects a couple, any couple, in any space and any place in time; one that protects the heart from the realities of life with all its messy trials. It's about commitment, and forgiveness, and self-sacrifice. And in this moment, I see how very wrong I've been about what Duncan and Mel have together.

I take Duncan's hands in mine, and the physical energy of his emotions almost knocks me on my ass. I wobble a bit and regain my balance before speaking. "Duncan, you have every right to ask me to step down as witness to your and Mel's handfasting. I don't blame you at all. Goddess knows, I've given you multiple reasons not to trust my intentions. But what if I told you that…just this very second…I had a major, Universe-sent-epiphany, would you believe me?"

He tilts his head and stares at me with those gorgeous, soul-sucking eyes, as if searching for the answers in my aura. I hope with everything I am that he sees or feels the major change in my thinking. Otherwise, I can only do as he asks and let someone else take the honored spot next to Mel. It takes nearly two minutes of his deep examination before he replies. "Aye, Lady Cousin. I can sense a shift in yar' aura. It is true, then? You believe that ma' Beloved and I are meant ta' be together? That we need ta' join our lives together for the good of the Universe?"

"I do, Duncan. I truly do. And I am so very sorry for not believing in the love between the two of you sooner. I'm not going to try to make all kind of silly excuses about my behavior and the awful things I implied, except to say 'old habits die hard' and I am ashamed of my actions. The Universe has a crazy way of kicking its children in the pants when they least expect it. Believe me, I personally can attest to that statement. But I also have first-hand experience that true, selfless love can weather even the biggest storms. I see now that you and Mel are gifted with that type of relationship, and... if it's okay with you...I'd like to stand as witness to your enduring commitment."

The bridegroom's smile breaks like a ray of sun through cloudy skies, and because I'm still holding his hands, his overwhelming joy runs through my tooth fairy magic and makes me again sway on my feet. My husband's cousin grabs tighter and helps to keep me standing upright. Grinning, he says, "I apologize for ma' exuberance, Cousin, but I am filled with such happiness that I ken barely keep it contained. You have made this day even better far' me, and ma' Beloved and I want nothing more than ta' have you and his Lordship stand for us this evening. Blessed be!"

TOOTHPICKS 29

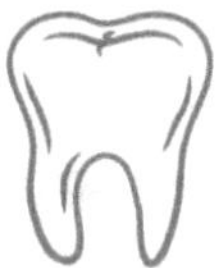

Love Conquers

I DON'T IMMEDIATELY SHARE what went down between Duncan and myself with my Tax Man, mainly because there isn't enough time for a long mental discussion of such a serious nature. By the time I return to our family quarters, our little entourage needs to start heading toward the Sacred Grove for the ceremony. Secondly, although I profess to be a follower of the Old Ways, I've never truly experienced what one would call a "spiritual revelation." Unless, of course, you count the moment I met Declan for the first time in my office that monumental June day, or the sudden realization that I was deeply in love with him in the midst of being kidnapped by Chechen terrorists. Because those things were happening to me in real time, amidst extremely trying circumstances, perhaps I didn't see them for what they truly were; a spiritual wake-up call from the Universe itself.

My conversation with Duncan felt less like the cultivation of magic, and more like a direct answer to the meaning of life from its higher source. I know. I sound like some crazy new age shaman. Very un-Rosie-like. I've always been a down-to-earth, practical sort. Maybe all this time in the Otherworld is having an effect on me. Still, my experience in the library with Duncan felt very real and I look forward to hearing what my beloved Tax Man has to say about being "tapped out" by the Universe.

For now, my focus is on witnessing a very special moment for our dearest friends. Mel squeezes my hand as we walk through the estate and out onto the grounds towards *Dun Siorai's* Sacred Grove. Each House has their own sacred place that is used for the practice of the Old Ways. I might have a slanted view because it's where Declan and I handfasted, but I think the grove here at *Dun Siorai* is especially beautiful. The branches of two giant oak trees, sacred to the Fae people, have been cultivated over many, many years to form a large canopy, while the circle itself is surrounded by full-grown Hawthorn, Ash, and Holly trees. The entire space is filled with lit lanterns, and because it is only April, the newly born leaves act like a curtain of lace, letting the light filter through them to cast a soft glow.

Unlike my own handfasting, there are no chairs or stadium-like seating enveloping the circle for attending guests. This is not a ceremony most of *I Idir's* population will attend. The reasoning has less to do with the family conflict surrounding their joining, and more to do with the fact that, politically and socially, Mel and Duncan are bit players in *Idir's* movers and shakers hierarchy. Even if

Duncan's parents weren't being complete jerks about his plan to handfast Mel, the guest lists would still in no way compete with ours. I don't mention this as a way of bragging. Quite the opposite. I'm a tad envious of our friends' intimate celebration of their love. If I can be honest, I felt like our handfast ceremony was more a spectacle than either of us would have preferred.

Mel and I take our place on the right side of the grove. Her parents and friends stand behind us, and I am pleased to see that there appears to be a nice sized crowd supporting my BFF. Sadly, it's a different story on the left side of the grove. There's only a small handful of guests on Duncan's side; most of them I recognize as the other members of Declan's intelligence team, but no actual members of the groom's family. During all the planning, no one has ever mentioned who will do the actual officiating of the ceremony. My Tax Man has been rather cagey about answering that question, so when a man arrives dressed in Druid robes with the Merlin symbols adorning his sleeves, I assume Declan has somehow managed to wrangle the High Wizard himself. And, once again, my assumptions are wrong.

The man pulls down the hood covering his head, looks directly at Mel and I, and, as if he can read my mind, smiles smugly. The Druid officiating Mel and Duncan's handfasting is not the Lord Merlin, but his heir, who just also happens to be the reigning Black Knight. He winks at me and I can't help but blush. I swear that man loves nothing more than to constantly fluster me. Still, I've never witnessed Ted Beckett in any role other than his one as the Throne's Hand of Justice, or as Sheriff of Essex

County back home, and the fact that he is here to officiate as a Druid is an interesting turn of events, since it's a known fact he doesn't hold much respect for anything deemed "spiritual." I ponder whether the Black Knight's presence here isn't The Morrigan's way of putting her "stamp" on this union without being overly open about it among the Ruling Council members. There is no facet of life here in *I Idir* that isn't influenced by its politics and The Throne itself.

The younger Merlin takes his position in the center of the circle at the same moment Duncan and my husband enter the grove. They make a handsome pair, the Tax Man with his fiery ginger hair and moss green eyes, the groom with his dark locks and sapphire blue ones. Those eyes go directly to Mel. It is the first time Duncan is seeing his Intended in her handfasting apparel, and as expected, he is...well...completely overwhelmed. It's hard not to be. Out here in the Sacred Grove, a nearly full moon shining down on her, my best friend looks like a goddess stepped out of an ancient past. No one can help but smile at the bridegroom because Duncan's passion for his soon to be mate is spilling from his aura like a cloud of genuine fairy dust.

"I do believe we need to begin this ceremony before the *fear na bainnase* (bridegroom) loses all sense of decorum," the young Merlin teases.

I'll admit to being surprised how confident the Black Knight appears in the family Druid role. Gossip being what it is in *I Idir*, it's common knowledge that although the 27th Merlin is to be wisely feared, his magical skills are nowhere near those of his esteemed *athair*. Still, he handles the words and actions of the handfast ceremony as if he's been doing them for centuries, and because it is after sundown in the Otherworld, I can feel his magical energy vibrate under my tooth fairy feet. When it comes time to seal Mel and Duncan's handfast knot with the wax, I catch my Tax Man's eye and hear him in my mind. *"If ma' cousin is even half in love with the Lady Sparks as I am with ya, Sweet Rosie Lass, then I swear ta' ya' no person or event will ever come between them."*

A late celebratory dinner in the new couple's honor is served in *Dun Siorai's* opulent formal dining room. Cook and her staff provide a lavish spread along with some of the estate's best wine and ale. Thus, by the time the main course is served, several of the male guests are deep in their cups. Though Duncan is titled through his position as Declan's second, at least until our son Dylan is old enough to take over the role, he isn't technically a Ruling Council member. Therefore, that whole ridiculous game of "bride stealing" isn't on the menu for tonight. That doesn't mean, however, that Duncan's close gentleman friends don't tease and torment him about the handfast night ahead.

Since the completion of the ceremony, my husband's poor cousin has been the butt of several practical jokes including pouring ice down his breeches, tying him to his chair, and attempting to lace his food and drink with licorice and chaste tree berries, both herbs that are believed to cause a decrease in male desire. Duncan good-naturedly takes it all in stride, but I can tell Mel is beginning to tire of the nonsense disrupting her handfast dinner. Being the good friend and Matron of Honor I am, I appeal to my husband on her behalf. "My Lord, do you think you can ask your comrades to tone it down already with all the silly pranks? Mel is starting to get upset over their nonsense."

"They mean no harm, Lass. 'Tis just a bit of traditional fun," Declan replies.

"It's gone beyond fun," I counter. "Now they're just getting obnoxious."

The Black Knight, who has stayed for dinner and is seated on my husband's left, chimes in. "Come now, Lady *Nuada*. Don't be such a party pooper. Let the boys have their fun. A few more drinks and most of them won't be able to stand anyway."

Royal family or not, his butting into a private conversation I'm having with my husband annoys me to no end. "Pardon my saying so, Lord Knight, but I was speaking specifically to my husband and not you." After I say it, I realize that I might have officially crossed the lines of formal protocol and embarrassed my husband, but then the two of them high five each other and start to laugh at my snarkiness, which doesn't do a thing to help my mood. "I think you're both being very rude, laughing at me like that. I am House *Nuada's* Lady, after all."

"I am sorry ma' Love. We don' mean ta' laugh. 'Tis just that ya' are so much like a wee tiger when ya' ar' wronged. 'Tis a wondrous sight ta' witness. Goddesses help the man that ever under estimates yar resolve."

"I concur, Lady *Nuada*. You are quite a force to be

reckoned with. House *Nuada* is lucky to have you at its helm," the Black Knight says, smiling with his white shark teeth.

"Hmmmm," I reply, not sure if I'm being played. "If that's the case, then as LADY *Nuada*, perhaps I should tell them to knock it off myself."

"There be no need, Love. Look around. The love birds have flown the coop...so ta' say. Off ta' spend the evening alone together," Declan explains.

I look back at the spot where I left just Mel and Duncan sitting at the table, only to find those seats now empty. "They've left already? They haven't even finished dinner," I complain.

"They are no hungry for food, Lass. Surely ya' remember how it was on our own handfast night?" my *Mo Shiorghra* recalls, as my mind is suddenly filled with misty memories of that amazing evening we spent together.

"I suppose you're right," I sigh. "But I didn't even get to say good-bye...or give them our gift...or tell them how much I wish the very best for the two of them."

My Eternal Mate looks directly into my eyes, and I instantly know that he's privy to everything that went on between Duncan and myself. "You have already given them everything they needed from ya, Love. 'Tis the vera' best gift they could have received."

TOOTHPICKS 30

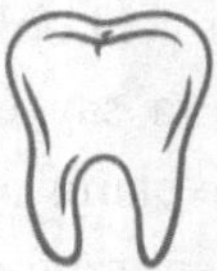

Past, Present, and Future

IF WEATHER IS a sign of the Universe's feelings, as many Otherworldly folk believe, then the Powers That Be were in joyful unity about what was to happen on this first day in May. It was as perfect as any day signaling the trek of days toward the Summer Solstice could be; not a cloud in the sky, a seasonably mild temperature, and every flower and bud in full bloom. There was an excited hum of magical energy as the staff, those who stayed on after the changing of the guard, hustled about readying the estate for the celebration to come. It was obvious that they were thrilled to see their young Lord take on the mantle he was born to wear. I am glad everyone is so happy. My *Mo Shiorghra* deserves better than an Eternal Mate who is decidedly less than thrilled over his new title.

It wasn't as if we hadn't hashed out this change to our lives on more than one occasion. Mutual communication is central to our relationship; it's hard for it to be anything else when our minds are often an open book to the other. I never minced words, relaying in detailed summaries how his being Lord of House *Nuada* would affect the peace of our family life. And Declan, being the ever-pragmatic Tax Man he is, listened attentively while offering logical solutions to some of my problems, while at the same time honestly admitting it was impossible to say how everything would work out unless we actually "talked the talk and walked the walk."

Personally, I am sick and tired of hearing about "walking one's path." Of late, I've come to decide that the Fae spiritual philosophy is really no different from any of the Mundane world religions: If there were no realistic solutions to life's difficult moments, one was just expected to walk blindly in faith and trust that what is happening was meant to be. Same old "cop-out" philosophy no matter what name you wanted pin to the cover of your belief system. If that sounds jaded or bitter, I apologize. Dr. Rosie Parker Fitzpatrick calls 'em like she sees 'em

Despite every one of my misgivings over this decision of life split between two worlds, it was May 1st, the Fae Beltane Festival, and here I stood; formally dressed and ready to be paraded among the cheering crowds, fake smile plastered on my face while crushing doubts settled in my heart, simply because I loved my mate with everything I was and could do no less.

A sharp rap on my door interrupted my gloom and doom. "Come in," I offer.

Lady *Siobhan* stepped into our bedroom, obviously dressed for the upcoming celebration. She looked stunning, as always, in leaf-green Shantung silk, but I was more than a little surprised not to see her decked out in the House's colors of maroon and gold as protocol dictated. Feeling mellow, I drop a respectful curtsy. "Happy *Beltane*, Lady *Mathair*. You look especially lovely today."

She gives a shrug. "Thank you, Rosalinda. I'm glad to see you took my advice and decided on the empire waist cut. It does a fine job of hiding some of that lingering baby pouch you carry in the front."

It's no use getting bent over my mother in law's lack of polite pleasantries. It's simply not in her nature to be anything but blunt. "I agree. It was the better choice," I say. "Though, I'm surprised not to see you in House colors, today of all days." Frankly, I'm not sure how she feels about Declan taking over her mate's position. She and I have never discussed it. My husband told her the news privately face to face and when I asked him how she took the news he'd only said, "Like you would expect her to."

"There's no use in playing games, Rosalinda. As of this afternoon, you will become Lady *Nuada*. I see no reason to hang on to a role that no longer suits me. *Dun Siorai* will have a new mistress. It will be you, for better or worse. To that effect, I will be moving out of the estate next week," Dragon Mama announces.

"Move out? For the love of Lugh, why would you do that? This is your home. You're always welcome here. There's no reason for you to leave," I say with surprisingly more emotion than I would have expected.

"'Tis best for all involved," she says, and as much as she

tries to hide the pain in her eyes, I see it there, plain as day.

"But where will you go?" I ask. "To Ballydonnely?"

"Gracious no," she answers. "The Mundane world is a charming respite from the politics of *I Idir*, but a human lifestyle void of any magic would be frustratingly dull for me."

"Then where?" I question.

"Herself has invited me to live at *Crann Bethadh* and be part of the Royal Circle. I have accepted her invitation," Lady *Siobhan* explains.

"Wow. That's quite an honor. I'm so happy for you, Lady *Mathair*," I say.

My mother-in-law laughs, but there's no joy in it. "You are still as naive as ever, tooth fairy. I am the bonded mate of the kingdom's most hated man. A traitor. What better place for me to be than under the watchful eye of The Morrigan and her equally ruthless Black Knight?"

I don't know what to say to that. Knowing what I know about the Queen of *I Idir*, it's hard not to agree with Lady *Siobhan's* take on her invitation to the Raven's Nest. I change the subject. "But what about Dylan? You'll still want to visit with your grandson, right?" I ask hopefully. Despite the wretched relationship between her and her only son, Dylan's grandmother seems genuinely devoted to our baby boy.

"I would never ignore *mo una beag* (my little lamb). I expect you to bring him to me for visits at least twice a week," she says.

"Of course. We'll set up a schedule next week," I promise.

"I'll expect that," she answers. "Now, before I leave for the fairgrounds, turn around slowly so I can double-check your appearance."

I do as she asks and she makes minor adjustments to the back of my chemise, which is cut low and open to showcase House *Nuada's* ink on my shoulder blade. "Master Finn did an excellent job adding the Eternal Bond link to the original sigil," Dragon Mama comments. "I hope you don't have regrets over taking your bond further," she adds, not hiding her bitterness.

"Me too," I respond. Truthfully, I don't have any regrets about adding the Eternal Bond, but saying so seems like rubbing salt in her own open wounds so I refrain from saying such a thing.

She gives my corset an extra tug then steps away. "You'll do fine, Rosalinda. Try to take whatever sweet memories you can of this day. Its joy is fleeting and you will soon be buried under a mountain of political *caic tarbh* (bullshit)." Then she's gone without a look back.

Her visit leaves me feeling even more anxious than I already was. I was counting on having Dragon Mama at *Dun Siorai* to help guide me through the unfamiliar protocols of my new role. Her moving to *Crann Bethadh* just adds another layer of worry to my growing unease. As I contemplate the multiple reasons I think this is all a bad idea, the air in our bedroom suddenly becomes too warm and stuffy, so I crank open one of the mullioned windows. The smell of green growing things and fragrant flowers floats into the space, and I inhale and exhale deeply, taking mindful breaths. Across the manicured lawns the staff mills about preparing for the large celebratory dinner that will follow Declan's installation, and it crosses my mind that perhaps hosting such a grand affair for a boatload of guests is far too extravagant for a recently reduced House treasury.

A large black raven flies to the open window and stares at me with strange green eyes. It wears no messenger collar, so I don't pay it much mind. I've never been much of a bird lover, but before I can shoo the pest away, it jumps to the floor of our Master suite. Without warning, the bird disappears, changing into the goddess of war and destruction, the Queen of *I Idir*, right before my unblinking eyes. Truth be told, I've never in my life witnessed a Fae shift form before and it startles me. I jump back and trip backwards over a small, square footstool, landing flat on my ass. Dressed in five layers of formal petticoat, I struggle to get up with any sense of decorum, and when I finally do, my curtsy is more of an embarrassed squat and dive than anything else.

"My, my…did I startle you, little tooth fairy?" she asks. It's hard to miss the sarcasm in her voice.

"Yes, Your Majesty. I'm…uhmm…not all that familiar with…uhmm…shifter magic," I stutter, sweating like a pig in a sauna.

"Well, I do apologize," she says with not the least bit of genuineness. "I wanted my visit to remain between the two of us. This conversation is to stay in this room."

"Of course, Your Majesty." I point to the most comfortable chair in the room. "May I offer you a seat and refreshment of sorts?"

"There is no time for niceties, little mother. Your

Lord's installation is set to begin soon and I need to speak to you before that can happen."

"To me, Your Majesty? May I ask about what?" I squeak, my voice three octaves higher than normal. There's no denying that The Morrigan gives me the "heebie jeebies."

"I have no doubt you already know why I'm here," she says.

"I'm afraid I don't, my Queen,"

"Do you think I am unaware of your doubts regarding your mate's path as Lord of House *Nuada*? Your infinite unhappiness regarding your new responsibilities to *I Idir*? Your head is an open book, tooth fairy. I have seen how you plead with your *Mo Shiorghra* to abandon his path and choose one that is more akin to your old dreams. You do him a great disservice by making him decide between his love for you and his duty to his kingdom."

As I mentioned, the goddess frightens me, but I'm not really keen on being scolded as if I were a mere child. "Is it not also my natural duty as a mother and mate to fight for my family, Your Majesty? Our life in *I Idir* will be far more complicated than one centered in the Mundane world, and flipping between both a logistics nightmare. There will be no steady routine. No sense of permanent home or hearth. Now that the Universe has gifted me with another child to raise, the stakes are even higher. You and I both know the prejudice *Oisin* will face here in *I Idir* because of his Elven heritage and the circumstances surrounding his birth. Is it wrong for me to want to protect him from that?"

For a second or two, she stares at me with those

piercing green eyes. When she finally speaks, she says, "Her name was *Dyr*. Her bones lie in *Nuada* soil."

I somehow know who The Morrigan means, but I ask anyway. "Who?"

She doesn't bother answering me. "It is the *Nordboerne* word for deer."

I turn away from that unblinking gaze. "That's why you named him *Oisin*…"little deer."

"Aye. She deserved at least that. The boy, like his unfortunate *mathair,* is forever tied to his destiny here. Hiding him away in the Mundane world will not alter his true path. Without proper training he will lose his way just as she did. His unique heritage makes him exceptionally magically gifted, which can be both a curse and a blessing."

I try not to think of that poor woman, murdered and deprived of ever knowing her child, because that's exactly what the goddess wants me to feel. Sympathy. To sway my thoughts. "You're using my feelings for the boy to keep us here."

"Is that what you think, tooth fairy? That I would resort to silly mind games over something this monumental? If you believe that nonsense, then you are not the intelligent woman I thought you to be. The path you walk has been set in place for more years than you have taken breaths. Nothing you say or do will change that. You can choose to fight the natural order of things and live a life of deliberate unhappiness. Or, you can accept the Universe's decisions for you and live the fullest journey possible. Either way, it will not change the outcome. You will never sway your *Mo Shiorghra* from his destiny. Your childish begging and pleading for a life you can never have will only cloud the happy, fulfilling adventure you might have together."

I turn back to face her, angrier than I should be toward a goddess who once controlled the outcomes of wars. "How can you be so sure that Declan and I wouldn't be just fine in the Mundane world? Lots of mixed-blood Fae live perfectly happy lives apart from the Otherworld. They don't need or want all the drama of your magical ways."

"Surely you are not as stupid as that, little tooth fairy? I am The Morrigan." She raises her hand and touches my forehead. "Open your mind so you may know."

There is a slight buzzing in my head and suddenly, I'm watching a fast-moving movie inside my mind. Images of the past, present and future tumble and race, some joyful, some shocking, and some so awful that I want to close my eyes, but there are no eyes inside my head to shut. I feel overwhelmed and slightly ill, so I put both of my hands to the sides of my temple. "Stop. Please. No more," I beg. And just as suddenly, the mental film ends. "That was cruel," I mutter.

"Cruel? No. Necessary? Yes," the goddess states. "This turn of events has been a long time coming. *I Idir* needs your mate to fulfill his destiny. You, tooth fairy mama, are an important part of it. Anya's daughter for Callum's son. It could go no other way."

Our discussion is interrupted by a familiar male voice in the hallway. "Rosie? Are you in the bedroom, Lass?"

"See the world with newly opened eyes, Lady *Nuada*," The Morrigan says. Then, she slips into raven form and flies out the same window she came in at the very same moment my husband steps into the room. "There ya' are. Are ya' ready to go, Love? I'd like to get there a few minutes earlier and see the layout of the stage before the Royal Entourage arrives." he says.

I don't answer because I'm gob-smacked. Speechless. Stunned. After ten months together, I'm perfectly used to seeing my husband in Otherworldly garb. There's no doubt about it. It's a natural fit for him. He always looks "vera" good in that apparel, like some cover model of a fantasy romance novel. But this afternoon, he, like Mel on her handfast day, looks...well...down right unearthly. Maybe, for the sake of my own mental well-being, I've always viewed my mate through my "Tax Man" eyes. Subconsciously, it must have made him seem more human to my senses. Or perhaps Herself has performed some magical juju to "open my eyes," as she so mysteriously put it. Whatever the cause, standing here in this room in this moment in time, Lord Declan Fitzpatrick *Nuada* looks every bit *Tuatha De Danann*, a throwback to the time when the "Shining Ones" ruled the land. It literally takes my breath away, and I find myself having to concentrate on inhaling and exhaling. The fitted breeches, the chemise with the embroidered cuffs, the platinum circlet with a large cut garnet resting on his forehead are all part of the vibe. But it's his aura that makes him so incredibly Fae, that shimmering green-gold filter of light that radiates around him like a magical shadow. I note that he is wearing the plain gold band from our Mundane wedding ceremony, a loving token specifically meant for me, as the wearing of bond rings by male Fae is not customary and considered an impediment on a sword hand. "You look amazing," I gush.

He gives me a huge boyish grin. "Thank you, Lass. Ya' look vera fetchin' yourself. That gown is fabulous. Vera' becoming with yar' red hair."

I give him a short curtsy. "Thank you, my Lord. You make a girl blush. I'm glad you're here, though. Can you help me fasten my choker?" I say, as I hold out the garnet and citrine necklace that was his handfast gift to me.

"Not today, Love," he says.

I look at him with confusion. "Why not? I love this necklace."

"I have somethin' I'd rather have ya' wear instead… if it so pleases ya'." He hands me a sizable carved wooden box. I tilt my head in confusion, to which my mate says, " 'Tis a gift for ma' beautiful Lady on this special occasion."

I open the lid and blink a few times in utter surprise. Inside, nestled on a bed of white velvet, is the rose gold and platinum torque from the shop in *Gleann Gas.* "How did you even know?" I stutter. "You were inside the other shop when I saw it."

"We had the bond open between us. I was too worried to close it, you bein' alone outside by yar'self. I saw and heard everythin' that wretched shop owner said ta' ya' that day and I wanted to crack his skull open far' it. Still, I felt how much ya' loved the necklace and I wanted to see it 'round your lovely neck. I sent Duncan to retrieve it far' me. My cousin is a fine negotiator. The old bastard is probably still weepin' over his lost profit."

"Oh, Declan. I love it! Thank you! But isn't it rather… well… expensive? Especially now?"

"As long as it pleases ya', Rosie Love, then I have no other worries. Here…let me help you try it on." He takes the heavy torque from the box and lays it across my decollete, then fastens the clasp. The necklace feels cool on my flushed skin. I turn to face the cheval mirror in the corner of the bedroom as the light from the window catches the oval emerald, making it shimmer with an unnatural glow. "Wow! It's stunning," I whisper.

"Just like the woman wearing it," Declan says as he kisses the back of my neck. "'Tis a perfect piece for House *Nuada's* newest Lady." Putting his arm through mine he adds, "Shall we collect the rest of our family and head toward the fairgrounds? The hour grows late."

I grin and drop another curtsy. "Aye, my Lord. As you wish. Let us proceed."

TOOTHPICKS 31

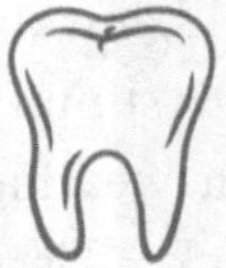

O La Shona Duit (Oh Happy Day)

THE FIRST DAY in May has long been celebrated by ancient peoples in both the Otherworld and the Mundane. Although different cultures have their own traditions, the celebration of May Day is traditionally set aside to herald the growing season, when soil, sun and rain work together to sustain life. For the Fae, this first day in the month of May is a time for spiritual renewal, a time for new beginnings, and the asking of blessings from the Universe for increased fertility within an ever-decreasing population. Along with *Samhain*, the celebration of *Beltane* is a key sacred holiday for the Fae folk, titled and otherwise, filled with dancing, drinking, and feasting, as well as an abundance of romantic and lustful behavior. It's no small wonder why Herself chose this day to install Declan as a member of *I Idir's* Ruling Council; the population of the kingdom was in a celebratory mood and ripe for rounds of partying, an atmosphere Her Majesty planned on using to her fullest advantage.

News of Callum Fitzpatrick *Nuada's* crimes had made the complete round of *I Idir*, and one would be hard pressed to find anyone who had not heard some version of the story. It was also common knowledge that The Morrigan had sent men out to hunt for Fae folk wearing the rebel ink. Gossip heralded that several people, men and women alike, had been found, arrested and imprisoned while awaiting trial for treason, causing a general feeling of suspicion and unease throughout the kingdom. To make matters worse, before disappearing, Declan's father had also failed to make payment to an abundance of those he owed, thus making a large contingent of merchants and money lenders out for *Nuada* blood and making the installation of his son in his place a "travesty" among some guild and business leaders.

Add to all of this, the ire caused by Declan's granting of *Riail an Tiarna* towards Duncan and Mel's handfasting, a point so strongly argued against by the *gancanagh's* parents. Their displeasure is apparent within the scowls and stink eyes we receive from that whole group of extended *Nuada* relatives as we pass by them. I keep a happy neutral face, but part of me is concerned that my Tax Man's unpopular decision might rear its ugly head today.

Despite a million eyes on our little family, my *Mo Shiorghra* appears unruffled by the scrutiny, while I myself didn't know where to look without someone staring back at me. "It will be fine, Lass," he promises me. "Ya' are nervous far' no reason. Herself knows exactly what she is doing. She would not have made ma' installation so public if she felt it would not go well. She has kept her Throne far' hundreds of years because she is vera' adept at readin' the moods of har' people."

As a group of musicians played a traditional Beltane song, I whispered to my husband. "Aren't you the least bit nervous?"

"Not really," he whispers back. "The ceremony is vera' simple. The Queen asks me ta' state my loyalty ta' The Crown and ta' the people of *I Idir*. I state ma' vows, and then she uses *Caladbolg* to draw some of ma' blood which I will smear on the sword's blade as a sign that I am willing to shed ma' own blood far' the cause. None of it is really difficult." Declan leans over and adds, "Though I will admit ta' ya' alone, Rosie, that I do have some minor anxiety over the 'testament' part of this dog and pony show."

"Testament part?" I ask. "What's that about?"

"Traditionally, after I take ma' vows and Herself announces my installation as Lord *Nuada*, Member of the Ruling Council, she will call far' open testaments from the people. That means the Fae in the crowd ken' stand up and say why I am a good choice far' the Ruling Council position. Testament Protocol, which focuses only on ma' positive traits, dictates that those doin' the testifyin' should be not be from ma' own House, lest it seem untruthful. The thing is, most common folk don' hold much ta' speakin in front of crowds, while the *Nuada* name is not a favorite at this moment. I am concerned no one will speak far' me. It changes nothin' in the way of ma' appointment. I will still be Lord. But 'tis vera' embarrassin' ta' have a silent Testament, and no doubt the other Houses would snicker about it far' years ta' come."

"Feckin' hell, Sweetie," I murmur under the cover of music, "that's awful! But you're a wonderful man; the most honorable and righteous man I've ever known. I have no doubt that tons of people will testify for you," I say, crossing my fingers as I speak it. I shudder at the kind of hostility I'm feeling from the crowd and hoping against hope that I'm right about someone standing for my beloved husband. I give his hand a squeeze. "I bet your testaments go on so long, Herself will need to declare a bathroom break in between them." The Tax Man smiles at me, and squeezes my hand back, but I feel a little wave of his anxiety crawl over me.

Eventually, the music ends, and a Lord from the Ruling Council gets up to speak. He explains to the crowd what will happen and then Declan is called to stand before the Queen. It all happens as Declan said it would, the vows and the sealing of the oath. Then, The Morrigan stands and addresses the assembled masses, "We will now hear testament of our newest Lord. Let your tongues be freed to speak only the truth."

I hold my breath as my poor *Mo Shiorghra* stands front and center, his chin held high and his back as straight and strong as an arrow, but the large crowd remains embarrassingly silent. I begin a litany of invocations begging every goddess I know, including the one that messed with my head this morning, to provoke someone in that large crowd to say something nice about the man I adore. I'm clenching my teeth so hard my jaw aches, when across the stage, sitting with his own titled family, *Cillian Mac Badh* stands up.

"I am Lord *Cillian* McDougal *Mac Badh*, heir to House *Badh,* and kin to Her Majesty. I wish to testify to the appointment of Lord *Deaglan* Fitzpatrick *Nuada* as newest member of *I Idir's* Ruling Council. It is the honest truth when I say Lord *Nuada* is a man of conviction and honesty. It is no secret that he and I have had our differences, but when I was put in a dire situation, accused of a crime I did not commit, *Nuada* stood far' me and spoke the truth in ma' defense despite any feelings of anger he might still have held towards me. I am grateful far' his ability ta' separate truth from emotion. That is the type of man we need makin' important decisions far' our kingdom. I heartily support his installation and am glad far' it. That is ma' testament." The young man sits back down and I try to close my gaping mouth.

I don't have to look behind me. I'm sure the other members of our entourage, including Declan's cousin, Duncan, who is no fan of *Cillian Mac Badh*, are as shocked as I am over the man's glowing praise. All except Herself, who deliberately looks my way while I hear that annoyingly familiar tinkling of bells in my head. Now I understand exactly what that interrogation of *Cillian* at *Crann Bethadh* was really all about. Whether you love or hate The Raven Queen, you can't deny her political and magical genius.

Mac Badh's testament sets off a chain reaction and soon scores of people in the crowd, both on and off stage, are asking to be heard. Maybe it's not long enough to require a bathroom break, but enough people speak glowingly on my Tax Man's behalf that I'm ready to get up and do the dance of joy right there on that stage. I look over and see the man I love so proud and happy in this moment and a little part of me wonders if maybe, just maybe, this is the right path for my family after all.

It's very late when I return to our personal quarters at *Dun Siorai*, leaving Declan and a handful of his friends still celebrating in the estate's solar parlor. The men seem in no great hurry to bust up the party so I politely excuse myself as the hostess, barely able to keep eyes open after the exhausting events of the day. The female companions of these men have already retired to their respective guest rooms, all except the Black Knight's, whose own mate was safely seen back to The Raven's Nest. It was my idea to invite his closest buddies and their ladies to stay the night at *Dun Siorai*, figuring that it would be best not to have them jumping back to the Mundane world overly tired and less than sober. Those who had pressing duties in the human realm and who needed to make the trip in the morning could easily do so after a good night's sleep and a hearty breakfast, and those who wanted to stay and enjoy an extra day's "holiday" were welcome to stay and enjoy the comforts of the estate.

I check in on the nursery, where both boys are sound asleep, with only *Birgit* and *Seamus* still awake. "'Twas a perfect *Beltane*, Lady Rosie. Everything was just as protocol dictates. I think even yar' Lady *Mathair* was impressed on how well you handled the hostess duties."

"Thank you, *Birgit*. I think it was lovely as well. And you're right. Lady *Siobhan* said as *Beltane* celebrations go, mine was 'adequate.' That's a high compliment from our Dragon Mama." We both giggle over that, and I add, "I know this sounds crazy, but I'm going to sort of miss her 'presence' here at *Dun Siorai*. She did make things 'interesting' in her own way."

"Aye. That she did. But I am happy that her Ladyship wants to keep up her visits with Dylan. The bonding is good far' both of them."

"Absolutely," I reply, covering a yawn with my hand. "Well, I think I'm going to call it a night. The 'Boy's Club' is still in the solar parlor, so don't be alarmed if you hear people moving about the corridors as they stumble off to bed."

"I will make note of that. Pleasant dreams, my Lady," the *scathach* says.

I make my way to our bedroom and undress, thinking I should have asked the nanny to help me unfasten the new torque. I struggle with the catch for a few minutes, then give up and leave it on. I'll have to wait until Declan comes to bed, or wear it until morning. At some point, I doze off until I hear my husband return, whistling a terribly off-key tune. Since returning from North Korea, the Tax Man's extended musical abilities have seemed to disappear, a topic neither of us has been inclined to discuss as of yet. He undresses and hangs up all his clothes, a trait I unfortunately don't share, then slides into bed naked which is his nightly norm.

"Done for the evening, Lord *Nuada*?" I say.

"I'm sorry, Love. I din' not mean ta' wake ya."

"No worries. I wasn't sleeping very soundly. Did everyone get to their respective beds okay?" I ask.

"Aye. That they did. 'Twas a vera' good plan ya' had, Rosie, invitin' everyone ta' stay the night. It makes me happy ta' know they are all safe and sound under *Dun Siorai's* roof."

"I'm glad to see you so happy, Tax Man. It makes me happy as well." I sit up in bed. "Can you help me unfasten this necklace? I tried on my own but couldn't quite unlock it."

"Is it vera' uncomfortable ta' wear?" he questions.

"No. It's not uncomfortable at all. Why do you ask?"

He grins at me. "Because I would really like ta' see ma' *Mo Shiorghra* wearin' that piece and nothin' else," the Tax Man replies as he begins to undo the pearl buttons on my nightgown while at the same time nuzzling my neck.

"You do realize we have a very full house," I comment.

"Aye. So what?" he questions as the nuzzling moves lower.

"I wish you hadn't told me about the...uhmmm...vibes you say we give off when we get...romantic."

"It should not matter what others think. You are ma' Eternal Mate, Rosie Fitzpatrick. I love you. You love me. 'Tis no secret among our friends and family that I ken' not keep ma' hands off of ya'. Besides, it is *Beltane*. They are all probably too busy doin' the vera' same thing to notice anythin' else," my mate explains as he continues his explorative trek downwards.

"It's a little embarrassing," I say.

Declan stops and looks up at me, just as a slice of moonlight filters in from the bedroom window and illuminates the muscles of his broad back and the handsome features of his face. "Do ya' truly wish far' me ta' stop, Lass?"

I glance down at the man who owns me body and soul. "Hmm…definitely not," I reply.

He gives me a wicked smile. "Good. I am plannin' on makin' these old walls shake with our joined magic so that everyone here at *Dun Siorai* knows Lord and Lady *Nuada* are celebratin' *Beltane* in the proper Fae manner."

And then that's exactly what we do. The Tax Man and I celebrate *Beltane*. Properly.

* * *

Find out what happens to Rosie, Declan, and their beloved family in Book 6 of The Tooth Fairy Chronicles: Missing Teeth And What Lies Beneath

More from Serenade Publishing

Songbird Series

By Sarah Williams

Songbird

Brigadier Station Series

By Sarah Williams:

The Brothers of Brigadier Station

The Sky over Brigadier Station

The Legacies of Brigadier Station

Christmas at Brigadier Station

Heart of the Hinterland Series

By Sarah Williams:

The Dairy Farmer's Daughter

Their Perfect Blend

Beyond the Barre

The Outback Governess

By Sarah Williams

About the Author

Victoria Rocus is a retired educator, accomplished miniaturist, and full-time author living near the home of country music, Nashville, Tennessee, USA. When she's not writing new adventures for her imaginary friends, catering beach parties for mermaids, or finding homes for orphaned dragons, she's building and rehabbing one-of-a-kind dollhouses and accessories, just like her favorite character, Dr. Rosie Parker. Many of her multiple miniature buildings are 1/12 scale replicas of settings from her unique fantasy stories.

Victoria started her writing career as a weekly blogger while still teaching middle school language arts. Now retired from the educational field, she's been able to make writing a full-time adventure, penning several fantasy and romance stories she hopes readers will enjoy with both a sigh and a smile.

Find out more at: victoriarocusauthor.com

instagram.com/victoriarocusauthor
tiktok.com/@victoriarocusauthor

Acknowledgments

Like Rosie's infamous lemon blueberry scones, putting out a new book requires a whole list of "ingredients" in making the magic happen. Foremost and always, I am eternally grateful to Sarah Williams and the team at Serenade Publishing for bringing Rosie and Declan into the wild. The fact that you believed in a book about a sassy tooth fairy dentist by an American debut author means more to me than I can say in these limited paragraphs.

A round of special thanks goes to my awesome Beta Reader Team: Carol Peden Fuller, Donna Gentile-Ruth, Daniel Caddigan, Kaia Vinney and Michelle Kaspar. You've been there from the beginning and are now willingly in for the long haul. I have no doubt you love these characters almost as much as I do. Your opinions and suggestions mean the world to me. Also, to my amazing fellow authors, Arla Jones, and K.C. Nord; there's no one more I'd rather be in the trenches with on his crazy writing adventure. Thank you for sharing this journey.

To my dear husband, Victor, my own *Mo Shiorghra*; I am grateful for your never-ending love and support. My years spent with you make writing realistic romance so darn easy. To Steven, Michael, Allison and Kaia; please know that there's a part of you guys in every fun-loving, often-loud, but ever-devoted family scene I write. Hugs and kisses to you all. Plus, an exceptional shout-out is definitely in order for our clan's own personal "Baby Tooth," Valerie James Rocus, whose Grammy loves her to *I Idir* and back, forever and always.

Lastly, a huge round of appreciative applause for you, dear readers, for coming back for each new adventure. Your support is surely the "frosting on the cake" within this recipe metaphor, and the main reason I keep mixing up new places to take our friends from the Otherworld. Here's hoping you'll continue to enjoy digging into these yummy stories created from the table of my imagination. *Bon appetit!*

www.ingramcontent.com/pod-product-compliance
Lightning Source LLC
Chambersburg PA
CBHW030608170726
48283CB00002B/512